THE SWORD AND THE HOUNDS

A.B. FINLAYSON

PARLIAMENT HOUSE PRESS

For Mam and Dad.
Who were so grateful when I eventually started reading (at the age of eleven) that they let me run unchecked through second-hand bookshops, school book fairs, and libraries with little to no concern about censorship or whether the books I hoarded were "appropriate."
I love you both.

And for my wife, Kel, whose contribution to these stories continues to be underwhelming :-D

AUTHOR'S NOTE

The places in this story are real but the people are not. Well, some of the ghosts are, but that really depends on your definition of real. I wrote *The Book and the Blade* when we lived in Richmond, and then I wrote *The Sword and the Hounds* when we lived in York, which probably tells you a lot about my organisational skills.

Richmond is stunning. In fact, it is one of my favourite places on the planet. We lived in the shadow of the castle for twelve months, and it was magic. I loved walking around the town and through the countryside, reading up on the history and legends, and talking to the many fascinating people who call the area home. They definitely added colour to the characters in this book, but for the most part, each person here is a complete work of fiction. The bar staff, the priest, the police officers, soldiers, dog walkers, and residents are all entirely made up, and any resemblance to real people living or dead is purely coincidental (or done so with kind permission). Some of the ghosts on the other hand—Richard and John Snell, Robert Willance, Potter Thompson, The Drummer Boy, and to some extent, the queen—are based on the real stories of real people, with more than a little artistic licence. Their lives make for fascinating reading. All other ghosts are products of my overactive imagination.

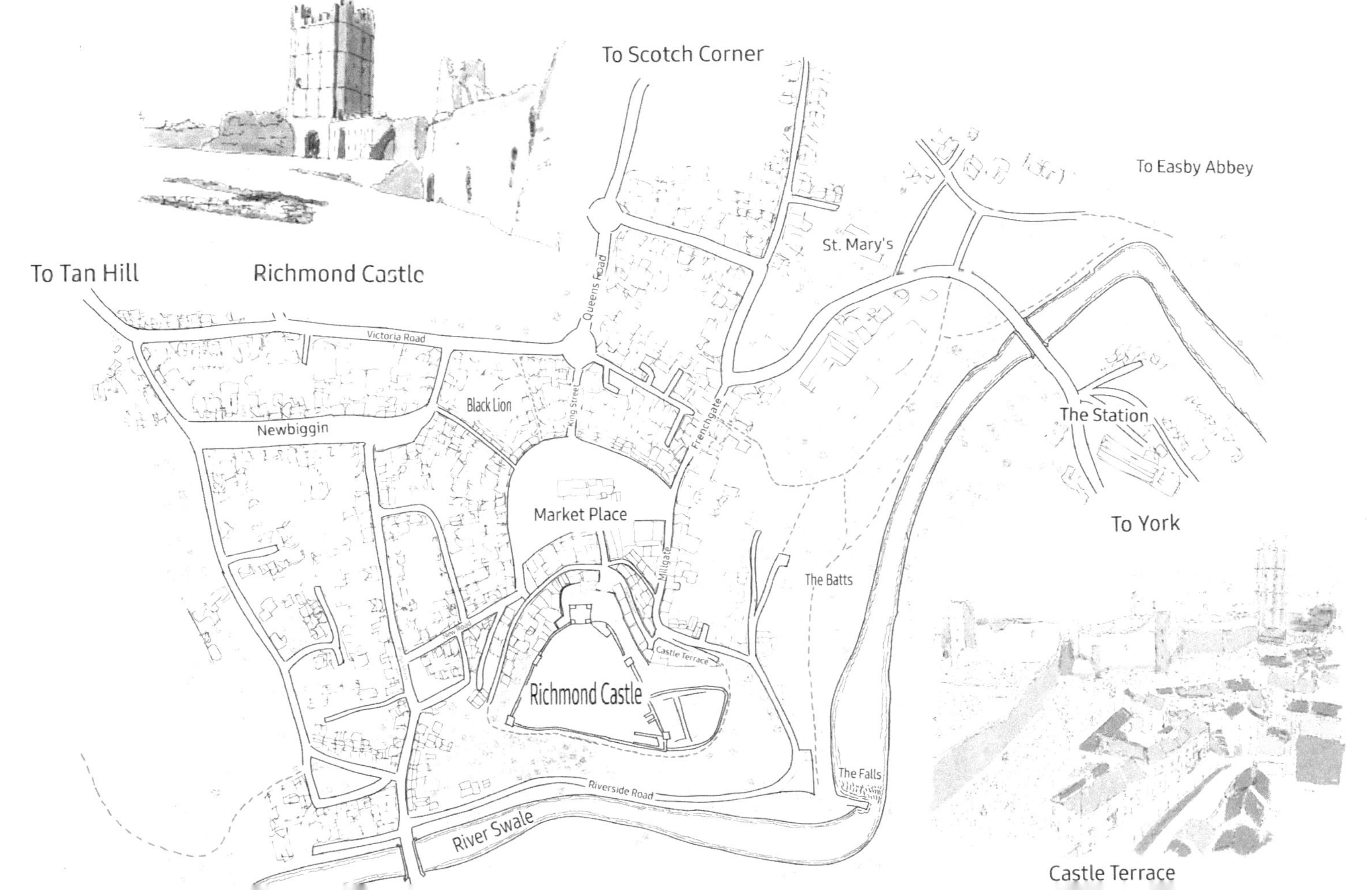
To Scotch Corner
To Easby Abbey
To Tan Hill
Richmond Castle
St. Mary's
Victoria Road
Queens Road
Black Lion
King Street
Frenchgate
The Station
Newbiggin
Market Place
Millgate
To York
The Batts
Richmond Castle
Castle Terrace
Riverside Road
The Falls
River Swale
Castle Terrace

PROLOGUE

"And they all lived happily ever after" is complete and utter bollocks. It is the wool pulled over children's eyes to let them know it all works out in the end. But kids aren't stupid. They know you just want to close the book, shut the door, and open the wine, and when you do, they lie awake wondering what happened next.

Why was the princess who slept for a hundred years perfectly content to jump straight into blissful domesticity a few days after waking up? Did she have no ambitions of her own? Then there's the psychological trauma of waking up to find that everyone she knew was dead, but somehow, she hadn't aged at all. She'd probably develop a pretty strong dependency on medicinal marijuana just to get through the day.

And what about this husband of hers? The type of guy who sneaks into a woman's bedroom and kisses her while she's sleeping! Okay, let's say he is a decent guy; they still got married too fast. What if he has rank breath? That could have been what woke her up! For that matter, what if she's a petty little sadist who likes to maim small animals, and that's the reason she was locked up in the first place and now that poor halitosis sufferer is stuck with her?

Some say the sign of a good story is that it leaves questions to be answered, mysteries to solve.

Others say this is a sign of a bad story.

Happily ever after, my arse.

The worst part is, as you turn that final page and read those words, you *know* it's a lie. You know fairy tales are only there to teach a lesson and make us all feel good about ourselves in the end. You also know they have been diluted and censored over the years to appeal to a more delicate audience, but Grimm's fairy tales were just that. Grim.

Stories don't all end happily ever after. And many of them don't start that way either. This is a story about what happens *after* the story.

It begins with a man in a pub.

PART I
CHRISTMAS EVE

CHAPTER 1

The last time Arthur got drunk, all manner of skeletons fell out of the closet. And it wasn't just skeletons either. There were ghosts, demons, witches, sprites, shadowmen, and shades. What had started as the usual "quick pint after work" quickly turned into a two-night bender that changed the young man's life forever.

That'll happen when you find out you can speak to the dead.

As it turns out, the hangover was worse than the party. The haze ascended but nothing made sense. People had died, the ghosts had gone, and the dead remained stubbornly silent while the rest of the world carried on as normal. Arthur had crawled home to his parents' house with his proverbial tail between his legs, seeking solace in the ordinary. This hangover had been going on for nearly six months. Six months under the watchful eye of mum and dad. And it's not like he could tell them the truth.

Arthur Crazy.

It was his name, not his nature.

He hoped.

"Another one, son?" his dad asked, rising from his seat with the empty glasses in hand.

"No thanks, Dad," Arthur said. "I've had enough of spirits to last me a lifetime."

He groaned inwardly at the crap joke and then smiled to himself. He'd love to be able to tell his dad why it was such a corny line. Of all people, Thomas Crazy would get a real kick out of such a terrible pun, but there were some things you just couldn't reveal to the people who raised you.

Seeing dead people while shit-faced sits quite high on that list.

Arthur smiled as his father walked to the bar. The grey-haired, slightly more weathered version of himself had never staggered to Arthur's recollection, but with the amount of beer they'd packed away, he was beginning to think today might be a day of firsts. Thankfully, the pub was so full Arthur figured you could pass out and remain upright, wedged between the press of bodies.

They had been lucky to get a small table in the corner of the long, narrow bar of the Black Lion, and it was a perfect spot for people-watching. From their perch, the two men could see the door, the restaurant, and the full length of the dark wooden bar top with its shining taps and assortment of glass bottles and snacks.

Arthur watched as his dad was swallowed by a rugby scrum of well-dressed farmers, ramblers, businessmen in ridiculous Christmas ties, and students in novelty Christmas jumpers. The television affixed to the wall above his head was an indistinct murmur amongst the hum of the packed pub.

Finding a table had been a stroke of luck. So, when they settled in, they didn't bother to move.

That was three hours ago. The pub was still full—full of Christmas cheer, full of laughter, full of life. People leaned in to catch shouted words, raised voices to be heard, or simply spoke over each other without being heard at all. Waitresses pushed politely through the throng of drinkers to serve those seated in the small restaurant. Then they vanished upstairs to the kitchens to return moments later, arms laden with steaming plates, all the while dodging proffered mistletoes with professional and patient smiles. It was a hive of activity, and the street outside looked every inch a Christmas card: dark, peaceful, and suffused in a soft orange glow from the streetlights. Decorations and fairy lanterns glistened in the shop windows, and the air gave the hint of frost, tapping at the glass with cold fingers. It might snow. It might not.

It *felt* like Christmas, Arthur thought, smiling to himself. There was something magical about it. Something that brought back all those memories from when the magic was real. *Really* real.

No one ever doubts the beliefs of a child.

"Here you go, lad." Arthur's father said, appearing from the throng with a glass of something amber in each hand. He placed the drink on the table in front of his son and settled back down.

"I said I'm okay, Dad," Arthur said with a grin

"Oh, I thought you said, *okay, Dad*," the older man replied with a slightly wrinkled yet identical grin. Arthur laughed. There was no point in arguing with an older version of yourself; they always knew every move you're going to make.

Arthur took the drink, and the two men tapped their glasses together. Thomas Crazy believed in large measures and no ice. Arthur sipped at the amber liquid and hissed as it burned over his lips and down the back of his throat.

"Thanks," he croaked, already considering how this "one for the road" might make the road rise up to meet him... but not in an Irish blessing kind of way. His head swam, and the edges of his vision blurred, but he was happy. For the first time in a long time, he was happy. So, he kept on drinking.

It's Christmas Eve.

I'm home.

What is there to be unhappy about?

Apart from the ghosts.

And the ghosts of ghosts.

Arthur had stepped off the bus in the cobbled Market Square of his hometown a little over six months ago. He was bruised and beaten, his eyes wide and unblinking. His mum gasped as she answered the door to his knock, and he just stood there, head bowed, awkwardly wondering whether it was still appropriate for a man in his mid-twenties to just open the door and walk into his childhood home. Everything was different, but it wasn't the eight years he'd lived away from home that made it so; it was the previous forty-eight hours. Arthur had changed, and his mum recognised it instantly.

"What happened to you?" she asked but didn't wait for an answer. She threw her arms around her little boy and drew him back into warmth and life and memories.

Arthur cried.

And over many a cup of tea and wonderful home-cooked meals, he found he couldn't quite bring himself to tell his parents why—couldn't tell them the truth. It wasn't that they wouldn't believe him; it was that they would want to.

And that was worse.

That made it all real.

Stories have power. They take lives and shape lives, and they live on long after those lives have ended. They say no one ever really dies while their story is still told, which is both oddly comforting and, depending on how literal you are, terrifying.

At around the same moment that Arthur rapt awkwardly on the door of his family home, thinking no doubt the main part of his story was over, another door opened. It was not a door familiar to the likes of most. To begin with, it wasn't attached to a house or even a wall, but it did lead from *inside* to *out*, and so in essence, it was very much a door.

High on the Yorkshire Dales—a barren and desolate moorland

stretching from horizon to horizon, full of deep shadows and hidden clefts—two stones about as tall as a man stood together as they have done since this part of the world was forged by ice. They were blasted smooth and round-tipped by the constant, scouring winds. Hidden in the foot of a rocky promontory, they were unmolested by the hands of man, but as the sun set, the darkness stretched across thirsty bracken and touched the first. It leached into the rock like ink on a sponge, climbing inexorably up the weathered surface before spilling across the ground and reaching for the other.

A man appeared between the stones as though stepping from the shadows themselves. This was not far from the truth. He was dressed entirely in black, a shade so deep and dark it seemed to be cut from the world itself. A peaked cap was pulled over his eyes, and his mouth cut a thin dark line across a pale face. He was tall and slender yet radiated power, his body poised and held in perfect control.

He was a Shadowman.

He emerged from the space between the stones with a bundle in his arms, and a large chain clenched tight in a gloved hand. Carefully, almost fearfully, he placed his burden on the cold ground and stepped back, holding the chain at arm's length. Ready.

All was still. Even the ever-present wind had died as if holding its breath to see what would happen next. The man knelt and laid the chain between the stones, not once taking his eyes from the inert form before him. He rose once more and then stepped back into shadow, vanishing through the gate.

The thing on the ground stirred, and the chains rattled dully as it turned towards the stones. There was nothing there. It was alone.

Doors open and they close. Many are locked... and for good reason. Some are designed to be a portal from one place to another and others are designed purely to contain. There is a reason we have developed the phrase "lock the door and throw away the key." There are some things that should never be set free.

Four powerful limbs rippled with corded muscle as the creature stretched and then stalked away into the night. It cared not for our rules or sayings. Not when there was hunting to do.

CHAPTER 2

The undergrowth whipped violently around the inert form as it shrank back from the thunderous passing of the Edinburgh to London GNER. Carriage after carriage sped past in a terrifying maelstrom of steel, oil, and thunder, beating like a mechanical heart as the small gap between each section tugged and pulled at the air. He whined. Every instinct told him to run but he had come so far. It had been the longest six months of his existence. The train vanished into whistling silence, interrupting his thoughts, and he rose on shaking legs. This was his chance. He darted onto the tracks, put his head down, and ran.

"Room for one more Crazy?"

Arthur and Thomas rose as Arthur's mum pushed her way through the crowd and took the seat they had saved for her. Thomas kissed his wife on the cheek somewhat clumsily, and Arthur leaned over the table to do the same.

"Hi, Mum," he said.

"Hi, love," she replied, taking off her coat and handing it to her husband, who went to the bar to get her a drink. "How was your day?"

"Not too bad."

"How was the appointment?"

"Not too bad."

"So, you'll see him again?"

"I don't think so."

Mrs. Crazy patted her son on the hand and changed direction. "Are you boys drunk?"

"Not too drunk."

She smiled at that. "Well, has your dad started singing yet?"

"Not yet," laughed Arthur, finally breaking out of the monotone brought on by his drifting thoughts.

"Good. We might actually get to Midnight Mass tonight."

"You know," Arthur said, leaning forward with a smile, "I've never understood that. You never go to church, as far as I'm aware you've got more belief in Odin than you do in God, but you go to Midnight Mass every year. Why?"

"It's the reason for the season," Mrs. Crazy replied with a grin that flashed into her green eyes and showed Arthur a hint of the mischief she mainly held in check. Though he, like his dad, knew it lay just a touch-paper's thickness below the surface.

"But you don't believe that!" he said with a laugh. "You've told me every year since I was a little boy that Christianity nicked it all from the Romans and the pagans. They stole Christmas, you said."

"Of course, they did, darling"—she smiled—"but that was a long time ago. Traditions change. And anyway, I like the songs."

Thomas returned from the bar with a bottle of wine in an ice bucket and a large glass.

"You've got some catching up to do," he said with a grin and laughed at the look his wife gave him as he poured her a very large glass.

Arthur smiled at his parents. He loved them dearly, and all he'd ever wanted was to find someone who made him as happy as they made each other. He thought he'd found that in Wendy, his university sweetheart, but that ended a year ago, and he knew now it had been destined to fail. They wanted different things. They were just two students who lasted slightly longer than most. Hindsight was a wonderful bitch.

At first, the loss had broken Arthur's heart and turned him to drink in a very unhealthy way, but then he met Sarah.

Sarah Brocklebank. The beautiful, wonderful, enticing woman in York. The epicentre of the two-day tornado of chaos.

True, there was a slight age gap of a few hundred years, and the minor inconvenience of her being mortally challenged, but something had grown between them during those two strange nights in the summer, something he had desperately wanted to explore, something that gave him hope.

Two nights of drunkenness, dead people, and destiny. Two nights during which he could speak to ghosts, and his feelings for Sarah seemed more real than all the legends coming to life around them.

But that all ended when he killed her.

Arthur grimaced at the thought—a fleeting moment of pain that flashed across his face and did not go unnoticed by the pair on the other side of the table. That wasn't fair... to his parents or himself. He hadn't killed Sarah. Not really. How can you kill a ghost? In fact, it was more likely he saved her. That's what he'd been trying to do after all. But the problem with releasing a ghost from this realm into another was having absolutely no idea where they went.

Arthur smiled at his mum and dad, but it didn't reach his eyes, and they all knew it. He hid himself behind his drink as he quietly battled his thoughts and memories. It was always like this with too much booze, but he just couldn't say no to his dad.

At the moment of release—at that horrible, final moment back in York—Arthur had felt everything. He felt the truth of each person he "set free." Flashes of their lives had landed in his brain fully formed, like previously suppressed memories suddenly released by hypnosis.

Three friends had been lost that night, three spirits whose extra time had finally come to an end. Steve was the ghost of a man who died by suicide, whose fear of life had been overridden at the last second by a glimmer of hope as the tie about his neck slipped. He desperately didn't want to go in the end. Lord Acaster, who held no fear of death but had been forced to relive the horrors of war over and over again, felt only regret that he would no longer be able to perform his duties to the dead. Then there was Sarah. Kind, loving, playful Sarah who entertained her sisters by playing hide and seek after their mother had died. Cast aside and thrown onto the streets when she lost her father's keys, she descended into madness when cursed to spend eternity searching for them. Sarah, who realized right at the very end, that the love she bore for Arthur overrode the supernatural ties that kept her returning each night to Micklegate Bar.

Sarah loved him.

Arthur knew it. He *felt* it. Among all the pain and suffering, the fear and horror of the creatures that attacked them, and the strange witch-child who controlled them... above it all floated Sarah's love for him. The power he discovered showed him the truth.

It was *this* that tormented him.

Arthur had never believed in fairy tales, ghost stories, or myths. When you have a mother who tells you about Odin at Christmas and Eaoster at Easter, it is difficult to maintain faith without empirical evidence. He loved the stories, but that's all they were: stories... entertainment before bed, fireside tales to warm the long winter nights.

No, Arthur had never believed in ghosts, until he fell in love with one.

The driver smiled as his passengers stumbled off the bus outside Darlington train station in a riot of laughter, flashing mobile phones, and a heady mix of alcohol and perfume. The bright headlights lit the road ahead in a white glow, and one of the women gyrated as if in a spotlight while her friends laughed and ushered her towards the pub, lighting hasty cigarettes as they went.

Good for them, he thought. One more run and he'd be done for the night. Done for the holidays. He'd got lucky this year and managed to get five days off. Sure, it meant working Christmas Eve, but he'd be home by seven and in the pub by eight. He glanced in his mirror. The bus was empty. He looked out of the door and then lowered his gaze. He smiled again.

"Didn't see you there," he said with a grin. "After a lift, are you?"

The passenger was breathing heavily and said nothing, just inclined their head, climbed aboard, and settled into one of the nearest seats without so much as attempting to pay. The driver laughed.

"What the hell," he said, "it's Christmas."

Then he closed the doors and drove away, heading to Richmond.

They were halfway through their pudding when the noises began. In truth, Arthur wasn't one hundred per cent sure they hadn't always been there, but the crowd had grown so loud even the television beside them was drowned out. There was a scream. He was sure of it. His eyes darted anxiously over the mass of people, and his parents turned in their seats to see what he was looking at. The scream sounded again from somewhere beyond the throng of people.

"You heard that, right?" he said to his parents.

"Heard what, mate?" his dad answered.

"There was a scream."

"They're all bloody screaming," the older man answered with a laugh. "Not one of them can carry a tune."

"Don't you start again," warned Mrs. Crazy with a smile and a nudge in her husband's ribs.

She had a red flush on her cheeks and was midway through a tequila and orange juice after seeing off the bottle of wine during the main course. All three Crazys had a warm glow about them, and their own volume had increased with the rest of the pub. There was indeed singing. Loud singing. Thomas Crazy had started it when "Fairytale of New York" came on over the speakers.

"They always get the words wrong if some bugger doesn't lead them," he'd said, then proceeded to stand in his place and conduct the customers of the pub like some bugger.

This type of behaviour used to cause a prickling embarrassment to crawl over Arthur's face when he was younger. He'd sink into his seat and pray for the earth to swallow him, but kids and adults see the world differently. He loved it now. His dad had the kind of magnetic personality that drew people to him. He had never seen anyone angry with his dad. Or rather, he had never seen anyone *remain* angry with his dad.

"It wasn't that sort of scream," Arthur said, leaning up in his seat to get a better view.

In true cinematographic style, there was another scream at just that moment, but it came from a young woman pointing to the ceiling with her overflowing glass of wine as she belted out "It's Christmas!" at the top of her voice.

"There's your scream, lad," his father laughed.

Arthur thought he might be right, but he kept glancing over their shoulders just the same. He'd heard screams like that before. There was a strange quality to them, something... different. He wasn't scared or worried; he was excited. Desperately, painfully, and hopefully excited.

CHAPTER 3

It was Christmas Eve in the city of York, and a queen sat on a throne looking down her beautiful hooked nose at the man slowly descending to his knees before her. She hid a slight smile behind a delicate hand as he let out a groan. To say that he was old would be like saying Stonehenge had been around for a bit. Leaning heavily on a shining sword, the man's skeletal fingers turned white on the hilt, and beads of sweat appeared on his forehead, tracing their way over the ridges of red flesh into his white beard. The queen was almost certain she heard creaking during his stately descent.

"Your Majesty," he croaked and bowed his head. Long white hair cascaded over his face, and the queen couldn't help herself. She chuckled, and her eyes flashed with mischief.

"You may rise," she commanded.

The man exhaled in what could have been a curse but stopped himself from mumbling. His head dipped slightly, and his shoulders sagged, but he moved, the sword shaking as his knuckles tightened. It was like watching a pile of coat hangers disentangle and rise slowly to become a man. A very old, very thin man, but a man all the same. His clothes didn't so much hang off him as hold him together. He was dressed like a monk, but the large belt around his waist held the scabbard for his sword and an assortment of other blades and pouches. The queen wondered at the miracle of that belt. Perhaps staying where it was out of sheer sartorial willpower.

"It pleases us that you be seated," she said as his bones finally clicked as straight as they ever could, and she nodded to one of the courtiers who rushed forward with a chair, placing it beside the elderly man, who, with some difficulty, was trying to get the sword back into the scabbard. The point kept missing. He swore under his breath and squinted, his tongue poking from the side of his mouth as he finally got it in. He let the sword drop home, and the weight of it pulled him sideways as the hilt hit his hip. He staggered, grumbled, and used the momentum to collapse into the seat where he panted, mopping his red brow with his long white beard.

"We believe you did not arrive in our city on your own, sir," the queen said. "Where is your companion?"

"He's parking the car, Your Majesty," replied the man. He had managed to get some of his breath back, and the colour in his face had faded from beetroot red to somewhere slightly south of crimson. At the very least, he was no longer sweating, though his long silver hair and beard glistened with moisture.

"You arrived in a car?" the queen remarked in surprise. "What are they like?" She leaned forward on the throne, her eyes bright with interest. "We have only ever seen them from the windows of this place, travelling at enormous speed, faster than the swiftest horse we would say. And some of them are impossibly large. Carriages for hundreds of people."

"Buses, Your Majesty," said the man by way of explanation.

"Buses," she mused. "We would very much like to journey on buses, but alas, our duty ties us to our manor."

The queen had died over four hundred years ago and had been surprised to find her ghostly form materialize in a place she had only ever visited once, a long-time prior, before it all went wrong. She remembered her death well—the imprisonment, the boat ride down the Thames in shackles, staring up into the unseeing eyes of her lover's dismembered head impaled upon the bridge.

She had died with his name on her lips. The ultimate betrayal to the one who ordered her death. "I die a queen, but I would rather die the wife of…" She closed her eyes as the axe fell and opened them again a moment later, staring this time in detached fascination at a familiar face looking up from a basket. She looked younger than she expected, the mirrors in the palace no match for the sight of her own eyes, or whatever memory now passed for eyes.

The queen had stood and turned to face the crowd. They flickered and wavered in the air, already faint and indistinct, but one man stepped forward, dressed entirely in black with a book in one hand and a blade in the other. He was more real than anything she had ever seen.

"Follow me," he said, not unkindly, and she had. They passed through the crowd like smoke, and he opened a large wooden door, holding it for the queen with a stiff bow. She dipped her head and passed through, and when she straightened again, she was here. In the Manor. Far to the north. In the place that held the fondest memories of her short life. And here she had remained, fated to spend eternity.

Of the many amazing things the queen discovered over the next few centuries, it was the existence of the few people—living, breathing people—who could interact with the dead that fascinated her the most. In her own life, she would have disregarded them as charlatans or deviants, and yet just six months ago, she had met Arthur, a young man who could not only talk with and touch the dead, but who also held the power to free them from their eternal wanderings.

Now, here she was again, sitting on a throne that held no substance in the living world, talking to an ancient man who still breathed, still sweated, still ached… still lived. And there was another. He had a companion.

She looked up at a commotion by the door. A man entered, and she blinked. She looked at the seated man and then back. They were absolutely identical. The newcomer strode forward, and her phantom entourage bustled out of his way as he came to stand beside his twin. He looked at the queen and smiled, brown eyes flashing beneath enormous grey eyebrows.

"Sorry, I'm late, love. S'a bugger t' park int city."

The bus rolled down the winding street and pulled up the narrow passage of French Gate, slowing as it entered the town. It rumbled over the cobbles of Market Place before coming to a stop outside the Town Hall pub. A single passenger got off.

"Merry Christmas," the driver called but received no answer. He didn't mind. He felt like he'd done a good deed, and anyway, his shift was nearly over. He closed the door and began to whistle as he drove away.

CHAPTER 4

"Don't stay out all night," Mrs. Crazy said to her son as she kissed him goodbye beneath the spire in the centre of the marketplace. The obelisk was covered in a curtain of small yellow lights and stood like a stone Christmas tree in the middle of the square. The town's real tree sat nestled beneath Holy Trinity Chapel, probably grumbling at being upstaged on its only annual outing.

"I won't, Mam. I'm just going to go for one more. See if any of the guys from school are out."

"Will you come to Midnight Mass?"

Arthur gave his mum a look that expressed exactly how he felt about that, but his look was no match for hers. She'd had longer to practice.

"Yeah, I'll be there," he conceded.

"Arthur, are you—" but whatever his mum was going to ask was interrupted by his dad singing at the top of his voice.

Thomas Crazy appeared from behind the obelisk in full voice, one arm on the stone, the other thrust dramatically to the sky as he belted The Pogues' classic "Fairytale of New York" to the world. Somewhere in the distance, a loud voice echoed around the town square in reply, much to Thomas's delight. He sang, or rather shouted, even louder, a look of sheer rapture on his face.

At that precise moment, the church bells chimed the 8:00 p.m. curfew, a tradition the town had kept going for many years, long after the rest of the country had given up. Thomas Crazy roared with laughter as the distant voice finished the chorus, and he danced down the steps to grab his wife by the waist, swinging her round in a wild foxtrot. "Curfew, my love. Time for the old people to go home."

"Who are you calling old?" she chided him with a smile.

Mr. Crazy hugged his wife and turned to his son. "Don't stay out all night," he said. "Christmas tomorrow. Best day of the year. You better have been a good boy or Santa might not visit."

"Behave, Dad."

"I always do"—his father grinned—"that's why Santa visits me."

He threw an arm over his wife as they walked over the cobbles towards the Market Hall, pausing to let an empty bus trundle past on the narrow road. Arthur smiled as they vanished out of sight. Rummaging in the pocket of his long black coat for his cigarettes, he mumbled as he lit one, then took a welcome drag in the cold Christmas air.

"Bloody twenty-six years old and still hiding cigarettes from my mum," he said to himself as he sat down on the stone steps at the base of the obelisk, the cold instantly seeping through his jeans. Arthur looked around the marketplace, the obelisk at his back, the old church in front with its round clock-face glowing like an eye over the streets. Tall houses lined the square on four sides with the church in the centre, now a museum for the local Green Howards Regiment. Over the rooftops behind the church nestled the rolling hills of the Yorkshire Dales, a dark smudge at the base of a dark sky.

Arthur sat with his elbows on his knees and smiled to himself. He liked being back, but it didn't feel like home. Not really. All the memories of growing up here seemed as though they belonged to someone else. He had made his home in York. *That* place felt like his. This just felt like his mum and dad's. There was something strange about leaving the town you grew up in and then returning as a visitor, almost as if you were trespassing on someone else's turf. Even stranger was the realisation that the *someone else* is a past version of yourself.

Arthur looked around and sighed. What was he going to do now? None of his friends were in town. He'd checked. He'd lied to his mum because he just didn't want to go home. Not yet. He didn't want to sit in front of the fire sharing a scotch with his dad and watching *Die Hard* after whatever Christmas Eve special gameshow had finished.

He paused.

Why not? he thought. That actually sounds pretty great. Why say no? Perhaps he just didn't want his parents to look at him with pity in their eyes as he sat beneath the three threadbare stockings hanging above the fire? Perhaps it was similar to his feelings about the town—the lurking sense that the happy memories belonged to someone else, and that going back was the same as defeat.

Or maybe he was just feeling sorry for himself and should stop being such a whiney little bitch?

As the thought entered his sluggish mind, Arthur knew he'd finally hit the nail on the head. He'd been feeling sorry for himself for the better part of a year now—half after Wendy left and half after the... incident—lamenting the fact he no longer had the gift that "made him special." The screams in the pub had brought a glimmer of delight to the lost young man—hope even. He had *longed* for it to be the screams of the dead.

Another part of Arthur's brain decided to chip in then—a part slightly more rational—and it told him in no uncertain terms how fucked up that was.

"Bugger this," Arthur said out loud. "I'm going home."

On the moors, the creature prowled. It was well beyond the gate now, and it had grown. Four powerful limbs rippled with corded muscle as it stalked through the night. It wasn't noiseless, although it could be when hunting, but it had recently fed and so it crunched across the frozen bracken with all the arrogance of one who knows no threat. Over the course of the last few months, it had left a trail of horrifying carcasses. Sheep, pheasants, foxes, and even a few cats. It especially liked cats.

People were beginning to talk. Rumours and dark superstition spread through remote farms like searching frost. Nothing killed like that. Nothing natural caused such horrendous wounds. And there were never any teeth marks, just the brutal work of rending, jagged claws. How could there be teeth marks when there was no head?

Lights glimmered in the distance, and the beast moved steadily towards them.

CHAPTER 5

"Archibald and Alexander at yer service." The man bowed with slightly more ease than his brother. He didn't bother to kneel, either out of discourtesy or pragmatism, but the bow was deep enough to cause a groan on its own, so the queen didn't mind. She sensed some of her courtiers bristling and wondered what her darling Lord Acaster would have made of it all if he were here. A sad smile crossed her face, and she shook her head to clear the thought of her absent friend.

"And we are at yours," she replied. "How might the crown assist?"

Alexander, who remained seated, cleared his throat with a noise like a dog coughing up a wasp and leaned forward. He paused—either to add a sense of tension to the moment or to catch his breath—then spoke in a low and earnest voice, each syllable rasping over his ancient white teeth.

"We have travelled long and far, my lady. Across mountains, rivers, and dales, through forest and foam, we have struggled to reach your side—"

"Aye, the A1 can be a bugger at this time o' year," grumbled Archibald, extracting a clay pipe from somewhere about his person and thumbing dark tobacco into the end. Alexander rolled his eyes and continued.

"We were called from our long slumber nearly half a year hence when the stars and planets aligned, and the shadows grew and spread from the dark vaults of their prison. We heard word of darkness descending in the north and we feared the worst. But we guardians have hope, for it is known that when the darkness spreads, a single light can be glimpsed across countless miles."

"Makes sense," said Archibald, striking a match and touching the flame to the end of his pipe. He sucked his cheeks until his face turned red with the effort, and smoke curled in tendrils up his face and through his hair. Finally, he breathed out a long plume of smoke and collapsed into a fit of coughing. His seated twin waited impatiently while Archibald hacked up a loud, wet cough and banged on his chest. "Bugger!" he said, finally, and waved his brother on.

Alexander rose from his seat in a surprisingly fluid motion and stepped forward.

"It is promised," he said, "that in a time of great peril, the saviour of this kingdom will rise again, draw forth his sword, and lead the forces of light against the forces of darkness! When all hope seems lost, he will return. When the darkness breaks the bonds that bind it, he shall be there! At the end of times and in our greatest peril, a saviour will step from the shadows and lead us to the light!" He was shouting now, his arms raised like a conductor as spittle flew through the air in sharp points of exclamation. "And we, my brother and I, have long waited to serve this valiant knight by bringing unto his hands the weapon of his destiny, the blade forged from starlight and earth's fire, the steel of the saviour! The—"

"We've come for the sword, pet," said Archibald with a wink.

Alexander swore.

"The sword?"

"Aye, pet. The sword."

Silence entered the room with as much force as a drumbeat.

"Pet?" the Queen said, slowly.

Alexander hung his head.

Archibald grinned.

There were some people for whom normal social conventions were simply strange eccentricities cared about by others. Archibald was one of these men. It made no difference to him if he stood before a queen or a washerwoman, a warrior or a waif. He saw no reason to change the way he spoke on account of the quality of their clothes. "We're all naked underneath" was another of his favourite aphorisms, one his brother fervently hoped he would keep to himself.

The silence stretched on, and then, confronted with his implacable face, the queen laughed. Loud and long. A lifetime (plus change) surrounded by sycophants had grown tiresome. Ephemeral tears rolled down her cheeks as a polite giggle turned into a chuckle, and then, via the medium of a snort, became a roar. Struggling to catch her breath, she patted her chest, wiped her eyes, and gasped.

"Oh, you wonderful man!" she managed with a twinkle in her eye that Alexander had seen all too often. Archibald inclined his head to the queen while his brother mumbled something that could have been "duck cake" but probably wasn't. The lady dabbed at her eyes with a petite silk handkerchief and asked, "Of what sword do you speak?"

"Big pointy one," Archibald said with a grin.

Alexander sighed and sat back in the seat. He crossed his legs with some effort and smoothed the folds of his robe as the queen stepped down from the dais and strode towards the brothers. It was always like this—insufferable. He'd been working on that speech for decades. That young chap in London had helped him with it—what's-his-name? The up-and-comer treading the boards? Ian McKellen! That's the fella. Promising thespian. Now *there* was a man who understood occasion. But no! Archibald comes blustering in like a drunk in a library, swears at the kindly lady stacking the shelves, and proceeds to tell a story to the mother's group that would turn milk sour. And they all love him for it.

If Alexander ever spoke to anyone that way, he just knew the result would be different. But hundreds—he paused—*thousands* of years of the same had shown him the sheer futility of complaining. No one ever listened. So, he just complained to himself. It was enough to drive a sane man crazy.

"Tell me, gentlemen..." said the Queen as she stood next to the brothers. She was taller than Alexander first thought, and he wished he'd stood up when she approached. He craned his neck, but she was looking at Archibald. "How is it that *this* is possible?" She prodded a finger towards the standing brother and poked him delicately in the chest. She gasped as she felt the pressure of flesh against her own form. "What sorcery is this that can make the dead and the living touch? You *are* living are you not?" she added.

"Oh, aye," said Archibald. "You've got yer full English 'ere, love. Two sausages and the blood pudding still fresh."

The queen roared with laughter again, and Alexander felt the life-proving flush of mortified embarrassment creep up his neck and through his cheeks. He had to intervene.

"It is entirely possible for the dead to touch the living, Your Majesty. It just takes... practice."

"Yes, of course, but there is something very unusual here," she said, poking the man in the side of the head and giggling as his silver hair moved beneath her touch. "You are not entirely mortal, are you, sir? The chair you so readily recline upon is, of course, not of your world."

Alexander's eyes opened wide, and he tapped the sides of the wooden seat.

"Don't think about it too hard, lad," his brother grumbled a warning.

"Too late," said Alexander and fell in a heap through a chair that suddenly became even less substantial than smoke. "Bugger."

"Now that is fascinating!" exclaimed the queen, kneeling beside the old man to peer closely at the chair, which to her now seemed to be sharing the same space as his stomach. She touched it delicately and raised an eyebrow as her fingers pressed against solid wood. Then with her other hand, she slowly touched Alexander. He, too, felt solid. "Fascinating," she breathed once more. "How is this possible?"

Archibald grasped the pipe between his teeth and spoke around it. "The rules work both ways. It just takes concentration. Like those islander lads who walk across hot coals. They don't feel a thing if they're concentrating on somet' else, but you can bet your arse to a barn dance their feet will burn like buggery if they look down. Silly sod looked down." He nodded to his brother who glared up at him. "In a manner of speaking, like," Archibald added with a grin.

Alexander shuffled unceremoniously to his feet with a sound like someone trying to unfold a pretzel. Then, he kicked at the chair. On the second attempt, his foot connected, and it skittered across the tiled floor with a loud scrape. He smiled with satisfaction, then turned to the queen.

"Sometimes, we all lose concentration, Your Majesty," he said with a small bow of the head. "We have had a long journey. Please forgive our intrusion and our impertinence." There was a heavy emphasis on the word *our*, and it was punctuated with a sharp look at his brother. "But we really must know where the sword is so that we might return it to the one who may wield it in these dark times."

"Yes, the sword," said the queen. She was thinking very quickly and trying to gather all the threads together at once. An idea was forming, and she almost dared not embrace it in case the thrill enveloped her completely. She rested one hand on the chair, the other on Alexander, and shook her head slightly as she tapped her fingers on both. "We imagine this sword is of special significance and holds some sort of wondrous power?"

"Yes, Your Majesty," the brothers said together.

"The type of sword handed down through the royal families of this great country for centuries?"

"Yes, Your Majesty."

"And one suspects that it was lost, oh, let's say roughly five hundred years ago when someone hid it to spite a gluttonous buffoon who didn't so much sit on the throne as fill it?"

"Your Majesty?" Archibald asked with a raised eyebrow.

"Big pointy one?"

"Aye, that's it."

"I gave it away."

"Shite!"

"But I know where it is."

CHAPTER 6

The wind whistled cold down the narrow street and whipped about Arthur's legs and arms. He shivered and thrust his hands deep into his pockets. The pulsing bass of the town's bars throbbed in the night, muffled now by the ancient stone houses that sat in a huddle beneath the grand castle, standing like a sentinel over them all. Huge, immovable, and unwavering. A symbol of Arthur's childhood.

"That's our castle," his mother used to say.

"You're always safe if you can see the castle," echoed his dad.

Arthur paused to watch a strange whirlwind of chip paper and crisp packets dance across the cobbles and wondered if he could be bothered picking them up and finding a bin. As he strode forward to do so, a sensation like a cool breeze on a hot day settled across his shoulders. He shivered involuntarily and looked around. There were eyes on him—he was sure of it. Just as you know when you're not alone in a dark room, Arthur knew someone was watching him.

He spun on the spot, the litter forgotten. The soundtrack of celebration in the town lowered to a dull pulse in the background. There was laughter in the night, the clink of glass on glass, muted singing, shouts, and swearing. All the noises that made the town seem like a living creature nestled beneath the castle were still there, but they came from far away. Arthur cast his eyes around the silent square beneath the towering keep and shivered. It was a crossroads of sorts, marking the spot where Tower Street ended, and Castle Wynd began. Four roads in. Four roads out.

And it was deserted.

There was nothing there but shadows and the huddled forms of three cars glistening with frost, parked at the top of the steep lane that led to his parents' house. A squat white cottage sat on the corner, and the streetlight glowed from the walls, though it was weak and fighting a losing battle against the night.

Arthur turned again. Quickly. Hoping to catch the watcher. A surge of adrenaline coursed through the sludge of alcohol in his veins.

"Anyone there?" he asked of the dark.

No answer. Not even an echo. The streets swallowed his voice and Arthur staggered. The sounds of life and laughter faded, leaching away into the cold stones, and, because the world some-times loves dramatic poetry, the streetlight above his head flick-ered and died. Arthur looked up, and the castle looked down. The colossal stone structure swayed against the inky black sky. He reached out a shaking hand to steady himself against the nearest car and took a deep breath, closing his eyes as he did.

Unseen, a silent figure padded into the square behind him.

"Woof," said the dog.

Arthur yelped, startled, and fell onto the bonnet of the car, setting the alarm off before landing in a heap on the cold ground.

If Arthur had been in control of his senses, he might have given more thought to that bark. As far as canine communication went, it was both perfectly accurate and stupendously false at the same time, but Arthur had no hope of figuring out why. Not yet at least. That probably had something to do with the fact his fingers were now in his ears trying to block out the sound of the car alarm as it shattered the night and bounced off the many stone surfaces with accusatory sharpness. His heart raced from equal parts shock and embarrassment.

He swore and looked down. Then he swore again.

After everything he'd been through, he'd been scared by a scruffy little Yorkshire terrier with white socks, a burnished copper chest, and the obligatory inside-out ear. Curtains of dirty brown hair hung over big sad eyes as they looked pleadingly at Arthur.

The dog wagged its tail. Arthur gave it the finger.

He wasn't proud of that, but he was sitting on the cold stones leaning against a car on Christmas Eve after setting the alarm off, so there wasn't much to be proud of. He certainly wasn't proud of the next bit either.

When the lights came on in Mr. Allott's cottage, Arthur scrambled to his feet, and legged it.

The dog looked at the young man's quickly vanishing form as he bolted down the cobbled street and shook its head. The rogue ear popped in and immediately popped back out again because some things are so ingrained, they can never be changed... much like this: the man was running, so the dog gave chase.

A rthur looked over his shoulder and saw the excited animal bounding over the cobbles. For some reason he couldn't quite explain, he felt compelled to run faster as though to get away, and so he bolted out of the alley, across the small car park at the top of New Road, and ducked down the narrow lane that led to Castle Walk. He wasn't running from the dog, not really; he was running from the car alarm. Mr. Allott was a right miserly old git, and he'd never hear the end of it if he saw it was Arthur who set it off.

But the dog was chasing, and when you're being chased, you run. Though, Arthur quickly realized that he had failed to learn one very important lesson from days past: never run on a belly full of beer.

He stopped suddenly, but the contents of his stomach did not. They erupted from his mouth in a plume that would probably have been impressive if delivered in slow motion but, thankfully, was not. Arthur spat and wiped his mouth with the back of his sleeve as he staggered over to a nearby bench and collapsed, closing his eyes and resting his head against the stone of the castle. He groaned softly. Beside him, the dog cocked its head and said, "Woof?"

Arthur looked down.

The dog looked up and wagged its tail.

"You said *woof*," Arthur said groggily.

"No, I didn't," said the dog.

Arthur stared for a moment, then his brain decided it'd had enough. It closed up shop, pulled down the shutters, and turned out the lights, leaving his chin to drop to his chest as he passed out. He began to snore. The dog cocked its head to one side, wagged its tail, and then whined a little. It stood on all fours and shook itself before padding around in a small circle and settling down beside Arthur. Fine, he could wait. It had been a very long day, and a nap would be nice.

CHAPTER 7

High on the Long Causeway that stretches over the barren moors of the Yorkshire Dales, the Tan Hill Inn braced itself against the biting wind. It was difficult to tell where the mists ended and the clouds began. Those people who, for whatever bizarre reason, had chosen to spend their Christmas Eve in a tent at the highest pub in the British Isles, were buffeted relentlessly by howling and whistling winds. They say there is a wonderful comfort to be had in the ebb and flow of canvas on a wild winter's night, which just goes to show that people will come up with all sorts of nonsense rather than admit their mistakes.

Zips remained firmly fastened and fervent prayers were offered to whoever might listen that pegs would stay fixed into the frozen peat beside the meagre shelter of the large rock formation at the rear of the pub. Small lights glowed from inside multi-coloured canvases, and dark shadows danced in the night as the tents moved violently in the high winds, here, at the top of the world.

There was one blessing to be taken from such a wild and tumultuous night, though it was a blessing none of the inhabitants of the tents would, thankfully, ever be aware of. The thunderous whip and crack of the wind against canvas was more than enough to drown out the sound of any dark creature stalking on giant black claws towards the light of the pub. The chain fastened around its ragged and open neck dragged and rattled, unheard, across the ground as it made its way between the tents.

~

"You're a dog," said Arthur as he re-entered consciousness by stating the bleeding obvious.

"Yes," said the dog.

Arthur didn't know what to do with this information and so he sat and slowly lit another cigarette. He had fervently hoped, for over half a year now, that his powers would come back and that he would be able to see ghosts and communicate with the dead once again, but talking to a dog wasn't exactly what he'd had in mind. His head swam as he sat up, and his mouth tasted exactly like mouths taste after throwing up a few pints of beer and some scotch. He hunched forward and looked around. He knew instantly where he was, though he couldn't quite remember how he came to be there.

Richmond Castle sat proudly atop a steep promontory with the river Swale roaring violently below. The high curtain walls circled the top of the hill, and Arthur found himself at the south-west corner beneath the remains of a tall, ruined tower. A cross-roads again. Castle Walk continued to his left, running beneath the outer wall and tracing the contours of the land and river, eventually leading to his parents' house. To his right was the road he had run down from the town, and just in front of him, a steep wooden staircase vanished down the embankment to the river far below.

Arthur sat on a bench beneath the postern gate, the hidden, secondary entrance to the castle, and tried to collect his thoughts. As a teen, Arthur and his friends had used this bench to climb onto the lower part of the wall and squeeze through the thick brambles and bushes to an iron gate sunk into the ground below the castle. It was here they would drink and smoke and laugh and fumble, safely hidden from the watching eyes of the neighbours and tourists. There could be anything in there, but from the path, you wouldn't know it.

Arthur stood up, and the dog whined on the bench beside him. Arthur sat back down. His mind was in turmoil. He looked to his left where Castle Walk stretched into darkness, but there was no one there. He looked to his right, craning his neck to see down the narrow and dimly lit lane of Castle Hill, which was also completely empty. He stood on the bench and pushed his head through the bushes, parting them with his arms to make sure no one sat in that hidden spot. It too, was empty, save for the usual array of abandoned bottles and crisp packets.

Arthur and the dog were completely alone.

"Not a ventriloquist then," he said, his hazy investigations completed. The dog tilted its head and somehow managed to raise one eyebrow. Arthur looked at it. "I mean, you really are talking, aren't you?"

"Yes," said the dog. "Sorry," it added, thinking it should offer more.

"But your lips don't move properly."

"I don't know what to tell you," said the dog.

"You shouldn't be able to tell me anything!" the man snapped, and he groaned as a wave of nausea washed over him.

Arthur's already tenuous grip on reality was slowly slipping, and he felt a strange compulsion to run down to the river and submerge himself in the icy water. That would clear his head. Sure, he'd probably die in what was, after all, the fastest flowing river in England, but at least his headache would be gone. He stood up suddenly and shook himself out, walking into the centre of the dark path, placing his hands on his head, and stretching to open his lungs.

He breathed the cold Yorkshire air and then undid his good work by lighting another cigarette.

The dog leapt down from the seat and trotted over to the iron railing that lined the path. Arthur watched as it sniffed one of the poles, then cocked a leg. When it was finished, it shook itself out and padded around in a little celebratory circle.

"Mine," it said.

The small animal turned to face Arthur and sat down, big eyes staring from beneath cascading curtains of lighter hair. It tilted its head, and somehow, Arthur knew it was about to talk again. Before it could begin, he lifted a hand and cut it off.

Without really knowing why, Arthur wandered over to the pole, unzipped the fly of his jeans, and peed all over the dog's meagre deposit. He grinned in satisfaction as he completely washed away any sign of the dog's urine with his own steaming stream. He shook himself and then turned back to the dog, the cigarette hanging loosely between his lips and a smug grin on his face. Whatever he was expecting from his unspoken challenge was not the response he got. The little dog rolled its eyes and sighed.

"God, you're a dick," it said. "Did that make you feel like a big man?"

Arthur was speechless, his momentary arrogance immediately stripped away and replaced with a flush of embarrassment.

"Sorry," he mumbled.

"S'alright," grinned the dog. "Blame it on the booze. I'm guessing from the smell you're hammered again?"

"Wha? What do you mean *again*? Do we—" Arthur paused here, knowing full well how ridiculous the end of this sentence was going to be.

Do we know each other? *That's right*, he thought, *you've forgotten about* this *talking dog because you've met so many of them and they all just blend into one after a while. I really am a dick.* He looked at the small animal, and something fired in the back of his brain. Drunk neurons flashed and fizzed as they tried to shake metaphorical hands with one another.

Arthur knelt down with his eyes wide, and the dog padded slowly towards him. The big brown eyes were downcast and flickered up almost shyly from beneath the curtained hair of his brow.

As the animal approached Arthur, it sat down and slowly, nervously, lifted a white-socked paw to the man it had been searching for since the moment it was born. Arthur took the offered paw and shook it gently.

"What's your name?" he whispered breathlessly.

The dog whined once, a soft, plaintive cry and said, "Steve."

CHAPTER 8

"We are coming with you," the queen declared.

"Who is?" Archibald replied.

"We."

"Who's we?"

"We... the queen."

"And?"

"And what?"

"Who else?"

"Just we."

"You've lost me, pet."

"It's the royal we," interrupted Alexander with a shake of his head. He knew full well that Archibald was playing with the young woman, but royalty was royalty and should be treated as such. Even when dead.

"Please, explain what happened to the sword, Your Majesty," he asked with a small bow, heading off any further nonsense. "We have travelled to London, Lincoln, and Pontefract before receiving word that the sacred blade may well be in the Manor House of York. It is of the utmost importance that we find it in order to deliver it into the hands of the one who can save us from the vile darkness that has been growing err this last year."

"Vile darkness?" said the queen. "Of what do you speak?"

"A force has awoken," said Alexander. "Surely you felt it, Your Majesty. At the height of summer, a great darkness was loosed upon this city. The ripples reached us all the way on the south coast. We would have arrived sooner, but we had to search for the sword first, not knowing that it was here all this time."

"I said it would be here, lad," Archibald said cheerfully.

Alexander ignored him and looked at the queen. Realisation dawned on the young lady, and she smiled at the twins, lifting her head high and looking down her angular nose at them both. They were talking about the witch-girl set free by the strange man, Arthur, nearly half a year ago.

"Oh, you need not worry, gentlemen. That danger has passed. The girl is no more." The queen thought of the brave young Arthur and how he had rectified his own mistake by sending the evil child from this domain. Her thoughts turned to the darling Lord Acaster, who was also a victim of the final conflict. She sighed. "It took a heavy toll, but the price has been paid. We are free from her evil once and for all. She has left this realm."

Alexander shifted his feet and scratched at his chin, unsure how to explain what he knew, what both he and his brother had learned long ago in a time before the country became so layered with stone and steel. As usual, Archibald had no such compunction.

"What about the dog?" the big man asked.

"What dog?" asked the queen.

"The barghest," said Alexander in a solemn voice.

The queen gasped and looked around the grand room. She had banished all her retainers from the manor hall as soon as the discussion began, and she now sat alone with the ancient twins, holding tight to a bunch of roses as Alexander spoke. For once, his brother remained quiet, sitting still, and smoking his pipe while listening through a great cloud of grey-blue smoke.

"You know the name, my lady?" Alexander asked. The queen nodded.

"The city of York has known of such a creature," she said. "It has sometimes made its way into the walls and prowled through the narrow snickelways and wynds. Though it hasn't been seen for some time. Lord Acaster always—" Her voice cut off with a sob as she thought of the absent giant. He had patrolled the city's dark places with his cats and made sure of their safety.

"Then you know how dangerous these creatures are," Alexander continued gently when the queen said no more. "You say the witch-child has been defeated, and that may be the case, but the war is not over until all the minions of darkness are forced back behind the gates."

"I don't understand," said the queen.

"When the witch-child was freed from her cage, she wasn't the only one released back into this world. You can feel it, can't you? You can feel the increased activity. Feel the darkness spreading. My brother and I are not part of your realm, not truly, and yet we can feel that the world has changed. The darkness spreads. It builds against the ancient barriers and finds cracks between worlds. When the witch-child broke free from her shackles, she set certain wheels in motion."

"Aye, she had a long time to plan," Archibald said darkly, "and she made certain... insurances."

"What do you mean?" asked the queen.

"A new barghest has risen," Alexander said. "We don't know where or even when, but we know it is somewhere near, and it is growing in power. They are dangerous, evil creatures, portents of death and destruction, harbingers of doom!"

"Steady on, lad," said Archibald, laying a hand on his brother's shoulder and lowering him back into his seat. "You'll do yerself a mischief. He's not wrong though," he said to the queen. "They're reet evil buggers, everyone one of 'em. Do you know why they're called barghests?"

The queen composed herself, she was frightened, which is a strange sensation to have when you're already dead, she gripped the roses tightly to her chest and tried to appear regal.

"We do not," she admitted, "though one might infer that the name derives from *burh* and *ghest*—a town ghost, perhaps?"

The twins were impressed.

"That's one interpretation," said Alexander, stroking his long grey beard. "And there are certainly barghests in many towns and cities. York has had its fair share as you say."

"Aye, and the one over Whitby way is a right bugger!" grumbled Archibald.

"Quite," said Alexander. "The Germanic people call the creature *berg-geist* or *bar-geist*—mountain ghost or bear ghost—but in the south, in Wales, they simply call it *Cwn Annwn*. The Dog of Hell."

"These are not all the same creatures," said Archibald, "though they now share the same name."

"We believe the witch-child has let loose a Dog of Hell. The worst of its kind."

"How?" gasped the queen.

"We don't rightly know," Archibald admitted. "There are some deals that should never be struck, some creatures never to be trifled with, but that girl has never been one to obey the blasted rules."

"Aye," Alexander said. "And it will look for her. It will search out the witch-child and kill everything in its path."

"But it won't find her," the queen said, a sudden, desperate smile appearing on her face. "She's gone. Arthur banished them all. Her and her minions."

"Arthur?" Alexander exclaimed in surprise. He turned to his brother, who had sat up straight and leaned forward at the mention of the name. "The man who smote the ruin of the witch-child was called Arthur?" he asked, his voice low and quiet.

"Yes," said the queen, not quite understanding their sudden agitation. A great smile had spread across the face of the normally taciturn Alexander, and his brother slapped him roughly on the back in jubilation.

"Ruddy hell! I think we're on the right track this time, brother!" he said and took a deep draw on his pipe.

"It would certainly explain the power of the call to wake us from our slumber after a mere fifty years. Where is Arthur now, Your Majesty?" said Alexander, barely able to contain the excitement in his voice. "Is he still in the city?"

"No," said the queen, "he left after he defeated the child."

"Do you know where he went?" pressed the brother, rising forward in his seat, all courtly manners now forgotten. "It must be him," he hissed to his brother before turning back to the queen. "This Arthur defeated the witch-child. He is the one that was promised. It was his power we felt after the darkness was released. We must find the sword and take it to him. Only then will the dark creatures be shackled once more. Only then will this nightmare end. Only then—" Alexander stopped mid-proclamation. He was standing again, spittle flying from his mouth as he declared himself to the room, but something had interrupted him once more. This time, it wasn't his brother. This time, it was the queen's laughter. Her beautiful face shone bright and clear in the dim light of the manor hall as she chuckled to herself.

"He already has the sword. It was to Arthur we gave the blade."

The outer door of the Tan Hill Inn opened and spilled more people into the thick, swirling mists of the high pass. The band had finished playing, and time had been called at the bar. It was Christmas Eve and time for those who weren't staying to make the long journey home. Cars crunched cautiously over the gravel car park and eased out onto the Long Causeway towards the A66 or in the opposite direction along the Pennine Way towards Reeth and Richmond. Twin lights of white or red shone dimly in the thick mist as they vanished out of sight. Laughter and singing carried far across the top of the moors, and the night was punctuated by sharp flashes of camera phones as people tried and failed to capture the ethereal views of the high country on their hand-held devices.

Tom Larochelle looked down at his own phone and stamped his feet in the cold. He showed the screen to his friend, and they grinned at each other. The famous hanging sign of the Tan Hill Inn stood out eerily between two old cartwheels while the world around glowed orange from where the flash illuminated the mists.

"That's cool," said Eric. "The guys back home won't believe where we are."

"I want to get a photo of the pub from over the road."

"You won't see anything."

"Maybe, but it'll still be cool. The time we spent Christmas Eve at the highest pub in the United Kingdom."

Eric pulled a joint from his pocket and lit it, passing it to his friend. "Happy Christmas, man."

"Yeah mate, happy Christmas."

They bumped fists and passed the joint back, staring into the swirling mists.

"You want this photo then?"

"Yeah, let's do it. It'll look awesome, and when are we ever going to get this chance again?"

"All right, but make it quick, yeah. It's bloody freezing out here."

"*Bloody*?! You're beginning to sound like an Englishman," Tom laughed.

"Let's just get going."

The two Americans walked swiftly across the main road and onto the dirt path on the opposite side. They could barely see a hand in front of them, but they knew where they were.

And so did the hound that padded across the marshy ground on silent claws.

CHAPTER 9

Arthur reached down in amazement and picked up the small creature to get a better look at him. His hands nearly fit all the way around the tiny body.

"Woah, Woah, what are you—" began Steve in protest, but the residue of his human self was fighting a losing battle against his new canine inclinations, and there was something deeply wonderful about being held by his friend. His best friend. He whined, and Arthur brought the Yorkie up to his face so they could look into each other's eyes.

"You're Steve?"

"Yes," said the dog.

"*Steve,* Steve?"

"Yes."

"Steve from York, Steve?"

"How many Steves do you know?" said Steve the dog in exasperation, lifting a leg and scratching behind his ear.

"It really is you," Arthur gasped with a smile and a catch of his breath. Tears spilled over his cheeks, and before the little dog knew what he was doing, he licked them clean.

Arthur dropped him and stood up. "Erm, that was weird," he said, wiping his cheek with the sleeve of his coat.

"Sorry," said Steve with a wag of his short tail. "I'm still getting used to it. I'm only a puppy."

"How?" Arthur stammered. "I mean..." he tried to finish the sentence but couldn't find anything remotely adequate. In the end he settled for repeating the same. "How?"

"Reincarnation, I guess," said Steve.

"So, the Buddhists and Hindus got it right?"

"I guess so, but I'm not a Buddhist or a Hindu.'

"Are you sure?"

"Of course, I'm bloody sure!" snapped the dog.

"I'm sorry, this is a lot to take in."

"You're telling me," said Steve, scratching himself again.

"I mean, this is amazing!" Arthur said, stepping over to the seat and sitting down with a thump. His hands were shaking, and he pulled out another cigarette, lighting it on the third go. Steve jumped up on the bench beside him and wagged his tail, though he wrinkled his nose at the thick smoke. Arthur reached out absentmindedly and scratched him behind the ears, and Steve's little doggy heart nearly exploded, the smoke completely forgotten. His tail became a blur as it drummed a staccato beat against the cold bench, his foot involuntarily thumping along with the rhythm.

"You came back." Arthur whispered. "I mean, you came back before, of course, but you've done it again." Arthur's brain was trying hard to process this new reality.

It had taken him the better part of half a year and a number of appointments with well-educated professionals to realise that he wasn't, in fact, insane. He knew as he was talking to each shrink that what he had experienced in York had been real, despite what they tried to make him believe. That meant, of course, that he *knew* without a doubt that there was an afterlife. Knowledge like that really puts a strange twist on things.

For the first time in his life, Arthur felt he understood what religious people were banging on about. If you knew something with one hundred percent certainty, then it didn't matter what contrary evidence or logical arguments presented themselves. So, when the shrinks all told him that his desires had been so strong, they had manifested themselves in experiences he only *believed* were real—despite it being a solid and logical argument presented by well-meaning people with certificates on their office walls—he knew it was bollocks.

Arthur *knew* that ghosts were real. He also *knew* that there was a place beyond this world and the ghost world. And now—he patted the dog beside him—now he *knew* you could come back.

"Sarah!" he gasped suddenly as the thought struck him.

Steve looked up, and his tail dropped. He'd been waiting for this. Dreading it. But a small part of him couldn't help but feel a little upset at how quickly Arthur had got there. It was probably a human part. He whined.

"If *you* can come back, then so can Sarah!" Arthur said, excitement rippling through his body like electricity.

"But she didn't," said Steve.

"How do you know?"

"I just know."

"How?"

The small dog whined again and shifted uncomfortably on the bench. He shook himself out, then said, "Because when you released us, I saw what happened. She went through the door, but I went... to the left."

"To the left?"

The dog shrugged, which was surprisingly hard to do. "It's the best I can do," he said. "It all happened so fast. One second, we were in that room with all those horrible creatures, and they were hurting us. I mean *really* hurting us. Then... you saved us. All of us." He rested his chin on Arthur's leg and looked up with wide eyes. Arthur didn't move him away. He just reached down and patted his head. The two friends stayed like that for a long time, each caught in their own dark memories of that horrible night, though Steve's were lightened by the pats.

Arthur was in turmoil. Thoughts leapt unbidden and fully

formed into his mind without seeming to pass through any intervening process. Why him? Why Steve? Why not Sarah? Why a dog? Why didn't that boy in the Bruce Willis movie go absolutely batshit crazy when he realised he could see dead people? What happened to him when he grew up? Did he go on to lead a normal life after everything that happened to him? Did he get a job? Get married? Live happily ever after? Or did he see dead people at every Christmas dinner? Every birthday party? How do you play pass the parcel with ghosts, anyway?

Arthur scratched Steve again. It felt nice. He wanted to be angry, though! He wanted to rage at the world, at the injustice of it all. He was tired, bone-weary in his soul, and he knew now that Sarah was truly gone. As certain as he knew that Steve had returned, albeit, in a slightly different form, he knew that he would never see Sarah again. It wasn't fair! Arthur closed his eyes and let out a sigh that quickly built and turned into a shout of frustration. He clenched his fists, tipped his head back, and roared all his anger into the night. Steve flinched away from him and jumped off the bench, turning in a nervous circle and whimpering as he looked at his friend. Purple crackles of electricity rippled over Arthur's whitened knuckles, and the air had turned heavy with the taste of tin. The angry shout echoed off the castle wall and bounced across the river, unheard by anyone with mortal ears but picked up by many, many others.

And he had been doing so well.

Without realizing, Arthur became a torch on a dark night, a struck match in the desert, a fart at a funeral. His roar unleashed something within him, and it lit him up like a beacon. For miles around, heads turned towards the man, towards the castle on the hill. Towards the power.

High on the moors, Tom and Eric made their way back down the frozen dirt path that ran in a straight line between icy pools of water and thick bristling heather. Neither man could see farther than a few feet in front and so the going was slow. They picked their way carefully along the hardened track towards the dim lights of the inn as the mists wreathed around them, thick and heavy, tangible, as though the clouds themselves clung to the earth to escape the cold of the endless black sky. The wind roared and ripped savagely at their coats, assaulting their ears, but there was no mistaking the sudden clank and clatter of metal chains rattling somewhere in the night, hidden in the thick grey blanket, somewhere terribly close.

There was no confusion, no nervous laughter, no "did you hear that?" Both men stopped dead in their tracks and gripped each other's arms in alarm.

There was something on the moors with them. Something big.

The chains moved, growing louder, the sound somehow coming from all directions. The men twisted and turned, narrowing their eyes as if to penetrate the shroud that had descended on them. A lull in the wind let the swirling tendrils settle into a wall of white for only a moment, and out of it stepped a monster. A coal-black beast padded from the thick bracken and settled on the path directly in front of the two men, poised and ready.

Large claws as big as a bear's gouged savage furrows in the ice-hard dirt as it gripped the ground and lowered its body. A heavy chain hung from its neck and rattled as the creature crouched. The tattered edges where its head should have been ringed a dark pulsing circle of horror; nerves twitched, and bone flashed dirty white. The muscles of its flanks glistened as it moved one large forepaw towards the men, then the other. The back legs were still shrouded in mist, but the terrified Americans could tell they were bunched and ready to leap.

It leapt.

There were no screams.

There was no time.

Somewhere close by, a man with a book in one hand and black-handled blade in the other watched as the headless monster ripped the throats and lives from the two men. He did not stop to watch it feed. There were some sights even the servants of death turned away from.

When it had finished, the creature sat, satiated and dripping gore until a sudden spasm tore through its body. It was followed by another. It slunk back, crashing through the bracken, spreading a bloody mess across the frosted grass as it thrashed in pain. Legs quivering, the beast bent low, straining and thrashing. The nerves, muscles and sinew in the dark hole of its neck moved and pulsed as the bones stretched and grew. The great beast writhed and flailed in the night, the heavy chain shattering the silence of the high moors, but it was nothing to the noise that followed.

A long, deep growl built and stretched and lifted to a rising howl as a monstrous head twitched and snapped violently into place, leaving the beast panting and snarling on the dark, bloody path. It raised its muzzle and opened its jaw, tasting the air for the first time. The great head snapped suddenly to the east as it caught a scent stronger than all the rest, and red eyes glowered out at the world.

Far away, Arthur Crazy lit up Christmas Eve like a star in the sky. And the barghest moved.

CHAPTER 10

The ghost of Queen Katheryn Howard stood poised at the door of King's Manor in York, staring out into the world of the bustling city. At this late hour on Christmas Eve, the town was beginning to slow down, but to her eyes, it was still a hive of activity. Buses and taxis picked up groups of people and ferried them away to warm houses and comfortable beds. Others walked, or swayed, or held onto each other as they sang Christmas songs in the frosty air. The city was alive while the courtyard of the old building was a dark and quiet haven from the world beyond the iron fence.

In all her years here, Katheryn had never left the grounds. She wasn't even sure she would be able to. For years after the man in black left her so far north, she had railed and cried against the injustices of being so far away from the man she had loved, from the world she had known, from the promised blessings of heaven. And yet, it was here that she had experienced the purest moment of happiness. Some might say that marrying the king of England would offer great happiness to a young lady, and for a time it did.

As besotted as he first was, Henry was not a man with whom to share a life. Thomas Culpeper, the king's groom, was different.

For one night only they had been together as husband and

wife, exchanging their own giggling vows before dawn while the corpulent king, her real husband, lay in an unconscious stupor at the far end of the building. For one night only, she had dared to live the life she dreamed of. Her darling Culpeper had knocked gently on her door and presented her with roses. Oh, true, the king had lavished her with gifts and land, but those flowers meant more to her than all the titles and fine linens thrust upon her by the ageing monarch.

Katheryn had been seventeen years old when she spent that wonderful night with her darling, a great risk, she knew, but not one she thought would cost her life.

After all the injustices she had suffered at the hands of men, and of the church, she had never once dreamed that they could simply command her life to be over. Oh, she knew of the terrible fate that befell her cousin, Anne, but those times had seemed like a different world, a story the ladies of the court told in hushed whispers late at night—never something to happen to her.

The queen looked out across the city, shielding her eyes from the bright spotlights that lit up the King's Manor building. Even in this vast city, she could still make out one or two stars suspended in the firmament above the majestic towers of the Minster. It seemed to the ghostly young monarch that all the truest moments of her life happened by the light of the moon.

She thought back to that night. That one night. The only time in her life she felt truly happy, truly loved. The night that ultimately led to her death and, she suspected, to this strange existence she now experienced. And yet it had all been so innocent. Thomas had been the one man who knocked on her room and did not demand entry, nor anything else. He simply presented her with flowers and bade her goodnight. It was she who had invited him in, her heart beating almost painfully in her chest. The young queen had perched on the end of the bed holding the flowers, as Culpeper, ever the gentleman, stood by the window, bathed in the silver moonlight.

They had talked, nothing more. And Thomas listened. On the

threshold, the queen sighed and lifted the roses to her nose in memory of that night with Culpeper. Oh, what it is for a man to listen and a woman to be heard. No one had ever listened to the young queen before. She had been a pawn in the games of men and high-born ladies—smiling their fake smiles while they waited to see how they could use her for their own ends. From the abuse of her tutor, the pressure of the young ladies at court, the forceful advances of Dereham, the manipulations of her own family who manoeuvred her like a chess piece, and then the whirlwind that was life with King Henry—young Katheryn had never felt as though anyone truly noticed her. The real her. Until Culpeper.

It often occurred to the queen over the centuries that followed that she might be living this strange ghostly existence as some kind of purgatorial punishment for what the courts regarded as treason, but as she grew in the afterlife, she dismissed the idea as a weakness of character.

Katheryn angrily ripped one of the rose petals from its stem and crushed it between her fingers. Five hundred years is a long enough time for one to change perspective. How can it be treason when she had no choice? How can it be treason when those men forced themselves upon her? And the only man who didn't, the only man who treated her with respect, was torn apart at the Tyburn.

She threw the petal and watched as it floated gently to the ground.

This wasn't justice, and if it was, then those meting out the punishment were the most unjust of all. It was for this reason that Katheryn had stayed behind when Arthur Crazy offered her a way out, offered her a chance to truly move on to the next life. As queen, she gave some semblance of stability and justice to all those trapped in this strange realm of existence. Lost souls came to her and served in her court. The dead citizens of York were still citizens, and citizens needed a queen.

She closed her eyes for a moment and gathered her thoughts. It was also for this reason that she had decided to follow

Alexander and Archibald on their quest to find Arthur. There needed to be justice, and Arthur, whether he liked it or not, could offer that justice in a far more meaningful way than she ever could. He could save those who needed saving, set them free, liberate their trapped spectral forms and send them on to whatever comes next. But right now, he was in terrible danger. The saviour needed saving. They had all felt it, everyone in the Manor and no doubt many others had felt the surge of power that could only have come from Arthur. The old warriors, Archibald and Alexander, had immediately run from the room shouting that they were going to fetch the car, and so she waited. Waited for the twins to return. Waited to leave this place for the first time in nearly five hundred years.

"Holy shit!" Arthur said in wonder, staring at his hands as purple and white lines crackled between his fingers. He clenched his fists, and the power died as if someone had pulled the plug. A small flutter of panic rippled through him at the sudden absence, but he opened them again and it came back. Arthur grinned, and then laughed. It wasn't particularly pleasant; there was a desperation there, like an alcoholic stumbling across a bottle of scotch after a forced abstinence. Even in his moment of joy, some deep part of his brain advised caution. He had no real idea what this was, what it could do, but it was a link to the past, to York, to the two nights that had tormented him since he stepped off the bus.

Beside him, Steve put his paws over his head and whined.

Arthur stood up and felt the power stir somewhere deep inside. The smile widened. He strode towards the metal railing and looked out over the river to the rolling hills that always reminded him of Postman Pat. The long ribbon of Slee Gill Road glistened in the reflected light of the streetlamps as it wound up the valley, but the world was dark and crisp. A few judgemental stars watched from deep in the velvet sky. Arthur blinked and shook himself. Everything was quiet and still as though the world waited with bated breath. His heart drummed painfully in his chest, and a shiver ran across his shoulders and up his neck. There was a pressure building in his head, but he wasn't sure if that was the alcohol or something else. He didn't care.

The power was back. It had come back! Perhaps it had never gone. The feel of it—like heat, like scotch, like goosebumps on his nerves—was intoxicating, and he was already worried that he might never feel it again. He closed his eyes and breathed in slowly through his nose, letting the air out in a long hiss from between clenched teeth. He did it again. And again. A technique his mum had taught him years ago when he was a child, when he had panic attacks, when he got upset.

At his feet, Steve grew ever more agitated, whining and turning in sharp circles.

Standing in the shadow of the castle overlooking the roaring river far below, Arthur Crazy opened his eyes, opened his hands, and opened his mind. He focused everything he had on the feeling of pressure within his head and his shoulders. He mapped it with his mind's eye as it moved and spread through him. He traced its path—following it, holding it, moving with it. It flowed like the river, quick and furious, the roaring in his ears no longer that of the Swale but that of his own heart. The sensation built within him, and he found he could direct it, manipulate it, flow with it.

He focused on his left hand and felt the wave reach to the tip of his fingers. Sparks crackled between them, purple and blue like in those big glass balls in the science lab at school. But this wasn't electricity. This was something else. Arthur curled his fingers slightly, and the sparks moved down towards the palm just as water flows downhill. He moved his hand and collected the sparks in the centre, a soft glow pulsing with energy. Arthur brought his two hands together, and his eyes opened wide as he felt the power condense between them.

Manipulating it, shaping it like a ball, making it grow, Arthur ignited a surge then patted it down and packed it tightly like a snowball. The smile that creased his face was almost manic. His eyes reflected the strange purple light as it magnified between his hands.

"I am fucking Ryu!" he whispered in awe as he twisted and turned the glowing orb in front of him, now the size of a small football.

Was it buzzing, or was that just the roaring in his ears? He didn't know, and he didn't care. He gave himself over to the thrill of power and pushed the ball together, squeezing it, building it, holding it close to his stomach until he could barely contain it. And then, with a roar, he thrust his two hands forward, palms out, and the ball fired across the river as he screamed "Hadouken!" at the top of his voice.

Arthur roared with laughter and joy as the purple ball rocketed over the river, over Slee Gill, over the houses and the Holly Hill Inn to vanish into the dark of the Dales. He stood there panting and gasping, utterly and hopelessly elated, gripping on to the cold fence to keep himself upright as he whooped and screamed in the night. Steve trotted up behind him and sat looking out over the river while his friend jumped up and down. He watched the ball of light vanish from sight, but his other senses kept track of it for a lot longer. It left a strange smell in the air that streaked like a line of colour into the dark night.

"Are you sure that was a good idea?" Steve asked when the man finally calmed down and stood panting against the railing. Arthur looked down at him and grinned.

"I'm sorry, did you want to fetch it?" he said.

"Dick," said the dog.

"Just asking."

The man and the dog stood side by side and looked out over the river, each lost in their own thoughts. Arthur was elated at the return of his power and could barely comprehend the emptiness its absence had caused in the past six months. It felt like a black hole behind him, an abyss he could so easily lose balance on the edge of. Steve, for his part, was dealing with something far more human than he had had to worry about in a long time. Anger. It took so long to find Arthur, all his will and tiny legs were bent to it, and then when he finally found him, practically his first words had been for Sarah. The little fella was in turmoil. Dogs, as a species, don't do bitterness.

But then Arthur bent down and scratched him behind the ear, and all was forgiven.

The crisp night air had grown colder, and down to the right, where the river flowed under the old stone bridge, a hint of fog rolled through the trees. Below them, where the imaginatively named Riverside Road ran beside the river, an old man shuffled along, bent-backed and limping as he leaned heavily on a walking stick.

"Bit late for a walk," muttered Arthur, looking at his watch. "It's nearly midnight." There was a pause as he continued to watch the old man who appeared to be muttering and gesticulating—one of those pauses where everyone else waited for the facts to fall into place and the person to find number thirty in their thirty-number join-the-dot puzzle.

"Fuck!" shouted Arthur suddenly. "Church!"

There it was.

Somewhere to the south, over dale and hill and town and village, a lone woman wept on the wind-swept moors of Middleham. The wind cut at her dress, but she couldn't feel the cold. She couldn't feel anything except heartache and the deep, gnawing regret of a decision wrongly made.

Dressed all in black and with a veil covering her face, she knelt on the frozen grass and cried her pain to the unforgiving night. There was no one there to hear; there never had been. Only the sheep shivered across this judgemental land, and they were terrible company.

The woman wept in pitiful mourning and railed at the wind as it whispered at her accusingly. *It's your fault. You strung them both along. You did this. It's your fault. What did you think was going to happen when he found out?* She sobbed and cried and screamed and tore ineffectually at the black cloth of her dress. *He'll come for me. He will. He'll come for me.* But he never did.

A light shone in the distance, but she paid it no heed. Just another of those strange carts she had seen over the last few years. Strange, unnaturally fast, and blazing with light, they were more and more common. But there was something about the approach of this particular light that finally caught her attention. It was moving faster than all the rest and not following any road that she could see as it headed straight towards her over the grass. Was he coming?

The woman lifted her veil as the small star streaked through the night sky and shot silently towards her. It was so beautiful. Purple. Dazzling. She felt no fear and no desire to move, though there would have been no time had she wanted to. She blinked once, and the ball of purple light struck her in the chest. There was no pain. The dark, barren moor vanished in light, and the lady blinked as the figure of a man appeared.

"You came back," she sobbed.

"Not me, love," the Shadowman said. He closed another door and checked his book with a shake of his head. This was getting out of hand.

CHAPTER 11

O fficer Boardman was not in a good mood. His shift was supposed to have finished an hour ago, but every time he went to make his way back to the station, he found some other drunk idiot to ruin his Christmas Eve. What was it about the birth of Christ that meant everyone had to get horrendously drunk to celebrate it, anyway? Shouldn't they all be at home with their families, in bed and waiting for Santa? That's where he wanted to be. Where he should be. In bed with his warm wife and with a beautiful, exhausted little girl snoring peacefully in the next room.

He smiled. The thought of his girls always made him smile no matter how difficult a shift he'd had, no matter how many drunks had nearly thrown up on him, or dickheads had got into fights. He clapped his hands together and blew into them to warm them up. He checked his watch, but he needn't have bothered as the bells of the Minster rang out over the city. Midnight. His shift was well and truly over. That's it. He was going back to the station come hell or high water. He yawned. It had been a *really* long shift. He hoped Santa brought him a sleep-in, but he knew his little girl would be up at first light. He didn't mind.

The short and stocky red-haired policeman had patrolled

York's streets for the better part of fifteen years, and he thought he'd seen everything. He'd even arrested a man for running around outside this very art gallery with a sword earlier in the year. It hadn't been anything to worry about. It was just a daft drunk man pretending to be King Arthur or He-Man or something. He smiled at the memory as he stood in front of the fountain that cut across the vast square outside the gallery, the bright blue water was lit from beneath and the shimmering pool glistened as small jets arced in from the sides.

Boardman rummaged in his pocket and pulled out a copper coin, balancing it on his thumb as he thought of his girls all safe and tucked up at home. Everything he did, he did it for them. He closed his eyes and made a wish, though it wasn't so much a wish as a thank you. When he opened them again, he tossed the coin and watched it spin in the air before landing with a gentle plink in the middle of the rectangular pool. The bells of the Minster stopped ringing, and he smiled. "Happy Christmas, girls," he said. "I'll be home soon."

It was at this exact moment a large car suddenly mounted the pavement no more than a few metres away from Officer Boardman, and if this had been any other story, it might have spelt the end for him. Let's face it, making a wish on Christmas Eve and saying *I'll be home soon* is just one cliche away from buying a boat called the *Live Forever* on the day before retirement. But this was different. And it was different because Archibald, although fast and breathtakingly old, was a very good driver.

The old man steered the car around the shocked police officer, skidded around the edge of the fountain, and spun the vehicle to a screeching stop near the gates of King's Manor. And it was all done under perfect control. Officer Boardman, who by this point was knee-deep in water and momentarily frozen in shock, was nevertheless a very observant man and couldn't help but appreciate the skill. He stepped from the pool as the car doors opened and couldn't quite believe what he saw.

The car was a beautiful old Jaguar MKII with all four head-lights blazing in a wide smile beneath a perfectly polished grill. The two men that jumped from the car were clearly ancient, but they moved so quickly. They were dressed in strange robes like monks, and both of them had swords strapped to their sides. Big ones. Police officers were trained to respond to any situation, and they spent their lives heading towards things that most people would run away from, but there was something about the scene unfolding in front of him that made Officer Boardman pause. Not only were the two old men seemingly identical in every way, but they moved as though they were twenty years younger. Hell, *fifty* years younger.

The driver dashed in front of the headlights, his impossibly long grey beard flowing behind him as he followed what had to have been his twin through the gates of King's Manor. Within a moment they were back, walking hurriedly and, to Officer Board-man's mind, seemingly ushering someone along with them, though there was no one else there. One of the men even went to the rear of the car and opened the passenger door, holding it wide like a valet with a proffered hand, and, as the policeman would later try to explain to his very tired wife, he *bowed* before closing the door gently and jumping in the front seat.

They were regal. They were gentlemanly. They moved as though their right to be there was as irrefutable as gravity. It exuded from them, the confidence of being completely, totally, and utterly in charge. Officer Boardman couldn't help but think they would make wonderful policemen. Perhaps they were? They were driving what looked like Inspector Morse's car, after all, though what department would employ Gandalf-bearded octoge-narians armed with swords, he had no idea.

Before he could respond, before he could do anything, the idling engine of the beautiful car growled and rumbled as the driver eased it forward. The window wound down slowly, and the passenger leaned out. He made a strange motion in the air with his hands, flicking his fingers towards Officer Boardman and then turning it into a crisp salute.

"Keep up the good work, Officer," the man said with a smile, and suddenly, the engine roared as the twin in the driver seat put his foot down.

The wire hub wheels caught the light as they turned rapidly, the old car leaping forward like a cat. Even the rounded wings looked like paws, the policeman thought. As he watched the car bounce from the footpath and swing onto the road, he wondered if that's why they were called Jaguars. He shook his head at having never made that connection. No wonder he wasn't a detective yet. The car vanished out of sight down Bootham Road, and Officer Boardman stamped his cold, wet feet on the pavement. Finally, he set off towards the station and home, completely forgetting to call it in, which was not like him at all. But then, it was Christmas, and they seemed like nice chaps.

Queen Katheryn Howard, by modern standards, was little more than a child—seventeen or eighteen years old, though even she was not entirely sure. She had a luxuriant childhood by the standards of the 1600s, but one ruined by the political machinations of her family and the unwanted advances of her tutor. Katheryn was a child thrust into an adult world, courted and adored, used and manipulated, pushed, pulled and ultimately executed for the *sins* forced upon her by others. She was destined, it seemed, to spend eternity as a ghostly queen in the King's Manor of York.

For nearly five hundred years, she wandered the halls of a place she had visited only once in her short life, but it was a place of happiness. For nearly five hundred years she ruled with grace and a firm but loving hand. The lost souls of York found comfort and solace in her court that was denied to them by whatever forces control the afterlife. The queen had truly become just that: a queen of incorruptible and regal standing, adored and followed and loved.

Ghosts broke their bonds to kneel at her feet, to receive a blessing from the green-clad, beautiful Queen of Roses. But she, in all the years that had passed since her untimely death at the Tyburn, had never once broken the ethereal chains that bound her to the Manor. Until now.

She sat in the back of the twin's car, the roses clasped tightly in her hands and a look of wonder on her pale, beautiful face. Long auburn hair was tied back in a long braid and she leaned forwards on the deep leather seat. Her eyes, perhaps blue or grey, stared with awe at the passing world. Katheryn felt the pull, the strange draw that bound her like chains to the Manor, but it was under control. More than that, it was almost forgotten.

Lights and buildings, people and parks, trees and tall hedgerows passed in a blur of speed never before experienced by the young lady. She leaned her ethereal form against the glass and felt a surge of emotion at the magic of the world.

"Wonderful," she breathed as they turned into a street of large brick houses and ornate gardens festooned with the dazzling lights of a modern Christmas. It was like nothing she had ever seen before.

Queen Katheryn leaned between the two seats and looked at the world that passed swiftly beneath the large car. The vehicle itself was fascinating, laced in leather, highly polished wood, and glittering metals that shone like jewels, but the sight of the open road being devoured so quickly filled her with a sense of excitement she had never experienced before. The road flowed like a river under the dazzling headlights, white lines flashing and vanishing beneath the roaring wheels.

Archibald glanced in the rear-view mirror and noticed the look of awe on the young lady's face. He grinned at her and winked at his brother, gripping the overlarge steering wheel, then lowering his hand to the lever that sat opposite the indicator arm.

He dropped the car into overdrive and pushed his foot down on the heavy accelerator pedal. The car leapt forward with a distinguished growl, and the strange company rocketed over the bridge and out of the city as the queen's joyful cry echoed through the night.

CHAPTER 12

Arthur ran through the town with the small dog trying his best to keep up. The strange companions dodged past the remnants of the Christmas revellers spilling from bars and restaurants, and cries of "oh, what a gorgeous dog" followed the pair as they ran. They jogged down the curve of the hill where Frenchgate turned into Station Road, and there, nestled in the crook of the horseshoe road, was St. Mary's Church. It rose majestically from behind a beautifully manicured garden and a slightly less beautiful council car park, framed in the night by towering ancient trees.

Jogging across the unusually empty road, Arthur made his way down the high stone wall, turning to check that Steve was keeping up. He couldn't help but smile at the little dog powering along behind him, tongue hanging out with ears flat to his head. He hadn't appreciated just how small Steve was, but a six-month-old Yorkshire Terrier was a tiny animal and, try as he might, he was dropping further and further behind. Arthur stopped and let the little fella catch him. He knelt down to the panting animal and stretched out his hand.

"Do you mind?" he said. Steve didn't answer but butted up against Arthur, who scooped him up with a smile and ducked through the narrow gate of the church with the dog under his arm. "Sorry, mate. I didn't think," he apologised.

Steve was panting so hard he couldn't reply, but even if he could, he didn't know what he might possibly say that could express the sheer joy he had just experienced running behind his friend. His very best friend. And now he was tucked up warm against his beating heart. All thoughts of bitterness and anger were left far behind. Steve had no idea how this night could possibly get any better.

"Good boy," Arthur said, ruffing the small dog's head, and suddenly he knew.

Canine neurons exploded with love, and Steve found that of all the human things he had left behind, shedding tears of joy was not one of them, which just goes to show that we do not deserve dogs.

Arthur tried to control his breathing as he walked up the narrow path towards the church. Still exhilarated, he felt that the world was made fresh and new. Not since his childhood had he so clearly felt the magic of Christmas. The beautiful church with its grand Georgian-style square tower glistened atop the hill like a scene from a Victorian postcard. A crowd of people gathered outside the wide doors and golden light washed into the night, lighting up ancient gravestones and the majestic towering trees. It was a tableau of perfect Christmas wonder, and Arthur breathed it all in. His dad stepped from the crowd and strode down the path towards him, tall, strong, and handsome, as he had always been, a broad smile across his neatly bearded face.

"You made it!" He grinned and clapped his son in a rough bear-hug, nearly crushing poor Steve, who let out a little yelp. "And who is this?" Thomas Crazy asked with a look of pure, if slightly drunk, delight on his face. "What a handsome little fella. Don't tell me you got your mum a dog for Christmas?"

"Not quite, Dad," Arthur laughed, then paused. He looked down at Steve, who looked up with adoring brown eyes. They hadn't spoken about this at all. There had been no time. Things had happened so fast, but Steve had travelled all the way from York to find him. That was a tremendous distance for a puppy. Arthur suddenly felt a wave of guilt, and his eyes widened with realisation. Steve was back! *Steve* Steve! And all Arthur had done was talk about Sarah and throw silly bloody fireballs across the moors. He looked into Steve's brown eyes and ruffled the hair on his head. Unspoken words flowed between man and dog, and somehow, he knew that it would be all right. Steve tilted his head, and the left ear popped out. In that moment, promises were made with nothing more than a look. "I'm sorry," Arthur said, then looked at his dad. "He's mine."

Cradled in his arms, Steve passed out with sheer joy.

The two Crazy men walked towards the church as the bells began tolling for midnight. "Close one, son," Thomas said. "You almost never made it."

"Sorry, Dad. Crazy night."

"Aren't they all," his dad said with a wink, ever the master of the family pun. "You're here, and your mum will be delighted. I expect you could have run a bit faster if it wasn't for all the cigarettes, eh?" he said with a nudge of the elbow. Arthur paused and stared at him with an open mouth. His father laughed. "Don't worry, lad. I won't tell your mother. I'd join you for one if I didn't think she'd kill me."

"What?!"

"Come on, time to get a damn good blessing," his father grinned, ignoring his son's indignation. "Your mother is saving our seats."

The two men and the unconscious dog passed over the threshold of the church, into a blaze of golden light and the warm sound of the organ. The place was crowded. People smiled and shook hands as they filled up the pews beneath grand arched columns that glowed orange in the glare of a thousand candles. There was hushed laughter and whispered conversations, a murmur of life not unlike that of the pub, only with a bit less swearing. A group of people in cheerful communion with each other. Thomas Crazy spotted his wife and pulled Arthur over by the arm. Maggie Crazy rose from her seat when she saw her son, and a big smile lit her face. She threw her arms around him and kissed him on the cheek.

"I'm so glad you came! Oh! Who is this?" she gasped as she noticed Steve, who blinked and looked around dreamily. "What a gorgeous puppy!"

"This is Steve, Mum. He's my dog."

"You know a dog is for life, son," she mocked with a smile, "not just for Christmas."

"Behave, Mum," Arthur laughed.

Mrs. Crazy knew full well that her son would treat any animal in his care with love and affection. She also knew, as the mother of a young man who had struggled terribly this last year, that the inclusion of a wonderful dog in his life could do nothing but good. Her heart soared as she saw the warmth of her son's smile. The lines and furrows that had creased his face so much since he returned home seemed to have vanished completely. Her boy was back. Her handsome, smiling boy. Tears welled unbidden in Mrs. Crazy's eyes, and she blinked them away before anyone noticed.

The family took their seats on the cold pews with Arthur and Steve squeezing in between his parents as the organ reached a crescendo, and the last lingering note echoed off the walls and drifted away. The chatter and clammer hushed as the crowd waited in expectant silence for the priest. Arthur let out a long, low breath. His shoulders fell, and the ache in his neck melted away. A feeling of contentment spread over his body like the caress of a warm shower, and he smiled to himself. He was home. This was home. And it was Christmas.

Arthur closed his eyes for a moment and listened to the priest as he welcomed everyone and reminded them all the reason for the season. The elderly grey-haired man in the white and gold vestments seemed particularly happy with that little rhyme and smiled at the dutiful titter from his congregation. This was the big one. One of the few times in the year he had a packed church and a truly engaged crowd. He had been nervous about it all day but soon settled with a few cans of Guinness in the rectory.

"There are slightly more of you here than we usually get for mass at St. Mary's," he announced with his broad Irish accent. "I wonder why that is? Perhaps I should conduct mass at midnight every week for all of you lovely night owls who just can't sleep. Of course, it'll be wonderful to see you all so full of spirit—" he paused with a glint in his eye—"and perhaps slightly less *spirits* at our usual Sunday service."

There was another polite susurrus of chuckles, but Thomas Crazy roared with laughter and loudly proclaimed, "He means the booze, son!"

Arthur went bright red though couldn't help but laugh along with everyone else who turned in their seats to look at Thomas. His dad wasn't the least bit concerned but sat there, straight-backed and grinning. The priest lost his thread for a moment and shuffled through his notes, then hiccupped.

"Crack on, father!" Mr. Crazy said loudly, and Arthur had to hang his head to hide the laughter. He glanced sideways at his mother and saw that she was hiding her face behind the order of service, but her shoulders were shaking, and her ears were red.

"Quite, quite," stammered the priest and then quickly moved on, announcing they would sing the evening's first hymn. There was a panicked ruffling as everyone turned from Thomas to fumble for their songbook and find the right page, but they needn't have bothered. Everyone recognised the tune as soon as the organ started.

As the first few notes of *Hark the Herald Angels Sing* filled the church, Thomas Crazy turned to his son and said, "Yes! This is a belter!" then got stuck in.

He was red-faced and roaring from the get-go, and by the time they reached the crescendo, Mr. Crazy had his hands in the air and had turned purple. The congregation around them, seemingly spurred on by his efforts, followed his lead, and the church filled with riotous noise as hundreds of people sang at the very tops of their voices. Poor Steve, with his exceptional hearing, squirmed in Arthur's arms and had to shout to make himself heard.

"I'm going outside!" he said to Arthur, who nodded and put him gently on the ground.

The little dog darted over Thomas Crazy's shoes and disappeared under the pews. Arthur suddenly realised that the dog had spoken very loudly in a very crowded place. He had no idea if other people could hear him or if it was all wrapped up in the strange return of... what? Magic? He glanced around nervously but not a single person seemed to have paid a blind bit of notice.

The hymn finished, and the crowd took their seats. An electric murmur of excitement filled the church as people chuckled and talked amongst each other. The service had turned more from a reverential mass into the buzz of a gig. There were a few grumbles from the die-hards, who went through the motions every week, but the priest himself was thrilled. He shook with excitement as he spoke and led the congregation through the opening prayers and the liturgy of the word, even venturing down from his platform and walking between the rows of pews—something he hadn't done for many years. When it came to the parts in the order of service program that were in bold—those bits the congregation had to say—Thomas Crazy was as enthusiastic in his responses as he was in his singing. His voice got deeper and more pronounced, and Arthur couldn't keep a straight face. He turned to his mum, but she was hiding behind the program again with tears rolling down her face.

By the time they got to the *amen* at the end of the creed, Mr. Crazy gave it full-throttle—their very own Monty Python sketch—that one word stretching out for as long as he could hold it in a deep, sing-song baritone. The priest looked at the tall man with what seemed to be unbridled admiration, and then made the long way back to the front of the church so he could get into the nitty-gritty of the mass itself.

Arthur soon lost the thread after that and zoned out as the priest fell into the sing-song oration of words he had heard a thousand times before. It was only when the people around them started moving that he snapped back to attention.

"What's happening?" he whispered to his dad.

"Bread and wine time," Thomas said softly.

"Aren't you going up?"

"Can't," he said. "Members only."

"Huh?"

"Anglicans, mate. You have to join their club before you can drink their booze!"

Arthur burst out laughing and tried to choke it back down, but it was too late. The two men were shushed from various sections of the congregation, and they both hung their heads guiltily, though big smiles still creased their faces.

From somewhere behind them, a deep Yorkshire voice hissed angrily, "Sacrilege!"

"Bit harsh," Arthur mumbled, looking round, though not a single person looked his way. He glanced at his dad, but the older man appeared not to have heard.

"Do you know they believe it actually turns into the blood of Christ, that stuff?" Thomas said quietly to his son, their heads bowed low and close together so as not to disturb anyone.

"You what?"

"It's true. It's called transubstanshy-something-or-other. Although that might be Catholics. I'm not sure, same stuff, different dresses. I get them all muddled up. Either way, they're supposed to believe that the wine actually, physically, turns into the blood of Christ when they swallow it."

"What? That's disgusting! And the bread?"

"Yep," Thomas Crazy nodded. "Jesus jerky."

"Jesus Christ! Dad!" Arthur laughed a bit too loud.

"Blasphemy!"

Another growl from behind. Arthur ducked his head in embarrassment. He probably deserved that one, but he had the giggles now and was finding it hard to get them under control. His dad had no intention of helping.

"There's something I've been meaning to tell you, son," he said conspiratorially. Arthur leaned closer. "It's about your mum," the older man said, nodding up to the front of the church where Mrs. Crazy had just stepped forward to receive a piece of bread.

The two men watched as she crossed herself and then placed the morsel in her mouth with her eyes closed.

"I think she might be a zombie!" he hissed, and Arthur snorted, clamping his hands over his mouth to stop himself from laughing out loud. The person behind them shouted again but neither man responded. They leaned against one another and chuckled while people returned to their seats and knelt in prayer. The Crazy men got themselves under control and listened as the priest led the congregation in some more prayers and then announced the closing hymn, *Once in Royal David's City*.

"Yes!" exclaimed Mr. Crazy, jumping to his feet before the rest of the church. "Go hard or go home, son!" he said, and the two men sang at the very top of their voices while Mrs. Crazy shook her head at her boys and smiled with utter contentment, completely oblivious to the angry shouts and cries of blasphemy coming from behind her.

In the churchyard, Steve the dog had marked a few graves, sniffed a few others, and was wandering around wondering what else he could claim as his own. There were so many smells. Cats, dogs, people, foxes, small animals, large animals, unidentified animals, and all the other smells associated with people. Bins were particularly fascinating, as were lampposts. A whole smorgasbord of redolent delights.

Being a dog had certain eccentricities that were somewhat hard to get used to, but so far, Steve had very few complaints. In fact, he realised, as he trotted over to a fallen stone, he had never been happier. What made this particularly strange was his lasting memory of being human. When he woke up—when he became conscious in this new form—he found he had all the hangovers and memories of his previous life. Plus a few from the space in-between. Those, in particular, were fascinating.

In fact, it was those memories that had borne in Steve the all-consuming desire to find Arthur Crazy, but the longer he was a dog, the harder it was to hang on to them. When he first saw Arthur, he knew he needed to tell him... something. But then Arthur had run, and a canine instinct had awakened within him and told him to chase.

Every moment since then was a blur of conflicting instincts and emotions, but there was something important Arthur needed to know, something Steve needed to tell him—something from that strange period between lives. But like the smells, drifting and shifting and mixing in the graveyard, whatever it was just wouldn't stay still.

The little dog stopped and thought hard, and he almost had it, but at that moment, a large black cat jumped from the church wall. All was forgotten as millennia of primal instinct took over. Steve growled and darted towards the offending creature. He had no idea what he was going to do when he got there, but he felt sure that yapping sharply and bouncing from side to side would feature heavily. The cat completely ignored the incoming dog and licked a paw. For her part, she had no intention of bathing in the dark churchyard, but the strange little creature running towards her was making such a fuss that she too reverted to millennia of instinct and so stopped to regard the excited newcomer with utter disdain.

Steve pounced forward and thrust his paws at the ground in front of the cat, his tail wagging furiously as he yapped and yapped for all he was worth. This was amazing! He had never experienced anything so wonderfully all-consuming as the sheer joy of the hunt. Another small part of his human self fell away as he attempted a growl, and the sensation made his whole body quiver with joy. Cats were great fun! And he... he was a wolf! A beast of the wild! A descendent of Fenrir!

The cat boxed him on the nose and hissed.

Steve ran so fast his back legs nearly overtook his front and he fell in a tumble of fur and ears and tail into the safety of the shadows behind the fallen stone. He put his paws over his head and waited, his heart beating furiously, his tongue hanging out as he panted in the cold night air.

Cats are bastards.

As if to illustrate the point, the sleek black feline lifted her tail, raised her head, and walked away as though nothing had happened.

~

"Wonderful service, Father," Thomas Crazy said to the elderly priest as they shook hands at the door. The old man looked elated and clasped Thomas's hand in his own. The big man had been the first to the door when the service ended, dragging his wife and son with him, but the priest had beaten them to it.

"Thank you!" he said with a hiccup he tried valiantly to stifle, "You know, we could use a man like you on Shunday. Get them all fired up! What do you say?"

"Oh, I don't know, Father," Thomas replied, tactfully ignoring the slur. "I think I'm more of a fair-weather supporter. Just here for the cup final sort of thing, you know," he added with a playful jab at the priest's ribs. The old priest laughed and said they were all welcome anytime. He clasped Arthur's hand and gave it a vigorous shake and then turned beetroot red when Mrs. Crazy planted a kiss on his cheek.

"Merry Christmas, Father," she said.

"Merry Christmas," he stammered as the family fastened their coats tight about them to ward off the winter chill. Arthur stepped from the shadows of the church to look for Steve, but Thomas Crazy put a hand on his shoulder to stop him. Arthur looked at his dad, and the older man nodded to the path where a black cat was sitting quietly, luminous eyes reflecting the lights of the church as it stared at the crowd. For a few moments, it just sat there, neither moving nor blinking.

"See," said the priest. "Best to stay in the sanctuary of the church. It's bad luck for a black cat to cross your path."

Mrs. Crazy smiled at the priest and patted him on the shoulder. "You're in Yorkshire now, Father. Nothing unlucky about a black cat crossing your path here. Quite the opposite in fact."

The cat regarded them all in the way that cats do, as though the gathering crowd of people were as interesting as dirt in a litter box, then it stretched and walked away. The congregation began to spill out of the church behind the trio, so they stepped onto the lamp-lit path to make room.

"A good omen, that," Mrs. Crazy said, as she huddled into her husband for warmth against the crisp winter air. "It's going to be a lovely Christmas."

Thomas leaned down and kissed his wife on the head. "Don't let the priest hear you talking about omens, love," he said with a grin. "He'll be devastated to find out you're a pagan."

"Please," she said. "Like I told him. This is Yorkshire. We're all a bit pagan round here. I mean, look, there's a Green Man right above his head."

They turned and sure enough, under the porch of the church, above where the priest was busy shaking hands and wishing the departing congregation a merry Christmas, there smiled down a familiar figure of a bearded Green Man carved from stone. He was wreathed in leaves with foliage hanging from his mouth, the old carving perfectly preserved in the shelter of the vaulted ceiling. The eyes seemed to follow them wherever they moved.

This was an illusion, of course, a clever bit of sculpture designed for just that purpose. The eyes didn't really follow you; it just looked that way. They certainly weren't following Mr. and Mrs. Crazy as they walked arm in arm down the frosty church path. The eyes of *this* Green Man were actually following their son as he searched among the gravestones for Steve. A stone-grey eyebrow arched in slow interest at the strange human who seemed to glow in the night. And perhaps he would have said something if he didn't have a mouth full of leaves. We'll never know.

Arthur found Steve cowering beneath a fallen grave. The little puppy was shaking but heard the small whistle of his friend, and so he bravely poked his head from the deep shadows. He made sure there were no cats around before letting out a small yap and running from cover when the man knelt to him. Arthur scooped him up, and the little dog's heart swelled with love and forgetful bravery. If any stinking cats came for him now, he'd show them what for!

"Why didn't you tell us you were getting a dog?" Mrs. Crazy said to her son as the older couple approached, the frosty grass cracking beneath their footsteps.

Arthur didn't know what to say, but he didn't need to reply because his mum was already snuffling her face against the little animal and speaking in an overly exaggerated baby-voice. Something about how cute he was and how she could just eat him all up. You know, the usual habit of perfectly normal and intelligent people when faced with puppies. Mr. Crazy hid a smile and affected a stern voice that no one believed for a second.

"We're not getting a puppy," he said with as much authority as he could muster.

His wife pulled the unresisting Steve from her son's hands and held him up in front of her face, speaking from behind as though she herself were the dog.

"But I'm shoo cute," she said in a sing-song voice. "And I'm shoo shmart. Shee, I wash shnuffling under Willance's grave looking for a leg bone."

Mr. Crazy couldn't help himself and burst out laughing at his wife.

"You laughed!" she cried. "I win. That means I get a puppy!"

"No, it bloody well doesn't!"

"But you laughed! Them's the rules!"

"I laughed at the Willance joke," Mr. Crazy declared, pointing in desperation to the fallen gravestone.

Robert Willance was a famous Richmond local who lost a leg in a bizarre riding accident and had it buried in the churchyard a full ten years before the rest of his body caught up. To be fair to Thomas, it was a good joke.

"We'll see," Mrs. Crazy grinned, handing Steve back to Arthur. "So, are we heading home? Santa will be doing his rounds soon and little boys who aren't in their beds won't get any presents."

"I thought I might take Steve down to The Batts first," Arthur said, meaning the narrow parklands on the west bank of the River Swale where most of the dog-owning locals took their pets for a walk. He was beginning to realise the situation with Steve wasn't exactly a straight-forward affair, and there were some things they needed to sort out. Up until quite recently, Arthur's "Christmas puppy" had been a full-grown man. Suddenly giving him cuddles, seeing him lick your mother's face, and inviting him over for a sleepover was a lot to take in. A conversation needed to be had first.

"We'll come with you," said Mrs. Crazy, linking her arm into her son's. "It'll be nice to have a walk." Arthur went to say something, then paused. What could he say? I'm sorry, Mum but Steve and I need to have a serious talk about sleeping arrangements, sniffing crotches, and humping legs? Thankfully, his father noticed the hesitation and jumped in. He winked at his son and mimed having a cigarette, thus adding more proof to the age-old prophecy that kids can never successfully hide smoking from their parents.

"Nah, come on, love," he said, gently pulling Mrs. Crazy away, "let the lad have a quick walk, and we'll go home and put the fire on. We can have a night-cap together after the dog has done his business. You'll only be a few minutes, right, son?"

"Yeah, right, Dad," Arthur said. "We won't be long."

"And anyway, I want to go wassailing," said Mr. Crazy.

"What's that?" Arthur asked.

"Wassailing!" said Mr. Crazy. "Proper carol-singing. It means something like *to be of good cheer*."

"Dad, it's daft o'clock in the morning. I don't think people are going to be too happy or cheerful about you knocking on their doors and belting out Good King Wenceslas."

"Ah, you don't need to knock on anyone's door to spread good cheer," laughed Mr. Crazy as he linked arms with his wife. "See you at home, son. Toodle-pip!" The couple walked arm in arm out of the churchyard as Mr. Crazy started singing at the top of his voice.

"We've been a-while a-wandering

Among the leaves so green

But now we come a wassailing

So plainly to be seen!

Come on love, join in," Arthur heard him say as they passed through the narrow gate.

Arthur grinned as his parents vanished out of sight, then looked down at the dog beside him.

"Come on, Steve. We need to talk. Let's go down to the river before we head home. I'm guessing you need to do your... business anyway."

He hesitated again. Richmond was the kind of town that took dogs very seriously. Nearly every pub and restaurant in the marketplace allowed dogs inside, and the council had installed a lot of bins specifically designed to deal with "business." Arthur often wondered what an alien species would think if they were to look down on the world and see humans following behind dogs, picking up their poo in colourful little bags and depositing them in purpose-built bins that, in turn, would then be emptied by someone specifically employed to the task. Who was really in charge?

The number of couples he had seen in the town with dogs that were more expensive than any car he had ever owned never ceased to amaze him. Or, as his father often pointed out, dogs were carried, and children were put on leashes. The world had turned upside down. But cleaning up your dog's shit was an entirely different affair when your dog can talk.

"First things first," Arthur said, making a swift decision. "If you need a shit, you do it somewhere private and you cover it up, so no one sees it, okay? I'm not picking up your poo."

"Okay," said Steve, who had to admit that the toilet habits of his new canine life had initially concerned him, but dogs were easier. If you have to go, you have to go. The only real issue was a nagging evolutionary holdover about predators catching you with your metaphorical pants down. That's why it was important to maintain full eye-contact with someone at all times. He was confident Arthur would understand.

"Secondly," Arthur continued, fumbling in his pockets for a cigarette and lighter, "there will be no sniffing crotches or licking faces, okay? I mean, I know it's a doggy thing and all that, but, well, you were a bloke not that long ago." But even as he said it, he knew it would be increasingly difficult to hang on to the memory of Steve as a dour, depressive office worker. As if to illustrate the point, Steve wagged his tail.

"Okay," the puppy said. "But look, I'm not always in control here. It's hard to explain but..." he wanted to say something about him not always being able to help some baser instincts, but a group of churchgoers walked past and wished Arthur a merry Christmas. Once they had gone, so had the moment, and Arthur knelt down.

"You stopped talking then," the man said, his mind whirring. "Can other people hear you?" he asked.

"I don't know," admitted Steve. "I think that was more a force of habit, you know."

"Let's test it," said Arthur, looking around the churchyard.

It was quite empty now as most of the congregation had made their way home already, but there were still one or two lingerers. Nearby, two men leaned against the trunk of an old elm, deep in conversation. They were shrouded in the dark shadows beneath the overhanging branches and facing away from Arthur and Steve.

"Run up behind those two and shout something," Arthur said, pointing to the tall gravestones that surrounded the tree. They would offer Steve plenty of places to hide. "If other people can hear you, then they should react."

The dog didn't need to be told twice. He happily darted away, and Arthur soon lost him in the shadows. After a few moments he heard a small voice shout out, "Hey you! You two!"

There was no reaction from the two men. Steve came trotting back out of the shadows and joined Arthur on the path.

"I guess it's just me then," the man said to the dog. He wasn't sure how he felt about that. On the one hand, it was like the powers—the magic—it was just *him*. How amazing it was to be unique. On the other hand, it was *just* him. There is a fine line between individuality and loneliness. Not for the first time in his life, Arthur felt the disconcerting idea that his name might be more than just a title.

"Come on," he said. "Let's go."

As the two companions walked along the path, Arthur glanced over his shoulder at the two silhouettes beneath the tree. One man was reaching into the low branches and straining with both hands. A loud snap carried across the frosty air, and the man staggered backwards. Arthur paused and watched as he stripped the twigs and leaves from a branch and handed it to his friend.

There were whispers of conversation on the wind, melancholy, and low, the sniffle of tears. Arthur wondered if he should go over and help, but the taller man put an arm over the shoulder of the other and guided him away. There was something strangely familiar about the way the older man moved, shuffling along using the stick, taking tiny steps. As Arthur took a step towards them though, the hunchback raised a fist to the sky, shaking it in anger.

"My brother!" he cried.

Arthur paused, struck by the grief of the words. "Poor bloke," he said, turning to Steve who sat patiently waiting by his feet.

"Probably best to leave them to it," said the small dog. Since all the talk of "business," he had other things on his mind, and he didn't think a graveyard was the place to take care of it.

"You're probably right," Arthur replied. "Come on."

The two friends walked side by side out of the churchyard and turned down the hill to the river. Above them, the Green Man watched as two shadowy figures shuffled away in the opposite direction. He chewed thoughtfully on his leaves as, below him, the priest locked the door of the church and tucked the large iron key safely into the folds of his thick winter coat. Soon, the church and its yard were empty, and silence spread across the world as the Green Man closed his eyes.

CHAPTER 13

Just as Arthur and Steve were walking down the steep path toward the bank of the raging River Swale, Queen Katheryn Howard was discovering the immense pleasures of the open road, a fine car, and Jimi Hendrix.

The Mark II Jaguar ate up the A1 at a blistering 120 miles per hour, a speed Katheryn was totally unprepared for and completely exhilarated by. The car was smoother than anything she had ever experienced, but the world flashed by in a blur that occasionally caused her to scream out loud for the sheer joy of it all.

The young queen had gone through all the stages of a road trip in a very short space of time. At one point, just before the A66 turned onto the A1, it had begun to rain, and Katheryn, like every other teenager in the modern world, rested her head against the window and watched the drops of water turn into rivulets on the glass. If she knew what a music video was, there was no doubt she would have imagined herself in one. But it was when she had asked about all the lights and strange buttons at the front of the car that her experience took on an entirely different dimension.

"What did you say this was called?" she shouted over the top of the raucous music.

"Voodoo Child, Your Majesty," Archibald called over his

shoulder as he eased the car into the middle lane and overtook a slow-moving long-haul lorry struggling up a steep incline just south of Catterick Garrison.

"Voodoo Child," the queen said to herself, nodding along with the alien but wonderfully perfect music. She gasped as the car raced past the truck as though it stood still, turning in her seat to watch the twin white lights fall quickly behind them.

"Cracking chap," Alexander said as she turned back. "We met him once down in London."

"Who's that?" asked the queen, who was frankly struggling to keep up with all the new experiences and wonderful sights and sounds they had come across since leaving York.

"Jimi Hendrix, Your Majesty. The musician."

"Jimi Hendrix," the queen repeated to herself again, in awe.

"I bet he's still going strong, passionate young lad like that," Archibald said as the song ended, and the radio moved on to an advert for something no one in the car understood.

"Can we listen to it again?" asked the queen.

"Sorry, your majesty. It's called a radio. We're not in control of what music is played."

"If only they had record players in cars," said Alexander.

Archibald laughed, "Ah, that's wishful thinking, brother. I doubt technology will have advanced that much. We've only bin' gone a few years."

"At least forty."

"Forty years," Archibald sighed wistfully, and the car powered on as the three strange companions fell into silence, each lost in their own thoughts and memories.

This was yet another universal impact of the road-trip: unbidden and intensely deep philosophical thought. Philosophy was not trapped inside a book, an alcove, a library, or a university. Sure, there were many things one could learn from the study of books and the works of those who had come before. But, without the space to put those thoughts into practice, they were just so many scratches on parchment. This was why the greatest living philosopher was not a dusty old tweed-donned don but, in fact, a middle-aged Australian woman named Ruth who drove road trains from Sydney to Perth. Imagine what Socrates could have achieved if he drove a truck?

The three companions of the Jaguar were, at this moment in time, considering their respective lives, each of which had undoubtedly stretched on far longer than anyone could have anticipated. The ever-receding sand of a person's time on earth was something the ancient gods were deemed to have gifted humans—a blessing to make the appreciation of our brief moment in the sun so much more profound. There were numerous stories of birds careening through dark windows into brightly lit rooms before vanishing out of equally dark windows on the other side—metaphors to explain such things. For Alexander, Archibald, and Katheryn, that second window had slammed shut before their bird could leave. Each person in the car remained trapped in a brightly lit room, fluttering about and bumping against the glass before settling in the rafters and shitting on the floor.

Metaphorically speaking.

After a long moment of almost painful introspection, Katheryn experienced yet another staple of the road-trip when Alexander leaned over to his brother and said, "You missed the exit."

"Bollocks!"

Somewhere to the west of the A1, beyond Richmond and high on the Arkengarthdale Moors, the barghest was struggling. It seemed that whichever direction it turned, the way was blocked by running water. Rivulets, streams, dykes, brooks, and creeks criss-crossed the Dales like scars on the shield of an ageing warrior. The great devil dog grew increasingly frustrated at having to turn back and retrace its steps. Occasionally, it came across a frozen stretch of a runnel and found that it could leap across if it took a run-up, and, of course, the humans were an industrious bunch with their stone and iron bridges, but the going was slow, and the beast was impatient.

The barghest had killed three sheep and one unsuspecting fox out of sheer frustration, but the wanton violence did little to quell the appetite that surged within. There was a man out there. A man who glowed. A man it needed. Every fibre of its being drew it on, and nothing, not even the strange and ancient barrier of running water was going to stop it. Its great lips curled back over savage teeth, and the brute snarled while all around it the creatures of the night hid in mortal dread. If there was anyone on the high moors to hear the strange noise that issued from the mouth of the beast, it might have sounded like the words "I'll find you," but there was no one there, so it probably didn't.

~

"I'm hungry," Archibald announced.

"So that's why you missed the turn-off?"

"Yes."

"Really?"

"Yes."

"Nothing will be open at this time," Alexander said, sitting back in the leather seat and folding his arms. His brother could be an obstinate man at times, and they sat in silence as Archibald eased the dark green car off the empty, brightly lit artery of the A1 and into the dark stretch of the slip-road. Giant, green and white signs indicated they were heading to Scotch Corner. Archibald grinned.

"There's always something open at t'junction," he announced. "It's where the Summer Road and the Winter Road meet Dere Street," he explained to the queen. "The Romans knew their stuff, I'll give 'em that. Even they needed grub on a long trip."

"It's barely been an hour since we left York," Alexander said.

"Aye, but we didn't eat, did we."

"If we're rushing anywhere, it should be towards Arthur. Heaven knows what is happening to the man."

"Well, we haven't felt anything since that first surge, have we," Archibald responded as he steered the car around the large roundabout that crossed over the A1. There were no other cars in sight and so all the traffic lights remained green. The trio gazed out the windows as they crossed over the main motorway they had just left, staring down at the modern six-lane highway that roughly followed the original Roman road known as Dere Street. There is a strange solemnity about an entirely empty, softly lit motorway, as though you are the only person left in the world, travelling ever onwards, alone.

See, the philosophy of the long-distance lorry driver.

"I'm sure we have time to get something to eat," Archibald said.

"Where? There's hardly going to be a place around here fit for royalty," hissed Alexander, nodding his head towards the queen in the back seat.

"Oh, I don't know." Archibald grinned, flicking the indicator and easing the car off the main road. In front of them, a large red sign shone brightly in the glare of the headlights. Alexander turned to his brother in disbelief.

"Really?" he said.

"Why not?"

"Here?"

"Absolutely."

Queen Katheryn leaned forward between the seats as the big car rumbled to a stop in front of a large glass and red-brick building. She looked up and smiled as she read the bright neon sign above them.

"Who is the Burger King?" she asked.

Half an hour later, Russell Law sat in his car and watched as the twin red lights of the old Jaguar vanished into the thick fog. The halo glow of the headlights shrank swiftly as the car roared over the bridge spanning the deserted A1, heading towards Richmond. He tried to make sense of the last few minutes, but the memories already seemed to be fading—as hard to grasp as the pea-souper that had rolled so suddenly off the hills.

He had been closing the restaurant. Of that, he was sure. Or was he? The lights were off, and the alarms were set, but then, for some reason he couldn't explain, he was back in front of the fryer fixing two large Ultimate Angus Mushroom Swiss meals for the charming gentlemen who had waited so patiently for their food. He was so sorry about the mix-up. He couldn't understand why the fryers had been turned off, and would they like extra fries on the house? They had been delighted.

Or had they? He wasn't so sure anymore. And they seemed awfully distracted, constantly talking amongst themselves and the... and the... and the third customer who didn't want anything to eat but was curious to know what a chicken nugget was. He'd cooked up a batch of those as well. Also on the house.

Now he sat in his car, and it was already later than he'd promised. His husband would be getting worried, but he couldn't help thinking the beard trimmer he'd bought John for Christmas was a mistake. Maybe they should both grow them out? Ease into it, Gandalf style.

The confused man shook his head and started the car. Christmas was always such a strange night.

CHAPTER 14

"What's that place?" Steve asked as he and Arthur walked along the dark path beside the river. He was looking at a large stone building with pointed rooftops whose wall he'd just peed on. There were so many smells here, he needed the conversation to distract him. He was already down to a trickle and wasn't sure he'd have enough left to mark everything as his.

Somewhere deep down inside, in some residual well of his human self that still existed, Steve thought he should be embarrassed by this, but the urge to pee on things that other dogs had already peed on was a nearly all-consuming part of his new life. It was a way of communicating that he just couldn't put into the language of humans. It meant something. It was important. To not pee would be like ignoring a high-five. But he'd caught the wrinkled look on Arthur's face whenever he cocked a leg, and so he was trying to reign it in, though he hadn't forgotten about Arthur peeing all over his scent marker near the castle. To pee or not to pee. There were indeed many things they needed to discuss.

"That's the old grammar school," Arthur said as he leaned against a gate and looked up the hill towards the grand building.

He often wondered what it would have been like going to school here. It had been closed for a long time, but even when it was open, and he used to see the boys in their pristine uniforms, it seemed to him a relic of a different time. Schools like that just didn't exist in his world other than for him and his mates to marvel at the large and expensive cars ferrying the boys to and from the gates. And, of course, in stories.

Arthur leaned against the gate and lit a cigarette, gazing up at the school across the narrow frosty field now littered with thick clumps of coarse meadow grass and rabbit holes.

The tennis court sat like an abandoned prison yard with its tall rusting wire-mesh fence glinting in the orange glow of the security lights and casting creeping shadows across the ground. Behind it, the sharp triangular rooftops of the main building pierced the sky like church steeples while the black windows peered out across the river. During the day, it was a beautiful, grand feature of the town's classic Yorkshire-postcard look, but at night, especially now as the darkness closed in and the mists gathered over the river behind them, it was the perfect setting for a gothic horror.

The cigarette dropped from Arthur's gaping mouth.

In all the excitement of seeing Steve, of his powers returning, he hadn't stopped to consider just what it was they did.

They let him see the dead.

Arthur shivered and stamped his feet. It is one thing to be excited about being able to talk to those who have passed on, but it is quite another to consider all the things that go along with that. He had been lucky at first; he met Steve and the beautiful Sarah without even realising they were dead. They talked, they laughed, they joked. They became friends.

After that, things quickly went south.

The trapped souls of the lost and lonely weren't the only things left in the realm between realms. There were creatures of darkness and shadow and malice Arthur could barely even comprehend. Arthur had experienced great joy with his strange gift but also unparalleled fear. He thought back to that first night in York and his headlong sprint through the narrow city streets and alleys, pursued by demons from the darkest depths—creatures from nightmares and legends, unspeakable horrors. And then the witch-girl. He closed his eyes and fumbled for the cigarette that smouldered on the cold stone wall. He took a deep drag to try and stop his hands from shaking. He failed.

It was the girl.

The girl who made him believe in evil.

"Are you okay?" Steve asked.

Arthur looked down at the small dog and smiled. It had been so easy to forget all the horror and fear when his gift, and his friend, had returned. But the world, he knew, was one of duality, which was both as comforting and disconcerting as that implied. But the witch-girl was gone, and Steve was here.

That was a win.

Arthur nodded and smiled at the little terrier who yapped and wagged his tail in response. There are few things as soothing for a troubled mind as a dog.

It's all a matter of perspective, Arthur realised. As his mum always said, sometimes you have to really search for the good. It might take a while, but it's always there. It just depends on where you look.

"You know," he said, "it's bloody awesome that you came back as a dog."

"It is, isn't it?" Steve grinned and barked for joy, jumping around in little circles as he did.

Arthur laughed. "You're happy, aren't you mate," he said. It wasn't a question.

"More than I can ever remember," the dog said, wagging his tail.

"Can you remember everything?" Arthur asked.

"Just about," said Steve and suddenly the thought that had been nagging at the edges of his mind began to itch. He scratched his ear out of sheer frustration of not being able to hold on to it. "There are some things I can remember very clearly, but other things are sort of... fading. It's like I don't need them anymore."

"Like what?"

"It's hard to explain," Steve said and paused to gnaw at his hip. He wanted to tell Arthur that all of the stuff humans spend most of their lives worrying about simply didn't matter, that life was really simple and really easy, and full of joy. But he also remembered that it wasn't as straightforward as that for most people. It certainly hadn't been for him. Depression had consumed him. Looking back at it now, it seemed an utterly alien concept. "Dogs are wired differently to people, I guess," he said. "The things that used to matter... don't."

"Sounds good."

"It is," Steve said, and then he ran round in a fast circle purely for the joy of it, the nagging thought momentarily forgotten.

"So, what are we going to do?" Arthur asked, walking away from the school and across the grass to where the river tore at the bank before thundering under the bridge. "I said to my mum and dad earlier that you were my dog but that, well, that was a bit presumptuous wasn't it, mate? I mean, you might have plans. Places to go, things to see—" He paused. This was getting a bit deep, and though Arthur was glad to be figuring out the nuances of man's best friend being a former man best friend, he was unused to talking like this to another bloke. He decided to lighten the mood a little. "...bitches to meet?"

Steve laughed, and Arthur felt it in the core of who he was. There was something wonderful about the sound of a dog laughing, and he realised right then and there, by the bank of the Swale, that he didn't want Steve to go anywhere. As luck would have it, and as we already know, Steve felt exactly the same.

"I came looking for you," the puppy said, and there was nothing else that needed to be added. Sure, there was something important nagging at the edges of memory, but as Arthur bent down to pat him on the head and scratch behind his ears, he couldn't for the life of him think what it was. Suddenly, however, Arthur stopped.

"This!" he said, lifting his hands. "Me patting you, isn't it weird? I mean, you were a man. You were my age. You were a grown man!" he said and stood up.

"But I'm not now," said Steve. "I'm a dog. Look, I'm a puppy!" he turned round and round on the spot. He loved turning round and round on the spot. It filled him with enormous pleasure for absolutely no reason at all.

"But you can talk!"

"Yes, I can. And how many dog owners wish their dogs could do the same?"

Arthur had to admit he had a point. "How many actually speak to them as if they do?" he asked with a smile, thinking of all the characters he had met in Richmond over the years.

The man who lived opposite his mum and dad in a small stone cottage at the top of Mill Lane was inseparable from his springer-spaniel, Charlie. Sometimes you heard Bob talking in the street and you could never be quite sure whether he was speaking to his dog or to a passing tourist. Bob spoke to Charlie in the exact same way he spoke to everyone else. And it was bloody great.

Arthur knelt back down to Steve and patted his back. "It's a bit weird at the moment because, well, you're Steve, but I'm sure we'll get used to it. Like we said in the church, though, we need some ground rules." He picked up a nearby stick and began to tear small twigs from it as he thought. "Number one," he said, standing up with a grin, "no crotch-sniffing or leg-humping!"

"No humping legs," Steve repeated, his eyes glued to the stick in Arthur's hand. He had never humped anyone's leg before, so he didn't think he'd be missing out on anything.

"Number two," Arthur went on, waving the stick to make his point. Steve's eyes followed it hypnotically. "I'm not cleaning up your shit. I know as a responsible dog owner, it's my job, but, well, it's just weird. So, make sure you do your business somewhere else."

"Done," said Steve.

"What about sleeping arrangements?" Arthur asked, thinking back to his childhood dog, Goldie, who always slept on his bed. He shook his head. "No, one thing at a time. We should be very clear about this." He knelt again to Steve and said seriously, "Do you want to live with me?" Steve jumped forward in excitement and licked Arthur on the face. There was a pause while both the puppy and the man looked suitably embarrassed.

"Sorry," said Steve, "I couldn't help it. Instinct."

"So, that's a yes," Arthur said with a grin as he wiped his face.

"Yes," said Steve. "Yes, please. Thank you." The little dog forced himself to sit down, but his whole body quivered with excitement. His tail thumped the cold grass in a blur.

"The talking thing is going to be hard," said Arthur. "It seems that other people can't hear you, but I can, so we're going to need to be careful, or people will think I'm a nutter. There might be times I ignore you. Or times you'll have to get my attention a bit more, well, like a dog, instead of just saying something."

"That's fair."

"What about dog food?"

"What about it?"

"Do you have any preferences?"

"I've never had any."

"What?"

"I've never had any dog food. I've just eaten what I could find."

"Ah mate, that sucks. Hang on." Arthur tucked the stick under his arm and pulled out his phone. He sent his mother a text asking if she could nab some dog food from Bob across the street. He always took Charlie for a last walk around midnight, so he was probably still up. Her reply came back almost instantly.

Will do x.

"Right, well, we'll work on food," he said.

"I have a rule if that's alright?" Steve said, tentatively.

"Yeah, mate, what is it?" Arthur asked.

"Don't wave a stick around unless you intend to throw the bloody thing!" he said. Arthur looked at the stick in his hand as if noticing it for the first time.

"Seriously?"

"Yep."

"Wow."

"I can't help it."

"But it's just a stick!" Arthur said, waving it around.

Steve didn't have the words or the capacity to explain what was happening inside him—the hypnotic pull or the all-consuming desire to chase—so he just started barking and yapping at the top of his voice and jumping from paw to paw. Arthur laughed and threw the stick high and long over the grass and another part of Steve's latent humanity fell away in the sheer joy of the chase.

"That. Was. Amazing!" Steve said breathlessly as he returned and dropped the stick at Arthur's feet. His whole being was aglow with pleasure, he wanted to chase the stick again and again, to teach it who was boss, but he had a more pressing problem to take care of. He ran away from Arthur and headed towards the thick tangle of bushes and scrub that marked the riverbank.

"Where are you going?" Arthur shouted after him.

"To take care of rule number two," the small voice came back.

Arthur laughed and turned away from the bushes to give the dog a bit more privacy.

He felt happier than he had in a very long time, and it didn't have anything to do with the amount of alcohol he had drunk that night. In fact, he realised, he was pretty sure he was sober. That in itself made everything different from the last time

Arthur was so happy and so full of joy that he barely noticed the weather closing in around them. The mists rolled along the river while clouds massed above to greet them, but the shrouded world just made him think of Christmas and the long, happy winter nights spent in this beautiful town when he was a child. He loved the cold, and the early dark nights, how the streetlights glowed a gentle orange in the mist and how the warm lights from the shop windows spilt out onto the shining cobbles of the marketplace. The smell of wood fires and coal chimneys hung delicately in the air, and people were just that little bit kinder to each other in the build-up to Christmas. It was something he had been aware of from a very young age. Even when the wonder of make-believe and fantasy stories drifted away, the magic of Christmas never left him. He loved this town, he realised, almost as much as he loved York.

Arthur was so full of nostalgic joy he didn't notice the figures watching him from beneath the trees. He didn't feel the eyes on him or the way the shadows seemed to bleed into the world like spilt ink.

But Steve did.

"We need to go," the little puppy said in an urgent whisper, returning quickly from the bushes. Arthur hadn't noticed him and jumped in shock.

"Sorry, mate," he said. "Didn't see you there. What were you saying?"

"We need to go."

"There's no rush," Arthur said, completely oblivious to the tone in the small dog's voice. "Did you know that Lewis Carroll went to the Grammar?"

"No," said Steve, looking around at the shadows that seemed to be leaching the light away from The Batts and slowly creeping towards them.

"He's the guy who wrote Alice in Wonderland," Arthur said. "Apparently, he hated it here. I often wonder if he came up with some of the ideas for the story here though, maybe even down by the river. That would be cool."

"Arthur?"

"Yeah, mate?"

"We need to leave."

"Why?"

"Something isn't right."

"What do you mean?" said Arthur, kneeling down beside the dog.

"I don't know. It's just... something isn't right. I think we should go."

Something about the dog's urgency got through to Arthur, and he scooped up the small animal, tucking him into the crook of his arm.

"Okay, mate. Let's get out of here. It's Christmas Eve and it's really late. Dad will have a fire going by now. We can warm up and then get some rest, yeah?"

"Sounds great," said Steve, glancing nervously around, but now that he was being cradled so close to Arthur, his other senses were beginning to wane in the face of the overpowering sense of love he felt for his friend. "Do you feel like you're being watched?" he asked.

"Not really," said Arthur. "Although when someone says something like that in the middle of the night and there are trees around, and it's misty, then I'll probably start to feel that way pretty soon."

He paused and then glanced around with a borrowed nervousness. He started to see the world a little differently. Trunks of trees became torsos, branches became arms and legs, the bushes camouflaged crouching beasts, and the dark places beneath park benches hid malevolent creatures. The encroaching shadows played tricks with his mind, and he laughed at his own nervousness.

"You're a bugger, you mate!" he said loudly—perhaps a little too loudly. "You ruined a lovely night and now I'm seeing bogeymen everywhere!"

"But you know they're real."

"What are?"

"The bogeymen."

"Fucksake, Steve!" Arthur laughed nervously, nevertheless picking up the pace and tramping across the grass towards Millgate and home.

There were two paths Arthur could take: one that ran along the western wall of the park and led through a stone gateway to a narrow lane that took him to the foot of Millgate, and one that ran beside the river and into the waterfalls car park. The first route was quicker, and Arthur made to cut across the grass and walk up the short hill towards Park Wynd, but as he did, the streetlamps marking the boundary flickered and went out. A thrill of fear crackled through him as the hill ahead plunged into darkness.

He didn't pause. He didn't say anything. He just turned and rejoined the original path, walking purposefully towards the gap between the leafless trees beside the riverbank.

The cluster of bare branches and brambles comprising the community garden rose in a steep, dark mass beneath the houses on the hill to his right. Arthur marched on, his eyes forward. The glow from the lights of the car park lit the world ahead, and he hurried towards it, unable to shake the feeling of dark shadows massing at his back.

But then a strange thing happened.

As he passed the circular ruins of the old mill, the tense atmosphere seemed to suddenly lift and then vanish altogether. It was as though something malevolent had been watching over the whole area and then suddenly away. The world became a little brighter, and the roar of the nearby waterfalls filled his ears with a familiar thunder. It was a sound he had heard almost every day since he was a child. If the castle was the sight of home, then the River Swale Waterfalls, or "Foss," was the sound, and Arthur immediately felt at ease. The tension fell from his shoulders, and he loosened his grip on Steve, rubbing the frightened animal on the head.

"Nothing to worry about, mate," he said. "Just being daft in the dark."

"Just be careful," Steve warned. Arthur felt the small animal shaking, and so he held him closer as they walked beside the empty picnic tables towards the entrance to the car park. He was almost through the small gap in the wall when he noticed the man standing above the falls.

CHAPTER 15

"You're lost."

"Am not."

"Go on, admit it. You're lost."

"I know exactly where I am, thank you, and don't you get any more ruddy sauce on my seats."

"Your seats?"

"I'm driving. My seats."

"You're driving and you're lost."

"You try navigating in this bleeding fog!"

Archibald leaned over the steering wheel and shifted in his seat. He had turned the music down as they entered the lamp-lit stone streets of Richmond and then turned it off entirely when the houses and shops turned back into hedgerows and trees.

"Bloody one-way systems," he grumbled to himself.

Katheryn sat in the back in rapt fascination. She had moved to the middle where she could lean forward with her head between the two men and watch the world go by. The roses were still gripped firmly to her breast, though every now and then she reached out to pass her spectral hand over the box of golden chicken nuggets on the seat beside her. She could almost feel the warmth. Almost. She closed her eyes and tried to imagine the smell, and the taste, though she had no real idea what it might be comparable to... chicken used to arrive on silver platters, not small boxes, and it certainly was never presented as golden "nuggets." Despite the lack of certain necessary senses, the queen knew they would be glorious. She smiled. The world was endlessly fascinating. Even the bickering coming from the front seats couldn't dampen her joy.

The brothers had been grumbling at each other since they left Burger King, but this short journey, in some impossibly ironic way, had given the deceased lady a taste for life, and she wanted to experience as much as she possibly could. Seventeen short, eventful years plus five hundred exceedingly long and boring ones were not enough. The world was a vast and glorious place full of Burger Kings, fast cars, Jimi Hendrix, and chicken nuggets. She wanted more. She wanted all of it. The young queen sat back and smiled to herself.

And Arthur Crazy was the key. He could help her.

An idea had been growing in her mind. There was something about Arthur's power—perhaps the same thing that steered the twins towards him like the magnetic pull of the poles. Something that blurred the lines between the living and the dead. She knew he could release her, send her off into whatever lay beyond the veil, but that was not her desire. Not yet. She wanted to experience the world around her, the here and now. She wanted to live.

What Katheryn Howard really wanted was to drive a car, and the desperate glimmer of hope had risen in her chest that Arthur might be able to help her with that.

After all, if headless horsemen could drive wooden carriages, why couldn't she drive a Jaguar MK II?

There are rules for the deceased as much as there are rules for the living, perhaps even more so. And it is these rules that the Shadowmen are, for wont of a better word, *employed* to police. Although it would be playing fast and loose with definitions to compare them to, say, Officer Boardman, who was at this moment gently stroking his beautiful sleeping girl's hair before helping his wife arrange the presents under the tree.

On entering the police force, a British officer takes an oath to serve "the Queen with fairness, integrity, diligence and impartiality, upholding fundamental human rights and according equal respect to all people."

The oath taken by the man in black—who is currently grasping a leatherbound book and staring with bemusement at the writing that has just appeared on the page—is not so different. There are distinctions of course. His wasn't exactly an oath given freely, and some of the adjectives weren't quite the same, but the gist was vaguely similar. He had a job to do. He made things right. He tidied up all the loose ends.

This particular man (and it is worth noting here that the word *man* is not a precisely accurate description either) was poised on the roof of Richmond Castle staring into the rolling mist and dealing with a sensation he hadn't felt for a very long time. It was the same feeling a junior manager has when the boss leaves them in charge for a week and everything starts to go tits up. It was the feeling of impending accountability.

The Shadowman closed the book with a snap and deposited it inside the folds of his dark, let's say, clothes. He sighed. It was a long and unpleasant sound.

The worst part about being left in charge was supervising all the incompetent idiots who could never seem to do their job properly... and then having no one to turn to when shit hit the fan.

The book was supposed to fix that.

That was the whole point of the it. But everything was mixed up and the damn thing kept changing. Writing appeared on one page then vanished only to reappear on another page. Names were crossed out, as they should be, but then the lines faded, and the names reappeared.

And it all revolved around one man. Arthur bloody Crazy.

For a human who lit up like a flare in the desert whenever he made bumbling use of the power he'd stumbled across, Arthur was annoyingly unreliable and difficult to find.

The Shadowman glanced around. Where were the bloody gargoyles when you needed them?! Not a single one of the useless buggers on this whole bloody castle! For the first time in his existence, he wasn't sure what to do. Accountability and trepidation. These were not feelings he was used to.

He had heard the story of his counterpart, of course, the one who had originally been sent to deal with Arthur. They all had. They all *felt* it. Well, he made a mistake, and he paid the price. He was gone.

Gone.

Never to be seen again.

A price paid in full.

The Shadowman pulled his peaked hat over his eyes and stepped backwards into the shadows of the imposing stone crenelations. The truth was, none of them ever really knew there was a price to pay. Not for them anyway. Certainly not by the hands of a human.

It was the curse of middle-management. You had to keep an eye on the bastards below as well as above.

The cat that had been watching the strange man blinked once and then entirely failed to react when it opened its eyes to see that he had vanished. It licked itself, then walked down the sheer wall of the castle keep, completely ignoring all rules of physics. But then, rules weren't made for cats, and even if they were, they'd just ignore them.

"Just admit you're lost, will you!"

"I am not lost! I know exactly where I am."

"And where is that?"

"Right here," said Archibald with a resigned snort of laughter.

"Right in the middle of this bleedin' road with no clue where the ruddy hell I'm going." He turned to his brother. "I think I might be lost."

Alexander laughed. "Well, I haven't felt anything from Arthur for some time now, so I figured you'd be struggling as well." He turned in his seat to face the queen. "What about you, Your Majesty. Can you sense Arthur at all?"

"Nothing," Katheryn shook her head.

Archibald pulled the car to the side of the road and turned off the engine. He opened the door and climbed out. Alexander joined him in the middle of the narrow country lane and so did the queen, though without the necessity of opening the doors. She sighed and stretched in the night. It had taken a lot of concentration to sit in the car. Like Alexander in the chair, a lot of concentrating on not concentrating. But it had been the car that got her thinking. Again, a bit like the chair, sharing two plains of existence. If she could sit in a real car for this long, there must be ghost cars. Ghost cars she might be able to control. It was a crazy, wonderful thought, and it consumed her.

The trio stood in the middle of the road and the truth was that they were indeed lost. The thick mist had obstructed their view completely in a way that only people familiar with the Yorkshire Dales, or Famous Five stories, could possibly comprehend. It had got so dense that for the last few minutes, the headlights of the car had only been able to pick up one white line at a time, and when the white lines vanished completely, they knew they were in trouble. They looked around but it was pointless. It was the same in every direction.

"Let's turn the car around," suggested Alexander. "At least we know the town is back the way we came."

"Aye, and we know the lad is down there somewhere," said Archibald. They had been following a residual trail left by Arthur when he cast the ball of power over the moors, but now that had faded, and they were left with only a vague idea of where he might be. It was fair to say, however, that he probably wasn't on a cold and mist-wreathed escarpment on the outskirts of Richmond after midnight on what was now Christmas Day. Archibald had a deep sense of pride that didn't often allow him to admit fault, but sometimes the truth points you in an overwhelmingly obvious direction. In this case, it was pointing back the way they had come.

"Let me try something first," Alexander said, pulling his robes tight to his chest against the cold. He stepped into the centre of the narrow road and turned back and forth, trying to get some sense of direction. He lifted his grey head as though smelling the air and closed his eyes. Katheryn watched, fascinated, as the octogenarian lifted his arms and traced intricate patterns in the night with his hands, his fingers creating eddies and swirls in the cloying mists. She moved closer, and he clapped once, his eyes snapping open suddenly. He turned to her slowly, the whites of his eyes wide and bright as he spoke three quiet words.

"We're not alone."

CHAPTER 16

"I'm a traitor! To Christ. To my brother. To my conscience!"

The old man stumbled forwards on the causeway above the Foss and staggered to the edge of the rocks. His walking stick dropped with a clatter that was lost in the roar of the waterfall. Arthur ran forward and dashed out onto the causeway, slowing as he neared the man, then easing closer as though approaching a frightened animal.

At first, he thought the man had been walking on the water itself, but when he moved closer, he realised the old gent was standing on the long stone ledge that ran out into the river above the falls. In the summer it was a haven for tourists to sit and dangle their feet, enjoying the cool reprieve of the fast-flowing tea-coloured river, but now the two men and the dog stood above a raging torrent that thundered over the rocks and roared away towards Catterick.

"Christ, forgive me," the man mumbled, rocking back and forth, the water so high it tugged at his feet.

"Hey, wait!" Arthur said, raising his voice to be heard over the roar of water. "Hey!"

The old man turned in shock and stared wide-eyed at Arthur's approach. Water sprayed cold in the sky, rising from the crash and thunder below to join the thick fog. The two men were barely a few metres apart but their view of each other was diluted and blurred by the elements. Arthur steadied himself and stepped closer. He grew up here. He knew the danger of these waters, the fastest river in England. It took many of those unsuspecting tourists by surprise, especially on this causeway. Upriver, above the falls, the water was often calm and crystal clear, a millpond almost. Young families swam and played in it, but even on soft summer days, the falls were fraught with danger. Deep pools and hidden rocks, whirling torrents, and trapped logs. On a night like tonight, where the heavy rain from previous weeks had gathered in the high places to swell the river on its rush downhill, the Foss was a killer.

"Be careful!" Arthur shouted over the thunder, reaching forward.

He concentrated on planting his feet firmly on the concrete, grounding himself against the pull and tug of the river, his trainers already drenched. He took hold of the old man's shoulder and gripped tightly as the old fella pulled away in fright. Both their feet slipped, and they stumbled slightly before righting themselves.

The man turned to Arthur. Frightened, red-rimmed eyes stared out from beneath unkempt hair plastered across the scarred face by the spray of the falls. Cracked lips and a broken nose protruded from a straggly dark beard flecked with white. He shook his head and tears spilled from his eyes to be dashed away by the spray.

Behind them both, Steve struggled and barked in fright. He backed away, too scared by the force of the river to come any closer. He hopped onto a higher stone, shook himself and whined, the plaintive noise lost in the night as he peered through the fog at the two men on the precipice.

"Have you finally come for me?" the man shouted, trembling in fear, but before Arthur could answer, he yanked his arm away and stepped back.

He was right at the end of the causeway now. One more step and he'd be lost to the falls. He looked at Arthur with an expression of utter pain and anguish on his broken face.

"I'm a traitor!" he screamed, and the river seemed to surge with the power of his emotions, broiling about his feet, coaxing and pulling and whispering and shouting all at once. The man looked into the tumultuous thunder, then lifted his gaze to Arthur once more. "Christ, forgive me," he said and closed his eyes.

Arthur realised too late and dashed forward.

"Jesus receive my soul," the old man sobbed and toppled sideways into the water.

The world slowed, and Arthur struggled to push down the instinct that told him to jump. The water beckoned to him, tugging at his feet and at his mind, telling him to leap without thought into the torrent, to swim, to save the man, to be the hero. It was a split-second compulsion that nearly cost him his life. But Arthur fought back and turned on his heel, slipping and staggering dangerously on the edge of the falls as he made his way to the bank. He dashed past Steve, who yapped in terror, and raced through the gap in the wall, swinging on a lamppost to steer himself down the path that led to the river.

He raced headlong through the dark towards The Batts, his feet thundering on concrete then grass as he re-traced his steps from earlier. He knew he could jump the low wall here and get closer to the water, but that would mean running through the trees where some unsuspecting rock or branch could reach out of the shadows to trip him. He risked a glance to the river and saw an arm clawing for the sky before the old man's body hit a protruding rock and vanished beneath the rolling black. Arthur took a breath and focused on running. The man had been a little way ahead of him and Arthur had to follow the path through the trees, but the curve in the river would mean they should reach the open sandy bank at roughly the same time.

Arthur was fast. He had always been fast, but he could feel his legs burning as he forced them on, pumping his arms in rhythm, willing his body to move. The cold night ripped the air from his lungs as he pushed himself harder and harder and his chest was burning when he burst from the trees and saw the man tumbling like driftwood a few metres ahead, a forlorn shape shrouded in mist and roiling water. There was just one chance before he was swept away completely, and Arthur took it. The only other option was to do nothing and watch him drown.

Arthur leapt from the grass bank onto the sand and raced into the water, keeping his legs high to get as far into the torrent as he could before the force of the river swept him up. He knew it was deeper than normal, but there were still plenty of rocks that could do a hell of a lot of damage if he didn't get far enough into the middle to swim. He burst into the dark water with a dazzling spray of white foam and was almost instantly enveloped and dragged away by the current.

A few moments later, a small black and tan terrier raced across the grass and leapt from the same rock to be swallowed instantly by the raging waters.

The man's breath caught in his throat, and an almost soporific terror stole over him as he leaned forward in the saddle to try to calm the skittish horse that twitched and moved beneath his legs. It was a calmness he didn't feel, and neither was it one he could fake. The horse lifted its head and snorted, shaking and quivering as it caught the scent of something on the hills with them. Something was close, something rancid—something evil.

They were not alone.

Here, high upon Whitcliffe Scar, Robert Willance found himself once more in charge of a nervous and inexperienced horse that was destined to race unchecked through the mists, but this time it was different.

When the Shadowman first took Robert, he had been delighted to find his body was made whole. Burying his leg in the graveyard had been the right thing to do after all, despite the number of people in the town who laughed at him. Even when he became Alderman, they hadn't stopped laughing, though they did try to hide it, especially if they needed something. And they *always* needed something.

Robert's joy had been short-lived, however, when he realised he was destined to relive that fateful November day over and over again.

Night after night he found himself back in the saddle and completely unable control the blasted horse. Oh, sometimes it seemed as though he had the beast calmed, but then the mists rolled in, the horse bolted, and away they went, careening across the clifftop. Every night, for hundreds of years, a headlong dash toward the inevitable... horse and rider plummeting over the edge of what was now known as Willance's Leap.

Of all the things Robert achieved in life, of all the obstacles he'd overcome and all the good he did for the ungrateful people of the town, he was cursed to be remembered as the man who lost his leg falling from a cliff on a stupid horse.

He blamed the townsfolk.

Bastards!

Had he not reminded them so often in life of the great trauma he had overcome, of all the things one could achieve if they put their minds to it... if they just persevered as he had. Was he not a perfect example of fortitude and bravery in the face of insurmountable odds?

After nearly four hundred years, Willance still felt betrayed. The bitterness ate at the ghost. Oh sure, his name lived on, but a small stone monument on the edge of a cliff was not what he had in mind. Most nights he railed at the infernal injustice of it all, raging at the man in black and all the ungrateful bastards who forced him to this torment. He was a force of righteous anger and indignation destined to charge across the cliffs and plunge into the abyss for eternity. But tonight, it was different.

Tonight, they were not alone.

Willance could see nothing in the deep mist but he could sense it, just as the horse could. It sent waves of nauseous fear through his ghostly form that almost caused him to fall from the saddle with the fatigue of terror. He twisted and turned but saw only mist and fog, though he knew there was something out there. Some creature—a monster shrouded in night.

A sharp noise broke the stillness, and the horse snorted and stamped. It was the sound of chains, bunching and rattling, then scraping as though being dragged. But dragged by what?

Willance felt the horse quiver, and suddenly it bolted. He could only cling on desperately to the ethereal reins as they raced through the night. The man clenched his legs tight together then rose forward on the stirrups, loosening the reins and giving the crazed animal its head. He screamed as a roar sounded in the darkness behind them. So close. So terrifying. The guttural howl of a demon!

He turned his head instinctively to the sound and saw a terror leaping from the swirling mist, a chimaera of sharp teeth, snarling lips and nefarious eyes. A nightmare made real, reaching for him with savage claws that missed his back by inches but ripped deep lacerations into the hindquarters of the terrified horse. The dark creature hit the frosty ground and was instantly swallowed by the mist as the horse raced on in terror and pain.

They were alone again, and for a moment, the only sounds were those of the horse's frantic breathing and the thunder of its own hooves, but all too soon the beast was back. Chains rattled in the mist and heavy paws thumped into the ground in pursuit. Robert crouched low over the horse's neck, letting it lead the head-long charge across the cliff tops with no thought of trying to calm the animal or change direction. For the first time ever, he actually wanted the horse to take those three desperate leaps that would see them leave the scar and tumble two hundred feet to the ground below.

Ahead of them, twin lights emerged in the mist, dancing in the night, small pinpricks growing larger as the horse got closer.

Peg lights to guide me home, thought Robert.

"What was that?"
"I don't know."
"Friendly?"
"Did it sound ruddy friendly to you?!"

Alexander saw the set of his brother's jaw and the way he stood, poised and ready. He nodded, walked to the car, and pulled the two swords from the boot, striding over to join his brother without a word. The two men buckled the sheaths to their belts and withdrew the blades with a sibilant hiss. They rolled their shoulders, loosening their limbs. Neither seemed encumbered by age as they had been just hours before.

"We should probably come clean about all the aching bones stuff, love," Archibald said to the queen. "All an act, I'm afraid, to stop people freaking out. Sorry to lie to royalty an' all that."

"I had guessed," the queen said, and there was another roar in the mists. Closer this time.

"Best you get between us, Your Majesty," Alexander said. Katheryn did as she was told with a nervous laugh.

"What could possibly harm me?" she asked as the brothers peered into the swirling mists, their swords held low and ready.

"You'd be surprised."

Another roar sounded in the night, and the trio spun towards the sound. Katheryn felt the thrill of fear and grinned. When you're dead, any sensation is a gift. But as the muted thunder of charging hoofbeats grew in the gloom, she suddenly remembered her darling Lord Acaster. He was gone. And as sad as that was, she knew now that she wasn't ready to follow. Not yet. Her desire now was to simply live, to experience life. She grinned at the irony. It was enough to make you mad.

The thunder of hooves grew louder and seemed to come from all around them, the mists diffusing the echoes over the hilltop as they swirled and danced in rhythm with the sound. The clamorous noise grew, and the mists moved in sympathy. There was a roar, then a shout, and suddenly a horse and rider burst through the billowing fog and raced across the road. For a moment, for just a brief snapshot of time as he dashed in front of the Jaguar's headlights, the silhouette of the rider was cast large against the wall of fog in the night sky. And, as though in slow motion, the shade of a giant claw followed after it, searching, reaching.

Time sped up. The horse hit the road, bunched its legs, and bounded away. It was followed by a huge dog, a terrifying creature of disproportionate size, massive like a bear but far from natural. It crashed from the shadows, missed the panic-stricken horse by mere inches and hit the vehicle with a smash, crumpling the left headlight and plunging half of the road into the dark.

"Bastard!" snarled Archibald as he strode forward, sword in hand, but the giant animal shook itself off and raced after the fleeing horseman with barely a pause. Within seconds, the mists had swallowed both rider and pursuer, and the trio were left in the single pool of pale light as the sound of hoofbeats and claws raced away over the cliffs. The twins didn't say anything, they didn't even look at each other, nor did they hesitate. They simply gripped their swords firmly and vanished into the mists after the horse and the beast. Katheryn followed.

R obert Willance cried out in dread as he heard the animal snap and snarl behind him. It almost had him. Two times it had lunged, and two times he had barely escaped. He saw the gaping wounds in the side of his horse and knew without a doubt that he could be hurt by this creature. Really hurt. Perhaps even killed. He had no time to consider the mechanics of this strange revelation; he just knew that he had to get away. Any creature that could harm a ghost was a creature to be feared.

This was different, he knew. This was not the same as the harm that came to him every night as he left the cliff. That was routine; this was terror. For the first time in four hundred years, Robert Willance drove his horse on with reckless abandon, hoping and even praying for that first leap. They must be close now, surely. He chanced a quick look over his shoulder and wished he hadn't. The creature was right there, bounding through the night, snarling and snatching with sharp teeth, a dark phantom of hell. He sobbed in mortal dread and then felt the muscles of the horse gather beneath him as it leapt.

Once.

Thank God.

Twice.

And all the saints.

A third time.

Christ preserve me.

The world fell away from Robert Willance, and he hugged the horse's neck in blessed relief as they plummeted, once more, to the ground far below.

CHAPTER 17

Cast the eye up now, away from the shattered body of the horse and the unconscious rider. Up the sheer wall of the cliff whose stones are dark and slick with moisture from the winter air. Up over the edge and above, further, to hang over the swirling, coalescing mists. They had a life of their own, dancing and twirling like blown smoke, eddies and currents tracing strange curves and intricate patterns across the top of the world.

A dark creature was left prowling and snarling on the face of the cliff, sniffing at the air and scratching at the frosty ground. Flesh and blood stuck to long talons, and steam rose from shuddering flanks as thick corded muscles rippled beneath the night-black pelt. It was a real creature. Flesh and blood and bone, but half in and half out. A beast of shadows. A hound of hell.

It leaned over the cliff-face and howled into the night; a prolonged and portentous cry filled with simmering malevolence. It was a cry that could stop the heart of the hardiest soul and steal courage from the bravest warrior just as ice steals warmth from the breast. Yet the mists parted, and two men stepped purposefully forwards, their silver-bladed swords drawn and ready. Behind them walked a queen. One of the men bowed.

"Here, doggy, doggy!" Archibald said.

"Really?"

"What?"

Alexander shook his head but did not take his eyes from the beast. The wind whipped at his cloak and lifted his beard over his shoulder like a scarf. His brother stepped to the side, putting space between the two men. Queen Katheryn stayed behind Alexander as he strode forwards. Though the trio could not see the edge of the cliff, they could sense that a few metres away, the world vanished suddenly into the dark abyss. It was the sensation of vast empty space, and perhaps more importantly, depth, that bade them move with caution. Unfortunately, the space immediately in front of the small group was filled with sharp teeth and glowing red eyes as the barghest turned. It sniffed and snarled, crouching low to the ground, a long chain winding back between powerful legs as it looked from one brother to the other.

Katheryn noted the way the two men moved, not unlike the animal itself, all the subterfuge of age and aching bones gone as they drifted over the grass with lithe steps. They were poised and ready. The sharp tips of the swords barely wavered as they pointed directly at the creature, tracing patterns through the swirling eddies of mist as they kept track with its movements. The barghest turned left then right, twisting its huge head to stare at one brother then the other, trying to keep track of each as they moved apart. Somewhere deep down, in the small part of the animal that was still tied to evolutionary instinct, a minuscule spark urged caution.

These were no normal men.

That instinct was quickly and violently overridden with dark malevolence. The beast shook its head and snarled, snapping at the air beside it as a dog does to an errant fly.

The two brothers looked at each other, Archibald with a raised eyebrow. The beast seemed to be fighting itself. This wasn't how either man thought this encounter might occur, but they would take any advantage they could get. Alexander nodded, then dashed forward with sword raised. He was fast. Much faster than his appearance would have suggested. He moved with the fluid ease and strength of a young man who trained every day, the sword an extension of his own arm. He sliced through the air with deadly precision, but despite his speed and skill, the barghest was faster. Unnaturally so. As Alexander's blade swept down, it hit nothing but the empty space where the creature used to be. The devil was already in the air, lunging for Archibald who only had time to lift the tip of his blade and hold hard, hoping to drive it through the neck of the diving animal and end this quickly.

The point of his sword smashed against the metal collar and was turned aside with a rending scrape. Claws flashed in the night and Archibald twisted his body to the side, feeling the skin of his ribs rip and tear as the beast caught him. He spun with a grunt, and his brother was there, standing over him as he rose once more to face the demon. Blades lowered, and the creature turned swiftly to meet them. It charged with a roar and suddenly the night was full of shouts and thuds as claws ripped, teeth snapped, and swords parried and blocked.

There was nothing Katheryn could do but watch the whirlwind in front of her as the two men spun and twisted in a savage dance of sword and steel and bone and claw. The beast moved like a shadow on the clifftop, darting and diving in and out of the swirling mists to rip and tear at the two brothers. They were so fast and so brave, never faltering, but Katheryn could see there was no way they could keep up with the frenetic pace of the deranged animal. Sooner or later, they would tire, and the creature would find a way through.

Archibald's sword flashed in a sudden shaft of moonlight that pierced the mists as he hammered at the beast, again and again, swinging his sword overhand like an axe, the exertion causing him to roar in rage, the blade flashing at each high stroke. He battered the creature back, and Alexander stepped in with a perfect wide swing of his own sword. Katheryn grasped the roses to her breast as the blade cut through the mist almost in slow motion, heading straight for the creature's snarling face. At the last second, the great head dropped, but Alexander's sword still found home, slicing through a mangy ear, hewing it clean off and carving a deep gouge into the black scalp of the animal.

The beast shuddered at the shock of pain and staggered back, growling and dripping blood onto the frosty grass. The flap of flesh showed bright white for a moment, then quickly turned bloody red in the moonlight. The animal stopped its movements and growled deeply, a sound of summoning rage and malevolence. The red eyes turned black, and suddenly, the world around them changed. The dancing eddies of mist twisted and turned in retreat as the dark shadows took on more substance. Katheryn stared in fright as the darkness closed in, gathering behind the devil-dog as it shivered and shook. She stepped closer to the brothers, and they moved back, panting heavily, swords still held low and ready. They had fought barghests before, creatures and men beyond reckoning, but nothing like this. There was something else at play here.

"We should've got the ruddy sword," Archibald gasped.

"No time, brother."

"Aye."

"You okay?"

"Grand."

The massed shadows behind the animal seethed and pushed as though spilling up against an invisible barrier, and the mists became stretched and thin, a veil between worlds. Furious and driven mad by pain, the great beast clawed at the earth and snapped at the sky, howling as spittle fell from its teeth and steam rose from its dark body, but the creatures in the shadows urged it on. It shook its head, splashing blood over the grass where it steamed in the cold night. It snapped once more and then tilted the bloody mess to the side as if listening.

The dark masses screamed.

"That's different," Alexander said.

"Aye," Archibald agreed through gritted teeth.

"Might've bitten off more than we can chew here, brother."

"Never."

The animal moved in a low crouch, the heavy chain dragging through the pool of dark blood as it stepped forward, eyes once more flashing red in the night. Katheryn stepped back in terror, and the brothers each instinctively put an arm out to shield her. She watched from between their shoulders as the barghest stalked towards them, noting how both men breathed heavily, the steam of their breath spiralling into the night as sweat plastered grey hair to red faces.

Blood dripped in a steady flow from the wound on Archibald's side and spattered onto the grass. Katheryn marvelled at the way it too steamed in the cool air. She stared at it for a long moment.

Many things were easily forgotten when you no longer need to pay attention to them. The warmth of blood was one.

Warmth.

Katheryn closed her eyes, and images of her short life danced in her mind. The joy, the heartache, and the pain. The whirlwind romance with the king that brought her to the attention of the entire world. The abuse. The manipulation. The control of her every move. The complete lack of choice. Her life had been lived for the whim and advantage of others and the only thing she ever took for herself resulted in death and an eternal sentence of loneliness. She gripped the roses and thought of the manor, of her one night of freedom, of her love. She thought of all the ghosts and spirits she had tried to help in half a century as the city of York grew around them—a hive of life surrounding the dead. She thought of her darling Lord Acaster and his cats, and she thought of all the courtiers who knew only how to serve and fawn and scrape, even in death. She thought how unfair it all was, and that thought was worse than all the rest.

"You are a queen," she hissed to herself.

Katheryn dropped the roses, opened her eyes, and stepped between the two brothers, her ghostly form passing through their outstretched hands. She glanced from one to the other—these brave men she had known for only a few short hours, who had shown her wonders she never thought possible, who were ready to give their lives for her.

That was not fair.

The barghest snarled and snapped, its back legs bunching as it readied itself to leap, and this time neither Alexander nor Archibald were fast enough, but neither was the beast. Katheryn lifted her hands, and a smile creased her face as she felt her ethereal fingers touch their robes and come up against solid mass just as they had done at the Manor.

Life. And warmth.

It took all her effort, but it was enough. Queer. Katheryn thrust her arms wide and shoved the two men away. She laughed. To touch is a wondrous thing.

She was still laughing when the barghest hit her, but she was ready. She wrapped her arms around its neck and threw herself back, falling over the cliff and taking the devil with her.

In the shadows of the swirling mists, the dark shapes fought and raged and blinked out of existence as though they had never been. Only one remained. It grinned. And closed a book.

CHAPTER 18

The world was a blur of dark rocks, black water, and misty sky. Arthur felt his feet drag painfully against the riverbed, and he pushed, striving to gain some semblance of direction. There was a moment of panic as he failed to break the surface, but then he gave himself over to the current. There was a big difference between fighting and tumbling out of control, and letting the river take you. Full of regret and fear, Arthur fought the weight of his waterlogged clothes, but there was nothing he could do now other than focus on working with the water and not against it.

He was going to die. He was going to die on Christmas Day because he had to play the fucking hero instead of dialling 999 like a normal person. He raged against the injustice, against his own stupidity, against watching too many damn movies, and tried to think. He remembered reading about people exhausting themselves fighting against rip tides when the best thing to do was go with it. He hoped it was the same for rivers. Arthur twisted as best he could, pointing his legs downstream, and used the momentum to launch himself upwards. He finally broke the surface and gasped desperately, the world a riot of noise as he struggled to tread water and keep his head clear. Suddenly, it all went dark, the sky and trees vanishing into a void.

He was at the bridge already!

The world came back, and the wildness of the river eased off. Arthur felt heavy and slow. Worst of all, he no longer felt cold. He had enough sense to realise this was not a good sign; he had to get out!

The river carried him through more fast gunnels as the waters passed between banks of trees and dangerous clumps of rocks. Suddenly, there he was—the man from the causeway, floating face down within arm's reach. Arthur rolled his body and lunged desperately, catching hold of the unconscious man, using every last ounce of strength to flip him over and lift his face from the water. He dragged and kicked and clawed his way closer to the bank, panting as he flung his free arm into the mass of passing tree roots. Finally, he managed to find a grip on a protruding branch. He tried to pull the man up, but he didn't have the strength. He cried out with the effort and shouted at himself and at the mist and the river, refusing to give in. Somehow, he managed to heave the old man's shoulders into a gap where his head was free. There they lay side by side, lifting and falling with the flow of the water while Arthur hung on. He gasped and spat and sobbed, his head resting awkwardly against the root of a gnarled old tree. His breath came in ragged gasps, and he closed his eyes.

The water lifted Arthur gently, and suddenly there was no pain, just a spreading warmth and the blissful pull of rest. He smiled as the river caressed him and washed the chills and aches from his muscles. The shivering stopped, and he gave himself over to it. Glad to be free.

"Don't give up."

A whisper in the dark.

His eyes moved behind closed lids, seeing something other than the river and the dark trees. He was in a room. A dark stone square. And he wasn't alone.

"Don't give up, Arthur."

Another whisper. A delicate voice on the edge of hearing. He spun in the dark but there was no one there, nothing to be seen.

Just him, alone in the stone room. He noticed a light at his feet, a soft rectangular glow, and he reached down to it, but as he grasped with slow fingers, the room turned and the light became a window.

"Keep going," a voice said, and this time, it was right beside him.

He spun on the spot and stared into familiar big brown eyes—eyes that had haunted his dreams and every waking moment for six months.

"Keeping going," she smiled, and he reached for her.

Sarah Brocklebank.

Arthur held the young woman's face between his hands and sobbed at the touch, his heart hurting as it beat hard once then slowed right down. He leaned forward to kiss her, but everything stopped, and he couldn't move.

Sarah's eyes grew wide, and she whispered, "Never give up," but then, to his horror, her face melted between his hands, the features distorting and twisting as the room spun. They whirled in a spiral of darkness, and Arthur could do nothing but hold on as the face vanished into a blank mask.

Slowly, horrifyingly, it took a different shape, pulsing between his hands.

Two dark spots spread like ink and became eyes... and then they opened. A flash of red as malevolent as dying suns in the centre of each. Black hairs crawled from the scalp and cascaded over his hands, writhing and working their way through his fingers, wrapping around his wrists like oily black vines. Arthur tried to pull away, but the hair held him fast as a dark slit opened in the mask and became a mouth that laughed and laughed and laughed.

The room continued to spin with the cackling face at the centre, and Arthur screamed in terror while a fear unlike any other rose within him. He realised the pain in his chest was different.

His heart had stopped beating.

Arthur closed his eyes and tried to shut away the howling laughter and the image of the tortured face. He shook his head violently and screamed again, but this time no sound came, and suddenly, the world was completely and utterly silent.

"Never give up." The faintest of whispers.

"Never give up." Louder this time.

"Get up!" a ferocious call to action that was cut off by a long, baleful howl.

Arthur's eyes snapped open, and all the pain of the world and his freezing body flashed back in an instant. In front of him, directly in front of his face, a soaking wet Steve shivered and barked and yapped for all he was worth.

"Get up, you bastard!" the dog shouted desperately. "Get up!"

Arthur gathered himself and forced his legs down against the push of the water. Planting his feet on rocks, he hauled himself from the river and onto the bank where he lay panting. Steve sat down and whined, his small form shivering and shaking in the cold night. Arthur looked up... at the dog and at the man half in and half out of the water. He was painfully and eternally tired.

Don't give up.

He pushed himself to his feet and took two stumbling steps to the old man, grasped him by the shoulders, and hauled him from the water.

He knelt beside the still form and thumped the thin chest with both hands. Nothing happened. He was shivering uncontrollably now. Each shiver like a stab of pain across his shoulders and ribs.

Never give up.

He closed his eyes and searched deep within, into the place that until so recently had been locked away. He summoned the power, and it came instantly, flashing through his body like static. There was pain this time. Piercing, stabbing pain like jumping from an icy bath to a warm one. He welcomed it. It was life. It coursed through his veins and ripped at his muscles as it spread like needles towards his hands, but it was a pain that felt unaccountably wonderful. Purple sparks crackled between Arthur's fingers, and he looked down at the inert form of the old man. And then, because he had watched far too many movies, he put his hands on the still chest and yelled, "Clear!" before pushing down hard.

There was a flash, and Arthur fell back.

A vision flooded him.

Two brothers sat huddled together in a dank jail cell, shaking pitifully and praying for the strength to maintain or the grace to die. Rats crawled over their naked legs and sometimes they just didn't have the strength to fight them off. Their weak bodies trembled, sitting as they were in an inch of fetid water. Their bellies churned and rippled with the spasmodic pains of starvation.

The image changed. There was a light. Soft hay. The smell of food. The pungent waft of incense. A gentle voice urged repentance.

"There is only one true faith. The faith of the blessed Queen Mary and the Holy Father. Just admit the error of your ways. Turn your face from the blasphemy of heathens and be welcomed back to the warm body of the living Christ."

The world turned again, and John Snell blinked at a thousand stars. It was warm and there was a choir. They looked like angels. A white-robed priest was talking, and the stars became candles. A voice was raised, loud and sonorous.

"Do you repent?"

A whisper by his ear, little more than a breath, "Your brother did."

John Snell cried in front of the congregation of St. Mary's and two words tumbled from his lips in mortal heartbreak.

"I repent."

Screams of "blasphemy" and "sacrilege" filled the church, and shouts of dissent rose in protest. John Snell could not see. The images were blurred. The lights painful. But his heart was heavy with anguish as he recognised the voice of his brother and realised he had been tricked.

"Sacrilege! Blasphemy!"

Two men leaned against a tree in a dark churchyard, and John Snell sobbed silently as his companion ripped a branch from an Elm to fashion a crude walking stick. His feet were rotten, his toes missing, his body ravaged by disease and abuse, but the torment in his soul was worse.

"I'm a traitor," he whispered.

Awake in a soft bed. Wracked by pain no doctor could cure. John Snell twisted and turned in torment. Blasphemy. Sacrilege. Traitor. Blasphemy. Sacrilege. Traitor. He had not seen nor heard of his brother in days. Blasphemy. Sacrilege. Traitor.

A long, slow walk to the river. Each step a stab of pain, but it was nothing he did not deserve.

A lone figure above a raging waterfall.

"I'm a traitor. To Christ. To my brother. Jesus, forgive me. Christ, receive my soul."

The dark, tumultuous torrent took him.

In the present, the ghost of John Snell hugged his knees and shivered on the riverbank. Arthur's watch had stopped, and his phone was missing, no doubt heading somewhere at great speed downriver. He had no idea what time it was, but it must have been close to two a.m. He hugged Steve tight to his belly, wrapped in the soaking coat. They were both shaking, and Arthur's lips had turned blue, but the old man just stared straight out over the raging water.

"I've never not died before," he said softly. The ghost knew Arthur had seen everything, but there were still things the young man didn't know. He suddenly felt the need to confess.

"Every night I die," he said. "Every night I'm either at St. Mary's or in the rooms above Trinity Church. Sometimes I'm in the cell and that blasted priest, Dakyn, opens the door to release me, but Richard, my brother, is never there." Tears fell from his eyes. "No matter where I start the night, though, I always end up in the river." He turned to Arthur. "I always drown."

"Not tonight."

"No," he said. "Not tonight."

Arthur leaned forward, and Steve whined. The poor animal was shivering uncontrollably. "I can set you free, you know," he said. "You never have to drown again."

"No." John Snell's voice was firm, even angry. "I deserve this. I hear my brother's cries in the church every night and it agonises my soul. I should have known Richard would never give in to that wretched priest." He broke off as he sobbed and then angrily kicked out at a fallen branch near his bandaged feet. "I can't rest without knowing that my brother is at peace. And when I hear him in the church, I know he is not."

"I can save him too," Arthur said in a quiet voice. John Snell fell silent. Deep in thought.

Steve shivered and whined in Arthur's arms.

"We need to go," the dog stammered. "We can't do anything tonight. It's so cold. You'll die if you stay out in this."

The mist had fallen heavily over the strange trio. It sat just above the raging water, the whole world covered in a blanket of thick white fog. There was no breeze amongst the trees of the riverbank, and so it just clung to the sky above their heads like fallen clouds. Arthur knew Steve was right. The power had given him a reprieve and a final burst of energy, but no amount of weird purple-sparked magic was going to be enough to fight winter in the Yorkshire Dales.

"I *can* save you," Arthur said, rising to his feet with a groan. "And I can save your brother, I promise."

"Be careful what you promise, boy," John Snell said. "A promise is a mighty powerful thing. Especially when broken."

"I do promise," Arthur said. "But not tonight."

He peered through the mist towards the embankment. He reckoned they must be about halfway to Easby Abbey, the old monastery that lay in ruins beside the river Swale. If he was right, the Drummer Boy Stone was just up the hill, and he was only ten minutes from home. The thought of a hot shower and warm fire was almost too much to bear. "What will you do now?" he asked the ghost of the old man, his teeth chattering.

"I don't know, I've never not died before," he said.

"Well, don't leave town. I'll find you in a few days. I'll help you and your brother."

"Promise?" the man asked.

"I promise."

They shook hands, the ghost and the man, and a deal was made between worlds.

CHAPTER 19

"Can you see her?"

"No."

"I wish we had a torch."

"Aye."

Archibald and Alexander picked their way carefully over the rocks at the base of the cliff. They had found a side road and driven the Jaguar carefully down the narrow strip to the bottom of the valley, but they could only hazard a guess as to where the queen and the barghest fell.

"Don't you know any jiggery-pokery to give us a bit of light?"

It always annoyed Alexander when Archibald called the magic jiggery-pokery. He was more than capable of grasping the power for himself; their entire existence was predicated on it, but he still spoke so nonchalantly and disdainfully about that which gave them life, that which gave them... everything.

"There's not exactly a lot to draw from," he snapped at his brother then instantly regretted the flash of anger. "I'm sorry," he said. "How's your side?"

"It'll heal," grumbled Archibald, though both brothers knew that was a lie. A wound from a barghest never heals. Not until the creature is killed. Both men were struggling. They had never seen anything like the way the barghest gathered the shadows behind it. It was as though a thin gossamer veil was all that held back a legion of shadow creatures and demons. They knew, of course, that the beasts sometimes found ways in. Weaknesses and gaps could be exploited, holes widened, but these usually occurred at the moment of death when the fabric was torn anyway. This had been different. This had been like looking into the abyss and realising it was looking right back at you. Their entire existence and purpose was to rid the world of the dark creatures that fell through the gaps, but they had never before come face to face with the painful reality that they were so crushingly outnumbered. Both men suddenly felt very old and very tired, and neither dared admit it. The barghest had been a match for them, perhaps even better. And that in itself was a worry. They had never had a problem with the dogs before, but this one seemed to be guided by a deep malevolence. It was driven, as though a terrifying master stood behind it with a whip of iron and silver. The beast had been afraid. But not of them.

Silver.

A cut from a silver-inlaid blade should have been enough to see the beast run and cower, but instead, it had stood its ground and fought back. Neither man wanted to think what might have happened had Katheryn not stepped forward. And both of them hated the fact that she did. The thought she might be truly gone sat like a stone in their hearts.

"Here!" Archibald cried, and Alexander raced to his brother's side, hoping against hope that Queen Katheryn was okay, and the beast was gone. He stopped and stared. At first, he wasn't sure what he was looking at, but then the strange image began to make sense. A twisted black head and four long legs pointed towards the cliff. Three of the legs were broken and the animal was quite clearly dead. A long, ragged slit opened across its stomach, the contents of which were scattered in bloody offal over the stones. It wasn't so much the stuff of nightmares as the stuff of an abattoir. Suddenly, the stomach moved and lurched, and a blood-red hand burst from the ragged wound, reaching and clawing. It grasped the upper flap of flesh and pushed it open to reveal a blood-drenched face gasping in the night. Despite himself, Alexander threw up in a small bush. *This* was the stuff of nightmares.

"Has it gone?" the face gasped, and the ghost of Robert Willance pushed his head and shoulders from the body of his horse, looking round with frightened eyes.

"What?" Archibald managed in a small voice.

"The beast? Has it gone? The—the devil dog!"

"We fought it on the cliff," said Alexander, wiping his mouth and spitting bile. He looked up. "It fell."

"I know! The blasted horror landed right where you're standing!"

Archibald and Alexander turned on the spot, swords at the ready. They searched the ground and pushed the bushes aside, completely forgetting the bedraggled and terrified ghost of Robert Willance.

"I said, has it gone?" he asked again with desperation in his voice. He didn't want to climb any further out of his horse if he was going to end up clambering back in. The first time had been hard enough.

Normally, the ghost of Robert Willance found himself re-enacting that fateful winter night from four hundred years earlier; when he had tried to save his shattered leg by opening the belly of his horse and thrusting it into the bloody warmth while waiting to be rescued. He never did save the leg, but the doctor reckoned the desperate action probably did save his life.

Tonight, when the beast crashed to the rocks beside him and began to twitch, groan, and shake itself back to consciousness, Robert grasped in mute horror at the stomachs of his horse, removed everything he could, and dragged it to the stones. There was no way he could move far with his shattered leg, and so he was left with only one option. He hid. Robert climbed inside his horse and lay there until he heard the great dog crash and stumble away. He lay for what felt like an eternity. To him, a night far longer and far more dangerous than any other that came before.

One of the tall grey men spun back and marched over to Robert. He crouched in front of him and pointed his sword at the terrified ghost.

"Was there a lady with the beast?'

"What?'

"A lady!" snapped Archibald, grunting at the pain in his side. "Was there a lady who fell with the beast?"

"N—no," stammered Robert Willance.

"Are you sure?"

"I'm sure, I'm sure!" he said, unable to take his eyes from the sword waving in front of his face. He was beginning to miss his normal evening ride and fall. Sitting with his leg in the horse could be strangely peaceful. Certainly, in comparison to this. But the sword point dropped away as Archibald slumped to the ground. Alexander walked out of the mist to join them. He held Queen Katheryn's roses in his hand.

"She is truly gone then?"

"So it would seem."

"Did the beast get her?" Robert asked. The brothers turned away, each lost in their own thoughts. Robert grimaced and pulled himself from the horse, panting with exertion and the phantom pain of his shattered leg. He noted the four rending claw marks on the flank of his horse and shuddered. "What a horrible way to go," he said. "You know, I had no idea until this night that ghosts can be harmed. I mean, I know my leg hurts, but I always figured that was my own memory of pain. I didn't think there was anything that could actually, truly threaten me. I'm dead! What can possibly harm a ghost?!"

"You'd be surprised," Alexander said, and then hung his head at the memory of the same words uttered not so long ago. His fingers turned white on the handle of his sword. "You'd be surprised," he said again, his voice cracking. "Fuck!" he screamed suddenly into the night. Brandishing his sword, he destroyed a bush with savage, uncontrolled swings, each cut like a hammer blow punctuating his words. "Fuck! Fuck! Fuck! Fuck you! Fuck this cliff! Fuck the mist! And fuck the horse you rode in on!"

"And I thought I was the angry one," Archibald muttered, taking a step back as his brother rounded on him, the sword raised and his eyes wild. "Peace, brother, peace. You fucking nutter," he added under his breath.

"Peace? Peace? She was just a kid! She was…"

"Hundreds of years old!" Archibald snapped. "And already dead. For all we know she just… reset. Or whatever the hell you call it."

The sword wavered. Alexander's eyes lost their frightening intensity for a moment.

"You don't know that," he said with a snarl. He tightened his grip and pointed the sword to the top of the cliff. "But you do know *that* wasn't normal. We should've gone straight to Arthur. We shouldn't have got out of the car. We should have got the sword first."

"Aye, well, we ruddy well didn't, did we!" Archibald snapped, his own emotions surging to the surface. "I went the wrong bleeding way, and that lovely lass paid the price!"

At the feet of the two seething brothers, Robert Willance felt an almost overpowering urge to crawl back into his horse. He watched silently as the temper leached out of both men, and the swords, then their shoulders, sagged.

"I guess it's fate," Alexander said, though he didn't sound convinced. He sheathed his blade.

"You know as well as I do there's no such bloody thing as fate," Archibald said. "Just other people's plans interfering with your own."

"Aye, well."

"So, what do we do now?" Archibald muttered, wiping his eyes with the sleeve of his robe.

"We keep going, brother," Alexander replied. "We find Arthur, we find the sword, and we use it to kill that blasted dog!"

"We should've had the damn thing first. I'm sorry."

"Maybe, but we didn't, and I have to believe the queen gave the sword to Arthur for a reason. Nothing happens without cause or design."

"Are you sure about that? After everything we've seen?"

"How can you *not* be sure of that after everything we've seen?"

"Sounds like fate to me."

"Sounds like piss poor planning."

The two brothers looked at one another, trying not to see the lines of age and defeat mirrored back at them.

"How will we—" but Archibald was cut off as something in the distance instantly grabbed the attention of all three figures below the cliff.

If this was a movie, the moment would probably have been marked by some dazzlingly expensive special effects—no doubt a powerful beam of light bursting into the sky and setting fire to the clouds. But this wasn't a movie, and that didn't happen. At best, it was a feeling, a prickling sensation of unmistakable familiarity, and instantly recognisable for what it was. The magic of Arthur.

"What the bloody hell happened to you?"

"Someone decided to go for a swim," Arthur said, holding out the shivering form of Steve to his dad.

"Christ almighty! You jump in the shower, lad, and I'll take care of your dog. What's his name again?"

"Steve," said Steve, but of course, Thomas Crazy didn't hear, so Arthur repeated it.

"Go on, get yourself upstairs and in the shower. It's after two but you need to get the cold out of you first. Lucky I've already put the Christmas log on the fire so it's roaring. We'll have a hot toddy before bed. That'll sort you right out. Go on. Go!"

Arthur couldn't argue with his dad. There was never much point anyway as they hardly ever disagreed, and he certainly couldn't argue with the idea of a hot shower and a warm drink. He dumped his soaking clothes in the small hallway at the front of the cottage that always reminded him of an airlock.

When he was a kid and going through an outer-space phase, that's exactly what it had become. The world outside was the vastness of space, the entrance to the house an airlock, and the doors to the dining room and living room two separate areas of the spaceship. In reality, the cottage below the castle was, like the other six houses on the terrace, a hodgepodge of much older buildings that had been built up, knocked down, and knocked through for hundreds of years. It always made visitors laugh that the rooms above the Crazy's dining room didn't actually belong to them but were, in fact, a little holiday flat only ever used in the summer.

Arthur discarded his clothes and shoes on the tiled floor and opened the door into the living room in just his boxer shorts. He was immediately hit by the warmth of home. Not just the physical warmth of the open fire, which was indeed roaring below the chimney, but the warmth of *being* home. The low white ceiling crossed with oak beams, the large wooden desk with its cracked green leather top in the corner, the deep L-shaped couch and the television, Christmas lights, candles, wreaths and decorations that had been with him since childhood. They were all there, eternal and unchanging. He breathed it all in and felt... wonderful. And then he felt like a complete prat for nearly throwing it all away by diving into a freezing river after a dead man. But even the dead needed their advocates, and he was here now. Home. Arthur smiled. For the first time in a long time, he felt both peace and purpose. It was intoxicating.

The moment was spoiled slightly when his mum turned in her seat and burst out laughing when she saw her shivering, nearly naked son standing in the doorway. Her mouth framed the question, but Arthur just said, "Don't ask," and jogged past her to the bathroom upstairs.

Thirty minutes later, the scene before us would not be so out of place on the front of a Christmas Card (if you have an open mind about all the Norse paraphernalia and knick-knacks accrued by Mrs. Crazy over the years. It's not often you see a manger scene with the little baby Jesus being watched over by a statue of Odin, never mind the array of Christmas Lego Star Wars figures because Mr. Crazy insists on a Lego Advent calendar every year). Arthur's parents sat snuggled together on the deep couch with Arthur on the thick rug at their feet. Each person stared silently into the roaring fire, lost in their own thoughts, a steaming cup in hand. The fairy lights flickered soft and warm, and the tree in the corner by the desk glistened with deep gold and red baubles. The fire crackled musically as flames licked at the traditional Christmas log. The first to be lit on Christmas Eve was always the last to be used from the year before, and each person (and dog) felt at peace. The house was full of tradition and warmth and love and life. The family stockings hung from the thick wooden mantle of the fireplace as they had every Christmas Eve for twenty-six years, but there was an addition this night—one that when Arthur noticed left him momentarily speechless. Next to his own threadbare red stocking hung an old football sock with a name written in permanent marker.

Steve.

On the outskirts of the mist-wreathed town, a creature prowled along the bank of the great river, looking for a place to cross, snarling and snapping in madness and pain. A heavy chain dragged behind it, catching on overgrown roots and forcing the animal to bunch the great muscles of its neck, then thrust and pull until something gave. It was never the chain. It howled in frustration and rage, a long, lamentable roar of obsession.

It was injured, but still, the barghest hunted.

PART II
CHRISTMAS DAY

CHAPTER 20

For a long time, Arthur simply lay still with his eyes closed and listened to the sounds of the world coming alive around him. The birds outside his window sang in celebration, and the house creaked and groaned as the cold night gave way to a slightly warmer day. Doors squeaked and stairs creaked as his parents moved quietly downstairs. A deep rumble from his dad and a hushed giggle from Mum. The click of the kettle and the unmistakable sharp chink of a teaspoon stirring sugar. He heard doors open and slam from the neighbouring houses, cars start, and tyres roll slowly down the terrace as families set off to visit relatives. The bark of a dog and a muted "Merry Christmas" from one neighbour to another. All across the town, church bells began to toll. Arthur lost track of how many chimes there were, as he was simply content to lie there in the deep comfort of his bed.

He used to think that coming home was some form of defeat, like he hadn't made it as a man if he had to crawl back to his parents. Indeed, that's how he felt when he stepped off that bus, and that's how he felt for a long time in the past half a year. His parents never made him feel like that of course. They welcomed him with open arms and gave him whatever space they thought he might need. The defeat was all in Arthur's own mind, and he realised this now as he stretched and smiled, happy to be surrounded by the magic memory of childhood.

His toes touched something.

It was cold and scratchy and moved slightly under his feet. He shivered and set a questing toe forward. He touched the object again and felt, rather than heard, something crinkle beneath his touch. Arthur's eyes snapped open, and he lifted his head to look at the foot of the bed. His toe rested on a familiar red shape, and he grinned widely. His Christmas stocking sat just outside his blanket, stuffed to overflowing with presents. He closed his eyes for a moment as the memory of fast-flowing water threatened to intrude on his happiness, but it simply floated away as he also remembered his power had returned. He flexed his fingers and grinned.

He was home. It was Christmas Day, and the magic was very much alive.

The morning passed into afternoon blissfully unaware it was riding the wave of the oldest cliche in the book, the calm before the storm. The Crazies exchanged presents in front of the fire, ate a breakfast of bacon and eggs, called in to the neighbours to wish them all the best and introduce them to Steve who, of course, was having the greatest day of his life. They opened the first beers just before midday as all four danced in the kitchen and helped with dinner. Soon the small brick house was full of the smells of honey-glazed turkey, sage and onion stuffing, roast potatoes, and veg. Steve's tail wagged so hard he had to sit on it but, even then, he found his whole body vibrating with pleasure. The smells. Oh God, the smells!

The family were sitting at the dining room table having a relaxing drink before serving dinner when they first became aware of the commotion on the terrace outside.

Mrs. Crazy wiped her hand across the condensation on the

dining room window and peered out. The town was still shrouded in fog, but she could see a car having trouble at the top of the steep hill right outside the house. This was not unusual. The narrow road of Millgate turned almost ninety degrees and descended sharply to the Foss car park. Many drivers misjudged the fork where the road split into the ramp of Castle Terrace, finding themselves on the narrow lane right outside the Crazy's dining room window instead of heading down to the river. Reversing back onto Millgate wasn't easy, and vehicles often got trapped, half on and half off the terrace.

"Someone's done it again," Mrs. Crazy said to her husband. "Nice car this time."

Arthur and Thomas stood up and left the dining room, the chill of the outside world hitting them as soon as they stepped into the "airlock." They opened the front door onto the terrace and stopped, completely stunned by what they saw. It wasn't the beautiful old car with one shattered headlight balanced precariously on the steep curb that gave them pause, nor was it the usual breathtaking view of the tall stone buildings hugging the hill below the castle shrouded in thick fog. Rather, it was the sight of two elderly gents in long robes with waist-length grey beards and matching hair arguing about how best to get the car free.

"Bloody hell! It's Saruman and Gandalf," Thomas Crazy whispered to his son, throwing his coat on as he stepped onto the terrace. "Merry Christmas, gents," he said cheerfully. "Would you like a hand?"

The closest man—and here Thomas and Arthur realised they were looking at identical twins—turned and forced a smile. He looked tired and angry, but he tried his best to hide it. He did not entirely succeed.

"No, thank you, good sir. We have it under control. My brother here just missed the turn is all. Merry Christmas to you," he added as an afterthought.

"You were bloody navigating," the other man said in one of those semi-quiet tones designed precisely to be heard, though with just enough softness for deniability. The two grey men glared at one another; a simmering anger almost palpable in the frosty air.

"Come on, fellas," said Thomas. "It's Christmas. No harm no foul. It happens all the time, trust me. That turn can be a right bugger if you're not used to it. Look, we've lived here for thirty years, and I could tell you a hundred stories like this one, but I'll tell you the most important." He strode towards the men, rubbing and blowing into his hands for warmth. "Lots of people get their car on here, but there's very few as can get it off. Luckily, you're looking at two who can."

The two old men looked at each other, and it seemed to the watching father and son that a silent conversation passed between them. The one nearest the car shrugged and strode over to shake Thomas's hand.

"Thank you," he said. "I'm Archibald, and this 'ere is my brother, Alexander. We'd appreciate your help."

"Pleased to meet you," said Mr. Crazy. "I'm Thomas, and this is my son, Arthur. Are you gents in town to see family?"

Mr. Crazy's question remained unanswered as Archibald held onto Arthur's outstretched hand, his eyes growing wide as the proffered handshake stretched on.

"Arthur?" he said in a small voice.

"Yes," Arthur replied with a raised eyebrow. "Erm, nice to meet you."

The other brother moved closer, slowly, rubbing his hand through the hair on his beard and cheek. It was an oddly nervous gesture. "Arthur from the city of York?" he asked.

Now it was Arthur's turn to stare. He tried to pull his hand away, but the old man's grip was like iron.

"What—"

"Arthur with the sword?"

"How—"

"Do you have the sword?" the brothers asked in unison, each placing a hand on Arthur's shoulders. There was no malice there.

No threat. Just pleading, desperate hope. Arthur swallowed and nodded.

"Yes."

"Then we've found him," Alexander said with a broad smile of relief.

"Aye, but it's not *him* him, is it. You know that."

"No, but he has the sword."

There was a polite cough, and all three men turned to look at Mr. Crazy, who was standing in front of the Jaguar in his bright red Christmas jumper with the Rudolph nose flashing merrily away.

"What sword?" he asked.

Picture your classic Christmas dinner. The family gathered around the table shoulder to shoulder with glasses of wine and bottles of beer, juice for young children, perhaps, and a festive table-cloth laden with platters and deep dishes full to the brim with delicious steaming food. Everyone dressed in their best and wearing cheap paper hats while plates are passed across the table. Shining cutlery clinking and scraping alongside the low murmur of a meal being enjoyed by all. Now picture the same scene with two elderly strangers sitting awkwardly to the side, holding swords at their waists while Mrs. Crazy, instead of eating in merry communion with her family, busies herself trying to unlock the eaves of a table that hasn't been used in quite a number of years. Arthur is clearing the plates his mother so recently laid down and organising things so that, when she eventually manages to "shift that blasted latch," the table will extend and they'll "all be able to fit quite comfortably, don't you worry. No, no, it's no imposition."

By the time Mr. Crazy rescued the brothers' car and parked it in front of his own, the room he entered does indeed look a little something like that picture-perfect Christmas scene. A large round table with places set for six: mother, father, son... two grey brothers and a puppy called Steve who can't quite believe his luck (because Mrs. Crazy is that kind of woman).

"No swords at the table," said Mrs. Crazy, then giggled to herself before taking a large drink from her wine. "Please," she added.

"Yes, ma'am!" The brothers bowed nervously in unison, unstrapping their weapons and, after an awkward look around the room, placing them in an umbrella stand near the door.

"Oh, don't call me that," said Mrs. Crazy with a laugh, though the red flush on her cheeks told both her boys she secretly loved it, but then, that could have been the wine. "My name is Maggie. Well, it's Martha, but everyone calls me Maggie. It's my middle name, you see. I much prefer it. Oh, look at me, babbling on."

"Dear Maggie"—Alexander bowed low—"we thank you for your hospitality. It is most unnecessary—"

"Aye, but most welcome!" said Archibald, who had been eying off the roast potatoes as they sat in a steaming mound with crisp brown edges and glistening white flesh on display. He loved roast potatoes.

"Right, gentlemen!" announced Thomas Crazy. "What can I get you to drink? We have beer, cider, wine, or something a little stronger if you prefer?"

"Oh, we'll be—" Alexander started but was instantly cut off by his brother.

"We'd love a beer, thank you kindly."

Arthur watched, unblinking, as the scene unfolded before him. His mother taking her seat at the table after bringing over a steaming jug of gravy. The two elderly wizards (that's what they looked like and so that's how he thought of them) standing politely as she sat and giggled her thanks. His father fetching four big brown bottles of Black Sheep Ale from the fridge and handing one to each man there—Arthur took his wordlessly—then pouring his wife a glass of wine. And Steve, Steve the dog, standing on the chair next to his mum with his paws on the table and his pink tongue lolling in delight.

The little black terrier looked directly at Arthur, tilted his head, and said, "This is awesome!"

Both Archibald and Alexander jumped slightly and glanced at the dog, and Arthur started to laugh. It began as a snort and then turned into a nervous giggle but quickly built into a full belly laugh he just couldn't rein in. Tears streamed down his cheeks, and he struggled to catch his breath. It was either that or descend into madness. When he finally got control and took a drink of his beer, he looked up to see everyone at the table staring at him, including Steve, and it was almost enough to set him off again.

"Sorry," he said, composing himself with some effort. "So, I guess there's a few stories to be told."

"Not now," interrupted Mrs. Crazy. "Now we eat. Everyone is hungry, it's Christmas Day, and everything makes more sense after a nice meal."

"And this is indeed a lovely meal, Maggie," Archibald said with a grin, reaching for a potato. Alexander slapped his hand away.

"Not before our hosts," he said.

"No, no, help yourself, tuck in, please!"

And so, the strangest Christmas Dinner Arthur Crazy and his family had ever experienced began in earnest. The turkey was carved and portioned out, potatoes danced from bowls to plates, heaps of vegetables were passed around and gravy splashed and mopped up with the mountain of dark brown Yorkshire puddings. People burped and sighed and laughed and thanked each other for passing unreachable plates, and Steve was hand-fed more food than he had ever seen in his whole canine existence. Crackers were pulled, jokes read, and thin paper hats distributed to all. The strange thing was the strangers didn't feel like strangers. Archibald and Alexander had perfect manners and charming smiles. They were gracious and polite at all times, and when everyone sat back in belt-loosening contentment, they rose from their seats and insisted on clearing up. There was a brief ruckus as the Crazy family told their guests to be seated, that they wouldn't hear of such a thing, but Alexander waved his hand and said a few unintelligible words. Somehow, the family sat back and watched as the two men made short work of the dishes. It was quite a sight to behold—identical twins with long robes and flowing hair hunched over the small sink, passing plates back and forth, one with a green paper hat and one with pink. When they had finished, Mrs. Crazy thanked them and brought out the desserts: a deep trifle, a Christmas pudding, and the biggest turkey bone she could find for Steve.

"We have a tradition in this family," she announced as she laid bowls on the table in front of the men. She lifted Steve to the floor where he happily dragged his bone to the radiator beneath the window. "Before we have pudding, we go around the table and we each say the things we are most grateful for. I'll begin." She smiled, raising her glass. "I am grateful for my husband's wonderful turkey—"

"Here! Here!" Archibald roared, banging the table with his bottle. He winced and held his side, but no one noticed. Alexander groaned at his brother's outburst, but the other two men laughed.

"—for you fine gentlemen joining us for dinner," Mrs. Crazy continued, "and for my son." She turned to Arthur and paused before finishing in a quiet voice laced with emotion, "whose smile has returned."

Arthur didn't trust himself to speak, so he simply leaned over the table to kiss his mother on the cheek. She threw her arms around his neck and held him tightly. He could feel the warm tears on her cheek.

"I'm grateful for you, Mum."

"And I'm grateful for my wife, my boy, getting to drive a beautiful Jag on Christmas Day, and Black Sheep Ale!" announced Thomas Crazy, sensing a shift in mood might be needed. Everyone laughed, and Mrs. Crazy let go of her boy. She wiped her eyes and sat back in her seat, smiling at her husband. She squeezed his hand and turned to their guests.

"Gentlemen?"

Alexander rose from his seat with beer in hand and raised it to

Mrs. Crazy. "To you, dear lady. For inviting us in. For new friends," he nodded to Thomas. "And... for finally finding you, Arthur."

Archibald rose to stand beside his brother. He lifted his glass to Arthur and said, "Aye, the same. I'm grateful we found you at long last."

"Why me?" Arthur asked. The question that had been on his mind throughout the whole dinner finally out in the open. "Why are you looking for me?"

"We've been trying to find you since York."

"Since the *girl*."

Mr. and Mrs. Crazy turned from their guests to look at their son. The handsome dark-haired young man they were so incredibly proud of but who was such a mystery. A closed book they had struggled to talk to for the better part of a year.

"Perhaps it's time to tell a story, son?" Thomas Crazy said.

CHAPTER 21

Arthur told his parents everything. Everything that had happened, everything he remembered, every painful detail and shocking mystery, every single thing he told the shrinks who tried to diagnose him with anxiety-induced delusions or put him on drugs to "even him out." He was terrified of their judgement. No, not judgement, that wasn't right. He was scared of something else. Their pity, perhaps? Their disbelief? That somehow, he had let them down. Arthur didn't leave out a thing, but neither did he look at his parents as he spoke. He sat with his head down, feeling like a child being admonished in the head teacher's office. His voice wavered as he told them about walking through walls, dark men with savage blades, and the demon girl.

He was telling his parents he walked through walls! Telling them he spoke to dead people! That ghosts were real!

Whatever happened next, there was no turning back.

The white coats are calling, he thought. *The white coats are calling.*

Arthur's voice grew small as he struggled to explain the depth of feeling between himself and the ghost of Sarah Brocklebank, of how this strange power of his allowed him to see the true nature of events that resulted in ghosts being trapped in the first place. And of how, at the moment he defeated the demon girl, he also felt the true nature and feelings of his companions. Sarah loved him, and he killed her. Lord Acaster was desperate to fulfil his duty, and he killed him. Steve wanted to live, and yet he died as well. Because of Arthur.

The story twisted and turned as he remembered bits and pieces and retraced his steps, trying to fill in the blanks. His parents sat still, their presence felt the way only a mum and dad's presence can be felt, but they never interrupted, they asked no questions. They just let him talk. It was only when he mentioned the creature known as the Fetch that Archibald rumbled,

"Aye, that'll be what started it all right enough."

The Fetch, Arthur explained to his parents, was a demon that took his form but more than that, it *was* him... and it tried to kill him. Even now he wasn't sure how he defeated it. He had a strong memory of punching himself in the face in a deserted street and something about a mirror, but it was all so jumbled and mixed together. This was the part the shrinks loved; it always got them scribbling with furious abandon in their little black books. Arthur Crazy fighting himself. There was something to diagnose there, surely, some sort of *Fight Club* style dissociation, but Arthur knew he wasn't delusional. He knew it wasn't a product of his mind. Over the last six months, however, when the power seemed to have abandoned him, the seeds of doubt had needled their way in. Logic tried to force its way back through the memories and provide explanations for fantastical events, and it had been tearing him apart. But now the power was back, and Arthur knew for certain it was real. He stretched his hand out on the table and looked up. His parents were staring, their faces unreadable, both sets of eyes rimmed with tears.

"I can prove it," Arthur whispered.

"You don't need to," his father said.

The Green Bridge crossed the River Swale, connecting the steep road of Slee Gill to the imaginatively named Bridge Street on the town side of the river. It was called Green Bridge not because it was green, which it wasn't, but because it led directly to the village green below the castle, which demonstrated, amongst other things, that the world used to be a far simpler place. A sharp right turn immediately after the bridge and before the green led to Riverside Road (it must have been a long day in the road-naming office)—the very same street that Arthur, from high above on Castle Walk the night before, had unknowingly watched the ghost of John Snell limp towards the waterfalls. The road swung in a wide loop as it hugged the bottom of the promontory upon which the famous castle had its home. When it reached the waterfall car park, the road followed the bend of the river and took a sharp left up the steep hill of Millgate where, at the top, sat the house of Arthur Crazy and his family. So, it was probably a good job that the barghest did not turn right along Riverside Road but instead slunk, unseen, into the deep shadows of Cornforth Hill.

The mists lay thick and heavy over the town, and from a distance, it seemed as though only the very tip of the castle peered out from above dense clouds. Streets, alleyways, snickelways, and wynds were all shrouded in a pallid heavy blanket that blocked out the meagre sun and plunged the land into a strange and sullen darkness. And through the silent streets, the barghest stalked its prey.

In a blissfully warm and content stupor, Steve dreamt. Mostly, he dreamt of smells and of running fast and of Arthur. His best friend. Each smell had its own colour and drifted across his world like floating rainbows. He chased them. He was happy. He was a good boy. People patted his head and scratched behind his ears and gave him food. He liked that. But there were shadows in his dreams. Flashes and images. Memories of a different life.

Glimpses of the spaces in between. He whined and tried to run. Away from the shadow and towards the voice of his best friend.

"You believe me?" Arthur asked, looking from his mother to his father. They didn't reply. They didn't say a word, and a pit threatened to open inside Arthur's stomach as the silence stretched on. His mother's face was a mask of worry and concern, but his father's was unreadable. This was what he feared the most. Their disappointment. Their shame. Their need to fix their boy. Thomas Crazy lifted his eyes to his son, red-rimmed and fathomless.

"It's a lot to take in, son. I mean, you don't lie. I know you don't lie. *We* know you don't lie! But, I mean... wow."

"I know, Dad. But it's true. Every word of it."

"And this is what you've been telling doctors and psychologists this past year?"

"Yeah."

"What did they say to that?"

"What do you think?"

Thomas and Arthur Crazy both took a drink of their beers, and the silence stretched on. Archibald shifted uncomfortably, and Alexander silenced him with a look. Maggie stared at the glass of wine she held in white fingers. In the corner, Steve whined in his sleep.

"I *can* prove it, Dad," Arthur said after a time.

"No. No, I don't want you to, son. I bet you can, but I don't want you to. I want to wrap my head around it before you do. I know, I know that sounds daft but... this is important. I've... I've not believed you before and..."

"Thomas," Mrs. Crazy said, taking hold of her husband's hand, knowing exactly what he was thinking. She often said she knew her husband better than he knew himself, and in this case, she was absolutely spot on.

Tears spilled over Thomas Crazy's cheeks, nearly disarming Arthur completely. The older man rubbed his eyes and looked directly at his son.

"Do you remember Hundred?" he asked quietly. Maggie looked away, her own eyes red.

"Hundred?" said Arthur. "Hundred what?"

"Not what. Who."

"I don't understand."

Thomas Crazy leaned towards his son and gripped the still outstretched hand. He held it tight and stared into the eyes of the person he loved more than he'd ever had the words to express.

"We believe you, son. That's not the problem. That's never the problem… anymore. What we need… is forgiveness."

"Forgiveness for what, Dad? I'm really confused."

"Hundred is… was… a ghost, darling," his mother said through her tears. "Here. In this house. Only—"

"Only we never believed you," Thomas finished, gripping his wife's knee with his other hand. "You were so young. Do you really not remember her?"

Arthur shook his head.

"When you were little. Maybe four or five, you used to tell us all the time of the little girl at the top of the stairs. She was called Hundred. We just thought it was an imaginary friend at first, you know. I mean, we read you all those stories. and you've always had a wonderful imagination. But you never stopped talking about her. She didn't say anything to you; you thought she didn't know how to talk, and she wore—how did he describe it, love?" He turned to his wife.

"Betty dresses," Mrs. Crazy said.

"That's it! Betty dresses! You thought she looked like the ladies who worked at Betty's Tea Rooms in York and Harrogate. You remember? We used to take you there because you loved the scones on the big serving plates. We went with grandma."

"I remember Betty's," Arthur said, bemused, "Gran loved it, didn't she, but I've got no idea who Hundred is."

Arthur looked from his mother to his father, hoping to find some clues in their faces, but all he saw was pain and regret. That drew a seed of doubt in his breast, somewhere deep down where most people don't like looking. Behind the doubt was a flutter of anger. He lifted the beer to his mouth and drained it, reaching for another one, knowing even as he did that it had only ever made matters worse. He set it back down. The new beer sat on the table, open but untouched. They had heard him out, the least he could do was listen.

"We thought it was just a phase or an imaginary friend or something," his dad said. "But you got to five, maybe six, and Hundred was still part of the daily routine. We'd find you at the top of the stairs in the middle of the night, talking to her or just sitting there quietly in the dark, and you were always so tired. You kept falling asleep at school, and your teacher was really worried about you. She thought we were bad parents or something, letting you stay up all night."

"We got so worried, darling," Maggie said. "You were so convincing. So, we... we told you to stop talking to her."

"We pretty much banned any mention of her, and we punished you or grounded you whenever you said anything about her."

"I don't remember any of this," Arthur said. It was like recounting a heavy night on the booze. He knew he was the main character, but the plot details were a complete mystery. He pushed the beer further away.

"That's when we changed bedrooms so your bed wouldn't directly face the open door," his mum explained. "The thing is, dear. You got so sad. You did as you were told but you were so sad all the time. You stopped talking to us, and it was like the light went out. You were such a happy boy, and then... then you weren't!" Mrs. Crazy stopped talking as the tears rolled down her cheeks. Alexander handed her a folded napkin.

"Mum, I honestly don't remember any of this," Arthur said. He thought perhaps he should be more upset, that he should tap into that hidden well of doubt and anger, but as he looked at the pain and love on his parents' faces, it just melted away. They did the best they knew how to do in, let's be honest, a tricky bloody situation. In Arthur's short experience with the supernatural, it was always the young ones that gave him the willies. He knew his mum and dad. They were good people. Good parents. He took his mum's hand in his own and squeezed it three times.

"I guess Crazy isn't just a funny name," he said. "I mean, it's just so bizarre. So, you're saying you think I might have had some of these abilities when I was a kid, and what, I just forgot about them?"

"Well, we never really thought it was true, son. Not really. Not until now."

"I wonder why they went away then? I mean, why could I not see other ghosts or do some of the things I can do now?" Arthur asked.

"Self-preservation," Archibald said. They all looked at him. He placed his beer on the table and leaned forward. "When you used your power in York, it drew us to you, Arthur. We were far to the south... resting. But you lit up the world like a flare in the desert, and we knew we had to find you. The problem is, we aren't the only ones. Your power, the things you can do—it will have drawn everything towards you... from both sides."

"Both sides?" Thomas asked.

"Good and evil," Archibald replied simply.

"Good and evil?"

"Well, perhaps it's not as simple as that, but you know for a fact there are bad things out there, evil things, and children are more susceptible and impressionable as it is. Trying to deal with"—he waved his arms in the air—"all of *this* as a kid would have been a nightmare. When your boy was a wee bairn, he had no control. It was all natural, see?" He turned to Arthur. "This... Hundred, must have figured you could see her, and so she made herself known, but when you were forced to forget her, you did. You probably didn't sleep because you were so scared. I know I would be. Imagine being a kid and seeing dead people. You would never grow up normal. No, I reckon something in you pushed it all back down and locked it away until you were ready to deal with it."

Or drunk enough to rip away the filters, Arthur mused to himself.

"No, hang on. What do you mean by *evil*?" interrupted Mr. Crazy, unable to let it go.

"Well look, maybe it's not as black and white as all that. We're all the heroes of our own story, right? What's food to the cat is murder to the mouse, that sort of thing," Archibald said. He turned to Arthur. "You mentioned the Fetch. That's a creature shrouded in myth and legend, and the buggers can cause all kinds of problems, but they're not necessarily evil. They just... are."

"I think I know what you mean," Arthur said. "It *felt* evil at the time. I mean, it was chasing me. It was terrifying, so of course it felt evil. You should have seen it, Dad; it chased me down Low Petergate, and it was this long black creature, sort of like a dog but more like a human running on all fours. I was too knackered to run, so I had to stop and fight—"

"Wait!" interrupted Alexander. "You actually stopped to face the Fetch? You never said that earlier."

"Yes, I did. Didn't I?" said Arthur. "Sorry, I thought I did."

"No, you just said you fought it."

Arthur was confused. "Is there a difference?"

"Yes! A bloody big one! Everyone runs from a Fetch! But it will always find a way to catch you, because, well, it *is* you! If you see one, it's usually a reflection, like in water or a mirror, and it takes you, usually right then and there. Or at least before the sun rises. They're sneaky, those buggers. They feed off fear and paranoia. They chase, then hide. Chase, then hide. Creeping into shadows and mirrors. But you're saying you just, what, turned around and faced it? In its physical form?"

Arthur nodded.

Alexander whistled.

"It wasn't like I was being brave or anything," Arthur laughed, as both Alexander and Archibald exchanged shocked but impressed glances. "I was shitting myself—sorry Mum—but I was too knackered and too drunk to run anymore, and when I turned to face it, it sort of, well, it sort of stopped being a weird devil-looking thing and turned into... *me.* It grew all tall, then shrank down like it was trying to figure out how to make its shape fit mine, and then suddenly I was standing face to face with... myself. So... I punched it."

Archibald spat his beer out and grumbled an apology whilst quickly dabbing at his mouth with his beard. "You *punched* a Fetch!"

"Yes... sorry."

"Oh, don't say sorry, lad. Punching a Fetch!" he grinned. "Have you ever heard the like?"

"Once," Alexander said, looking at his brother, and the laughter died instantly.

"Don't."

"I'm just saying—"

"No."

"Look!" interrupted Maggie Crazy, a slight edge of anger rising in her voice. "This"—she waved a hand between the twins indicating their back and forth—"this isn't getting us anywhere. This isn't one of those bloody movies where everything goes wrong because people are too stupid to say what's on their mind. We talk things through in this family, we always have. Now, instead of speaking in code and riddles and half-sentences, why don't you two gentlemen tell us exactly what you know and why you're here. It's no coincidence your car got stuck outside our house, no coincidence at all. Not when you spent half the night looking for my boy. If it is, well... well that's just lazy writing! You were looking for Arthur, and now you found him. Kindly tell us why."

After a long pause, Alexander looked at his brother and then leaned forward, placing his elbows on the table. He clasped his hands in front of him as he faced the Crazy family and swallowed.

"It is promised," he began in a deep rumble, "that in a time of great peril, the saviour of this kingdom will rise again, draw forth his sword and—"

"Stop!" barked Archibald. "Stop that bloody nonsense. You'll give the lad the wrong impression with all that claptrap. You know full well it's not him." He turned to Mrs. Crazy and then to Arthur as his brother crossed his arms, sat back, and grumbled in his seat. "It's not really *you* we've come for, lad. I'm sorry. We thought it might be at first, but it's not. We do want the sword, though."

"What sword?" Mrs. Crazy asked.

"The sword Her Royal Highness gave your son in York. When the... when Arthur's power woke us, we knew we had to find it. The search led us to York, but by the time we got there, the queen had already given the sword to your son."

"The queen?" Maggie said. "What queen?"

"Queen Katheryn."

"Katheryn who?"

"Howard."

Mrs. Crazy sat back. "As in, Katheryn-killed-by-King-Henry Howard?" she said in a low voice.

"The very same."

"What the fuck?!"

"Mum!"

"Sorry. Did you *really* see Katheryn Howard?" she asked her son breathlessly.

He nodded. "Sorry, Mum. I left that bit out."

"She's my favourite," Mrs. Crazy said. "I always thought there was more to her than meets the eye. She was only a bairn, bless her. The poor thing didn't stand a chance in that court, but she seemed to have some steel in her."

"That she did," said Alexander in a hoarse voice, and everyone stopped and stared at him. There was something in the way he spoke. Something horribly final about his use of the past tense. Something more than the recognition that she had been dead for over four hundred years anyway. Alexander hung his head and couldn't meet their eyes.

"She's gone," Archibald said softly. "Lady Katheryn came with us from York and late last night she—" He couldn't finish the sentence, and the catch in his voice brought a shocked silence to the room. Archibald grimaced noticeably and clasped his hand to his side. Alexander pulled a red rose from within his robes and laid it on the table.

"She gave herself so that we might live," he said, and tears spilled from his eyes and dropped into his beard.

Arthur was shocked. The queen had been so lovely and kind to him. His mother was right, there was some steel to her, but she had also been playful and interesting. Arthur had been in awe as he knelt before her in King's Manor in York, the giant Lord Acaster by his side, Sarah Brockelbank and Steve there also. So, she too had died. If you could call it that. He shook his head. Ghosts can die, he thought. It didn't make any sense. It wasn't fair. When he left the queen, she had declared her intention to stay in York, to look after the dead who found their way to her. It was grand and noble, and now she was gone, ripped once more from everything she knew. Arthur reached for the beer and took a drink. A small one. Then he drank some more.

Arthur glanced at Steve in the corner of the room and realised he hadn't told his parents the truth about him yet. He wasn't sure how. That just might be one thing too many. First, the queen.

"How did she... die?" he asked.

"A barghest," Archibald growled.

"I know that name," Thomas Crazy said. "It's a... a big black dog or something. Whitby is famous for them. And there's one supposedly in Manchester."

Archibald nodded. "That's right. We believe the witch-girl released a barghest before she died, or, at the very least, she set the wheels in motion for one to be released."

"You see," interjected Alexander, "it wasn't so much *you* that woke us, Arthur. It was the awakening and release of the dark power of that girl. You simply lit the way. And then, when we got to York and found that you were in possession of the sword... well, we were convinced you were—" he trailed off.

"I was what?" Arthur said.

"Someone else," Alexander finished.

"You said you woke," Maggie Crazy said in a level voice. She was rapidly losing patience with the story as it danced around and around without ever quite getting to the point. She had had enough. "*What* are you?" she demanded, placing deliberate emphasis on the first word.

Archibald paused and took a drink, then it was his turn to lean forward. "We are guardians," he said.

"And what do you guard?" asked Mrs. Crazy, meeting his gaze and refusing to be cowed.

"We guard the sword."

"And he who wields it," added Alexander.

"But you lost the sword?" Mrs. Crazy said, working out the bits and pieces in her mind as she thought two or three questions ahead. She had an idea where this might be going and wasn't entirely sure if she was prepared for the arrival.

Archibald nodded. "It has always been kept safe by the royal family of this country," he said. "Until—"

"Until Lady Katheryn stole it," Alexander finished.

"And she stole it from... the royal family of this country," Maggie said slowly, her mind whirling. "She stole it from Henry the Eighth!"

"Yes."

"Why?"

"He was a right fat useless bastard," grumbled Archibald.

"Brother!"

"What? He bloody well was, and everyone knows it. Oh, he started out fine, of course. Fantastic even! A man to follow all right, but sadly, there are few as can keep it up it seems. The fatter he got, the worse he got, and poor Katheryn didn't deserve any of it."

"Neither did the others."

"Aye, that's right enough."

"So, you served in the court... with Katheryn?" Mrs. Crazy asked.

"Nope. Only met her last night. Lovely lass. Bloody lovely."

"Wait, I'm confused. If you are guardians of the sword, then why weren't you with the sword?"

"We were... busy," said Alexander.

"We were asleep," Archibald corrected.

"For how long?" Mrs Crazy asked slowly, guessing the answer was going to raise more questions than it answered.

"Not sure. A hundred years or so?"

There was a very long, very tense silence as everyone in the room processed that piece of information. Each drink was slowly lifted to lips and then just as slowly lowered. The brothers waited patiently as the three Crazies considered and dismissed a myriad of potential questions. Only Steve carried on as normal, hugging his bone and dreaming beside the radiator.

"So, let me see if I've got this right," Mrs. Crazy said, raising her hand and ticking off her points one by one. "You two gentlemen are guardians. You guard the sword. A sword you say my son now has. You are... old"—she lifted her hands and shrugged—"really old. You sleep for a really long time, but six months ago, you were woken up because Arthur here released a... a witch in York. But then Arthur dealt with the witch because"—and here she turned to her son—"because you can talk to ghosts and free the dead from *being* ghosts." Arthur nodded and she continued, "But all this craziness is still not over because the girl got a dog—"

"A barghest."

"A barghest... right. And that's evil too, or it might just be the hero of its own goddamn fucking story—"

"Maggie!"

"Mum!"

"—and so, you came up here to stop it. Am I right so far?" demanded Mrs. Crazy. The men at the table were shocked and a little speechless, though Thomas Crazy had a small smile stealing on the edge of his mouth. "Stop me if I'm wrong!" Mrs. Crazy said angrily, and they all jumped a little.

"You are correct, lady," Alexander said with an inclination of his head. "Although I feel I should point out, we don't always sleep for hundreds of years at a time. We're not Snow White. No, we pop up and down as we need, when we need, we just... missed that one."

"Aye, we're not completely bone-idle," Archibald said. "It's not like we napped during the wars, ya' ken? That thing with Henry and Katheryn was just a grand tour. We weren't to know some wee slip of a thing was going to half-inch the bloody sword."

Maggie chose to ignore that. "About the barghest," she said. "I'm guessing if you were looking for Arthur, it will be looking him as well?" She stared the men down, daring them to contradict her.

"Correct," Alexander nodded. Among many things, he was a good judge of character.

"Because of his power? And probably because he *got rid* of the girl?"

"Indeed."

"And you need the sword so you can give it to someone else—*not* my Arthur—who will stop the barghest?"

"Not just the barghest, Ma'am. The release of the girl unlocked a powerful darkness in the world. It is beyond our ability to resolve, so yes, we need to return the sword to its rightful owner."

"And the rightful owner is?" And here Maggie Crazy finally played her trump card.

"Arthur."

"But not my Arthur."

"No," Alexander said slowly. "Not your Arthur."

Mrs. Crazy nodded and leaned forward in her chair, reaching for one of the bottles of wine on the table. She poured herself a very large glass and had a very long drink. "Well, one thing's for sure," she said with a sigh.

"What's that, love?" asked her husband, utterly perplexed.

"It's got to be true. No one in their right mind would make all this shit up."

CHAPTER 22

A stone arch rests at the top of Cornforth Hill, stretching between two twin houses. It serves no function other than to stand as a reminder of a time when the town needed a medieval wall to keep the danger out. The stones shiver with the memory of forgotten purpose as the barghest passes through unchecked and vanishes into the dark of the alley beyond. A man in the shadows smiles and makes a note in his book. Finally, things are getting back on track.

❧

"I'm so sorry about the queen," Arthur said after no one had spoken for a long time.

All the men were staring intently at their drinks and casting the occasional furtive glance towards Mrs. Crazy. Steve began running in his sleep, so he was a happy distraction for a few moments while everyone sat lost in their own thoughts. Mrs. Crazy had gone quiet, but no one really wanted to speak until they were sure she was finished.

So, it was Arthur who broke the silence in the end, his thoughts full of images of the green-clad queen in York. "I didn't even know which queen she was," he said, more to himself than anyone else. "She never said. I mean, I tried to research it but never got anywhere. You're right. She gave me the sword and I never really thought how strange it was that she could hold it and so could I. Is that rose one of hers?" he asked Alexander.

The old man nodded in reply. "And you can touch it?" Arthur said quietly. "I wonder—" he leaned over the table and picked the rose up gently, marvelling at the strange sensation of the touch. "I always thought the roses were... ghosts as well," he finished, knowing just how crazy that sounded.

"No, lad. They're very much real. Often there are objects that tie spirits to the places they died. Roses are... *were* Her Majesty's."

"Are they always real? The objects I mean, the things that tie the ghosts to the places of their death?"

"No, not always. Most times they belong to the world the spirit departed and so they don't really exist in this realm."

"What about the sword?"

"What about it?"

"Is the sword real?"

"You held it didn't you?"

"Yes, but... well, I was also walking through walls and touching dead people, so now I'm not so sure. Although—" he said, casting his mind back. "The policeman held it when he arrested me."

"You got arrested!" his mum said quickly. "What for?!"

"For waving a sword around in the middle of the street," Arthur said.

There was a moment of silence and then a slow spread of telltale grins as people looked away from Arthur, unsuccessfully hiding their amusement.

"But you *do* have the sword?" Alexander asked.

"Yes," said Arthur. "I, erm... I got it back. I don't really remember how, but it was the last thing I did before all these powers sort of, well, vanished. I remember walking through the city and then trying to hide the sword in the luggage rack of the train. It's under my bed. Hang on."

Arthur ran out of the room, and Mr. and Mrs. Crazy both noticed the nervousness that descended on the two brothers. They sat up straight, smoothed down their robes, and even ran fingers through their beards, though their eyes never left the door. It was a strange reaction, almost like a fan who is nervous to meet a celebrity and fidgets with unease. Archibald kept plucking at the robes on his side as though worried they were sticking to him. It was an absent-minded gesture, and he immediately stopped when Mrs. Crazy caught his eye. Arthur returned a few moments later, a long bundle wrapped in an old coat under his arm, and Mrs. Crazy could have sworn the brothers were both holding their breath. Arthur unwrapped the bundle to reveal a short sword sheathed in a nondescript scabbard, which he placed carefully in the centre of the table. Alexander sighed and Archibald grinned widely, clapping his twin on the shoulder.

"We did it, brother. After all these years we found it!"

"And in the hands of a man called Arthur."

"Nice round table, too," said Archibald.

"Now who is filling his head with nonsense?" Alexander said.

"Oh, it was just a joke!"

"It is *his* sword though, there's no denying that, brother. You can feel it."

"Whose sword?" Thomas Crazy asked. He was always at least half a step behind his wife. When watching mystery movies, she'd taken to writing down "whodunnit" on a post-it note to hand to him when he eventually got there himself. Now, she folded her arms across her chest and glared at the two old men as if daring them to answer.

"Arthur's."

"*Arthur,* Arthur? My son, Arthur?" Mr. Crazy asked.

Alexander and Archibald both shook their heads silently and Mrs. Crazy took another long drink. She was smiling, but there was no humour in it. All eyes dropped to the sword on the table.

"Then..." Thomas Crazy didn't or couldn't finish the thought. In the corner of the room, Steve whined, and his legs kicked in his sleep. For a moment, the small gathering looked at the dog, but soon all eyes were drawn back to the sword resting with portentous weight in the middle of the round table within the house below the castle.

"You said something about a coming saviour," Mrs. Crazy said to Alexander with a carefully measured voice. "Would you care to explain who—" but even she couldn't finish the thought. It was bad enough—ridiculous enough, even—that she was considering who this sword might have once belonged to, but the crazy notion that was dancing around her head was enough to drive anyone insane. Even in the face of everything they had just heard. This time her husband was the one who got there first.

Well, aloud anyway.

"I'm guessing the sword needs to be used," Thomas suggested.

Archibald nodded.

"By... Arthur?"

The twins lifted their gaze to Arthur Crazy who had been growing increasingly bemused by the back and forth across the table and finally snapped.

"Arthur's sword but not Arthur's sword," he said, banging his hand on the table. "Mine but not mine? Arthur needs to use it but not me. I don't get it! Will you please tell me what the fuck is going on?!"

"Arthur!"

"Sorry, Mum."

"Well?" she said pointedly to the twins, and at that exact moment there came a single harsh tap on the dining room window.

The barghest killed a man in the back alleys of the town just near the marketplace. It was lost and confused, and no matter which way it turned, it did not seem to be getting anywhere. The itch in its mind that dragged it to and fro had increased like the buzzing of flies, and so, when it saw the elderly man placing a black bag in a large plastic bin, it sunk its teeth into the back of his head just because it could. The man made no sound other than a strangled gurgle as his skull cracked and he choked on his own blood. The barghest let the body fall and watched the lifeblood drain away in dark, warm rivers that traced the cobbled stones of the streets. It was still watching when a scream split the air. The black creature looked up at the old lady standing in the doorway of her home wearing slippers and a yellow paper Christmas hat. The distraught woman tried to take in everything she was looking at, but there was nothing in her world of experience to prepare her for the vision beside the bins.

As she clutched her chest and fell to the frosty ground, the last thing she heard was the sound of laughter.

Long, mocking, and feminine.

The man watching from the shadows tutted and checked his book. Two names appeared on the dark pages, and he nodded, looking up to see a now youthful man and woman run into each other's arms and vanish together through a sizzling purple door. He drew a fine line through the names and then closed the book. All was well.

As it should be.

The Shadowman smiled. It was a rare occasion, but he liked the neat ones even if they were unexpected. He didn't even need the knife this time.

There *was* something unusual, though—something he couldn't quite figure out. He wouldn't be doing his job properly if he didn't at least give it some thought.

The laugh had been unexpected, and he wasn't entirely sure where it had come from. The man's hearing was never in question, and neither was his sight. In fact, he saw and heard things on a daily basis that would make most people run for the nearest padded cell.

He was confused, and he didn't like confusion. It was messy.

The Shadowman watched the creature carefully as it sniffed

around the two bodies. The beasts were always unnerving (not to him, of course, but to lesser beings) but there was something particularly off about this one. Sometimes, he got the impression it knew he was there, but of course, that was impossible.

He stepped back into the dark alley and watched the barghest as it got bored of its afternoon's work and moved away.

Through the black paths, the Shadowman followed.

CHAPTER 23

Steve's dreams had taken a turn. He was no longer the one doing the chasing. He was being chased, and no matter how fast he ran, it simply wasn't fast enough. A dark shadow rose behind him, growing larger and larger, and he was moving so slowly. So painfully slowly. He looked down and saw he was on two legs. He wore trousers and a white shirt with a red tie. He tried to run, but he couldn't move at all now. Something had him by the neck. The shadows grew. There was laughter.

Steve could run no further. He was blocked in on three sides by tall stone walls, and behind him, the shadows reached out. The pressure on his neck had increased, and he was struggling to breath, grasping and clawing at his throat with long white fingers. Suddenly, a purple light exploded in front of him and covered the whole world with painful brightness, the darkness banished in an instant. Steve blinked and tried to clear his vision, but there was no time. He was already moving, slipping and sliding on a steep slope. Now falling—falling deep into black, and there was laughter. Laughter all around him. Laughter following close as he fell.

~

"I t's just a robin," said Arthur, who had got up to check the window. He wiped the condensation to reveal a beautiful robin sitting on the white window ledge outside. As he leaned closer it rapt its beak sharply on the glass once more. "He's beautiful. Wow!" he added, noticing the world outside. "The fog got really thick out there. It's really dark."

The little, red-breasted robin tapped again, and Arthur knocked on the glass in reply, smiling as the bird sang out and flew away in a quick dart across the street.

"Nothing to worry about," he said, closing the curtain and tucking the ends behind the radiator to "keep the heat in" as his mother always said. He turned to the room and caught the look on his mother's face. "What is it?" he asked.

"How many times did the robin tap on the window?" she asked.

Arthur laughed. "I don't know, three, maybe four? Why?"

"That's really bad luck," she said. "A robin tapping on your window three times. Terrible luck."

"Nah, it's all right, love," said Mr. Crazy. "I know that one about the robins. It only counts if someone in the room is sick. No one here is sick, are they?"

Archibald pulled his hand away from his side and took a long drink of his beer.

"I'd love something a little stronger, if ya don't mind?" he said to Thomas.

Suddenly, Steve snapped awake in that way dogs do, from zero to one hundred in an instant. He was up on his feet, barking and leaping at Arthur in a mad frenzy. He ran round in a tight circle and leapt at Arthur again, growling and whining, his tail tucked firmly between his legs.

"What's got into him?" Thomas Crazy said, handing a glass of scotch to Archibald, who took it with a grateful nod. "Must've been a bad dream."

Arthur knelt down, and Steve scrambled up, climbing onto his knees and forcing Arthur to take him into his arms, where he nestled in as tight as he could. Arthur stood up and carried Steve to the table, sitting back down in his seat. "He's shaking," he said, patting the dog's head. "What's wrong mate?"

There was something in his tone of voice that caught the attention of his parents. It wasn't how a person normally spoke to a dog. They realised, almost at the same time, that their son was expecting a reply and as they stared, they couldn't help but think Arthur was listening to one.

"Son," Thomas Crazy said slowly, his hands shaking slightly as he reached over the table then thought better of it. "Why did you decide to call your dog Steve?"

"I didn't, Dad," said Arthur, not really thinking. "That's his name."

"Aha. And, erm... would this be the same Steve from York?"

Arthur looked up. He saw their faces. Their wide eyes. Well, in for a penny, in for a pound. He nodded.

Thomas and Maggie Crazy looked from their son to the dog and back again. They were white, and a small twitch gnawed at the corner of Maggie's mouth. Other than that, they didn't react at all. Neither did they blink.

"I think now might be a good time to prove it," Alexander said quietly.

"What do you mean?" asked Arthur.

"Use your power."

"To do what?"

"To build a bridge. That's what magic does. It connects."

"How do I—"

"Just try."

Arthur looked down at Steve, who had been talking to him, but who honestly hadn't been making a whole lot of sense. Something about being chased, and a door, or being chased *by* a door. He was very excited. Arthur concentrated on the young dog and looked deep into his strange eyes. He had never noticed before, but they had a slight blue tint to them. He thought they were brown. Arthur shifted his concentration to his own feelings, reaching into the warm place that seemed to be just behind his stomach. He drew the power up and through his body with no real idea how, but he brought the prickling, crackling warmth up to his chest and down through his arm to his left hand.

His parents blinked in slow unison when purple sparks jumped from finger to finger. Arthur concentrated on the feeling of the power within him, trying to connect it to Steve. He imagined a wire running from his right hand, which still rested gently on the side of Steve's face, through his body, and into his left hand. He had no real idea what he was doing, but he could feel the surge within him. If anything, he struggled to stop the power from spilling over. It built and built, and he thought it might burst completely, and so he simply let go.

Nothing happened.

Nothing continued to happen.

Then Steve said, "What the shit was that?!" And Thomas Crazy started to laugh.

Across the street, in the cottage at the top of Millgate, Bob was getting ready to take his dog, Charlie, for a walk. He had finished a lovely Christmas dinner and one or two more glasses of wine than he normally enjoyed, so was feeling a little unsteady as he pulled on his coat.

"Ball," Charlie said.

"What's that, mate?"

"You forgot the ball."

"Oh, right. Sorry."

He reached onto the top shelf in the little foyer of his cottage and pulled down one of the many worn tennis balls. This one was red, or rather, it used to be, and seemed to be Charlie's favourite.

"That's my favourite!" said Charlie, wagging his tail enthusiastically and darting in a quick circle at Bob's feet.

"I thought so," said Bob.

"I love you," said Charlie.

"I love you too, mate."

Bob was halfway across The Batts waiting for Charlie to run

back out of the mist with his red ball when he suddenly decided he needed to have a little sit down and think about what just happened.

Just outside the Crazy's house and directly opposite from Bob's, where the terrace ramp leaves the road at the top of the hill, a set of steep stone stairs lead up to the equally steep road known as Castle Wynd. The elderly people who live in Richmond have calves like Roman soldiers because, no matter which direction they take, everything is uphill. Castle Wynd runs from the Crazy's house up to the courtyard outside the castle itself, where, the night before, Arthur had run away from Steve. The street is lined with high stone buildings and low stone cottages. Inside the squat white cottage of Number 1, Mrs. Ormerod (there's always a Mrs. Ormerod in cottages such as these, no one knows why) was spending Christmas Day with her parrot, Dave. She fed him another cracker through the bars of his cage and crooned,

"Who's a good boy then? Davey want a cracker?"

Dave took the cracker delicately in his beak and then dropped it purposefully on the floor before turning one beady eye to Mrs. Ormerod. "No, I don't want a fucking cracker!" he said. "I want some of that cheese you've been guzzling, and would it kill you to open this bloody cage and put Coronation Street back on!"

At the top of the hill, in the low house near the parked cars, Mr. Allott sat smoking his third joint of the day. Nothing beat getting baked at Christmas and watching old movies. It had been his private little tradition for as long as he could remember, and he loved it. His cat, Betty, sauntered into the room with complete indifference and sniffed, flicking her tail in typical feline disdain.

"Where's my food?" she demanded.

"In your bowl," Mr. Allott replied.

"It's empty."

Mr. Allott leaned over his chair to look at her bowl. It was almost full, although she had eaten the food from the middle and the green plastic showed beneath, a small circle licked clean.

"There's still half a tin in there," he said.

"It's empty."

"Oh, piss off."

"You piss off."

Just then, a dark shadow passed by the window, and Betty leapt into Mr. Allott's lap. She turned one way then the other and slunk into a low crouch, her eyes fixed on the net curtain that entirely failed to move creepily in any breeze. The room was perfectly normal, nothing out of place, but Betty grew ever more agitated, seeing something no one else could. Her fur stood on end, and she growled as she gripped sharp claws into her human's leg. Mr. Allott swore and put his hand on the frightened cat to lift her up, but, as he touched her, he realised she was shivering. He stroked her back and scratched behind her ears, but she refused to move, her gaze fixed on the window. He reached out and tweaked the net curtain to peer outside.

"Better not be any bugger messing with my car again," he grumbled, but there was nothing there, just a heavy mist shrouding the world in a dark blanket intermittently lit by the faded orange orbs of the streetlights. Mr. Allott sat back, took a long draw from his joint, and sighed in contentment, closing his eyes for a moment and relaxing. It took a long time for the residual fear of whatever had passed the window to make itself known and creep through the fog of his mind. He shivered at the latent memory, but then another more pressing thought presented itself front and centre.

"Wait a minute," he said, sitting up slowly as the cogs began to turn. He scratched his cat behind the ear again and gently lifted her face to look into her eyes, clasping the joint between his teeth and her head between his hands. "Did you just talk?" he asked. The cat and the man stared into each other's eyes for a moment and Mr. Allott blinked as her pupils grew from narrow slits to wide black holes.

She completely failed to react.

Oh, she could have done, if she wanted to. She just didn't want to.

Halfway down the hill, in the first house on the terrace, Maggie Crazy rose wordlessly from her seat as her husband laughed, paused to look at the dog on her son's lap, and then walked slowly into the kitchen. She reached up to the top shelf and brought down an old metal tin with the famous Yorkshire Tea logo on the front. She opened it, retrieved something from inside, and walked back to the table where she quietly sat beside her husband and lit a cigarette before passing him the pack. Thomas took one in shaking fingers and lit it on the second go, never once taking his eyes off Steve the dog. They both sat back in their seats. They both took deep drags from their cigarettes. And they both blew long plumes of smoke that swirled up to the ceiling to wreath around the large oak beam that crossed the room. The question formed on Arthur's lips, but he suddenly found himself speechless. Steve did not.

"It's her!" he barked at them all, shaking in Arthur's arms. "It's her!"

Thomas Crazy let out a small, nervous laugh.

Maggie Crazy smoked half a cigarette in one go.

Arthur Crazy stared, unblinking, at his parents.

Alexander and Archibald took a drink.

"It's her!" Steve said again, and barked for real this time, snapping Arthur's attention away from his smoking parents and back to the terrified animal on his lap.

"What do you mean, mate? What's her?"

"The... the thing. The bad one. The big one. It's her!" Steve said. This had been the thing he had desperately tried to remember, the main reason he set out immediately to find Arthur. It was to tell him this—to warn him before it was too late.

He was too late.

CHAPTER 24

The front door exploded in a rending crash of splintered wood and shattered glass. Before anyone had even risen from the table, the door to the dining room was ripped from the hinges and smashed beneath giant, powerful claws.

Mr. and Mrs. Crazy found it almost impossible to process the creature that stalked into the room. They had no frame of reference other than in the books and movies they enjoyed. The great joy of fiction, however, is that you are merely a passive observer and can retreat to the safety of the real world at any time, safe from the nightmare.

There was no retreat from the beast that steamed and vibrated with menace in the doorway of the small dining room. There was nowhere to go, nowhere to hide. It stepped through the broken mess, one giant claw at a time, shifting huge shoulders to squeeze through the gap. The shadows of the old house gathered around it as it breathed heavily—a sharp, rasping growl like stone dragged over stone. Deep, red eyes glared at them from within an inky, black face as it moved deeper into the room.

Shaped like a wolf but the size of a bear, the beast's body rippled with powerful muscles. One ear was missing, and in its place, there ran a thick, ragged scar across the top of the head—a glistening line of congealed blood knitting tattered flesh together.

The barghest sniffed the air then lowered its head slowly, though it kept its eyes trained on the humans, flitting from one to the next, watching, judging, sizing them up. It looked at them as it crouched, hackles raised, muscles taught, legs ready. It opened its wide mouth to reveal two rows of glistening white teeth, and a purple tongue flicked out as though tasting the air. The black lips curled back in what seemed to be a smile, and suddenly the beast roared. The avalanche of noise was an explosion in the confined space, and it forced everyone to their feet. Chairs fell as they staggered backward, and glasses smashed to the floor as Arthur stumbled into the table. Steve fell and disappeared between the legs of people and furniture. After the echoes died down and the gasps of shock and fear fell into strangled sobs, they were left with nothing but the sound of mocking laughter.

And then, even worse, the creature spoke.

"Little people," rasped a voice, heavy with malice and savagery.

"No!" Arthur gasped. "It can't be!"

The barghest laughed and Arthur heard it this time, he heard the familiar mocking arrogance, the strange and terrifying mixture of impossible age speaking with a child's voice.

It was the girl from the window.

The witch-child.

Arthur backed away in fear and loathing, his legs shaking and his stomach leaden with terror. The giant head turned toward him, and the great eyes narrowed.

"You," it said in a sibilant hiss. "You think you beat me. You think you brought an end to who I am, *what* I am. I can see it in the way you cower, the way you hide. You don't deserve what you have!"

The beast roared, and Arthur backed into the kitchen counter with a strangled sob of terror. He was trapped, and his parents stood beside him with nothing but the round table between them and the beast. Alexander and Archibald were against the far wall on the other side of the table, their swords scattered to the floor along with all the brollies, and suddenly the creature moved.

It was fast, unbelievably so, but someone else was miraculously ahead of it. He had been waiting.

Thomas Crazy flipped the table with one great heave and shoved it forcefully across the room like a giant shield, crashing with a roar into the barghest. He caught the creature off balance and screamed at his family to run, but his wife was already by his side, stepping in front of her son and slamming her shoulder into the table, forcing the snarling beast back into the shattered doorway.

Alexander and Archibald moved as one, reaching for their swords, but the creature was too quick and too strong. Black claws gripped the side of the table, and the giant teeth clamped into the rim. There was a brief moment where it seemed like it might hold, but then suddenly and violently, the table exploded in a shower of splinters and broken wood. Mr. and Mrs. Crazy fell to the floor and scrambled backwards over the detritus of their dining room. Thomas pushed his wife behind him and looked up in terrified defiance as the barghest bore down on them, red eyes flashing, mouth open wide.

"Run, son!" Thomas screamed, raising a futile arm as the barghest lunged.

Archibald hit the great beast from the side, a rugby tackle around the neck that did just enough to drive the snapping teeth away from Thomas Crazy and into the ground, but the animal roared and twisted its neck with such speed that the brave guardian didn't stand a chance. The sharp teeth scythed into Archibald's already bloody ribs and clamped down over his chest as he let out a roar of agony and desperate defiance. He kept shouting as the beast shook him from side to side as though he weighed nothing. The old man reached desperately, plunging his fingers deep into the bloody mess of the devil dog's missing ear, and gripped a handful of flesh, pulling it back. The beast roared with pain and flung Archibald hard against the brick wall, where his body smashed with a heavy thud and dropped, unmoving, to the ground.

It all happened so fast, and Arthur was watching as though through someone else's eyes. He was frozen in place, a passive observer unable to think or move or react as his parents scrambled away, bloody and bruised. Archibald's body sailed through the air and hit the wall, and Alexander plunged his own sword deep into the side of the animal that didn't even flinch. A giant claw shot out with lightning speed and simply punched Alexander away, the sword still quivering from its side.

All this and Arthur remained frozen, the different parts of his brain taking it all in, processing and retreating in horror and disbelief.

This simply did not happen. Not this. Not his home. Not the world of his childhood.

Not his mum and dad.

He stared in mute terror as the barghest put a giant foot on Archibald's chest and brought its gaping maw close. The old guardian's eyes snapped open, desperate and wide with pain. He gasped in agony, but there was no air to take in, the world only full of shadows and teeth. He spat at the devil and used what breath he had left to curse it one last time,

"I hope I give you the shits, you bitch!"

And the barghest bit his head off.

The room spun in a maelstrom of shadows and a malevolence so thick it hung like coal smoke against the low ceiling as the dark places writhed. The Shadowman watched it all with what, on any other being's face, might have been considered a smile. But even this dropped when he noticed the man known as Arthur Benedict Crazy finally begin to stir and move. Lightning crackled at the man's fingertips, and to the Shadowman, it seemed as though he was glowing from within.

Arthur was furious. It was an anger so deep and primal that it overrode all sense of fear. Oh, the fear was still there, but it suddenly wasn't as important as the rage that fed him—the anger that drove him forward and finally made him move. He let the power surge without trying to control it and laughed as it coursed through his body. He built a ball between his hands and let it fly with a shout of wrath.

And the barghest... the barghest laughed.

"Child!" it spat, shrugging off the hit as though it was nothing more than a slap. "You can't hurt me. You can't end me. There is no end. There is only next. And I? I am what comes next!"

The creature took a step towards Arthur over Archibald's decapitated body and Alexander's unconscious form, and the young man suddenly felt completely and utterly alone. As quickly as the rage built, it fell away. His parents were huddled in the corner. His father, he realised, frantically trying to stem a profuse flow of blood from his mother's shoulder. She was hurt. She was really, seriously hurt by a creature that should not even exist. And there was nothing Arthur could do.

"There is nothing you can do!" the barghest said with the voice of the girl, echoing Arthur's own thoughts. "I gave you the chance to join me, and you spurned me. You will never get that chance again, though I will make you long for it!"

"Fuck you!" Arthur managed to scream.

"Did that help?" the girl-dog sneered. "I doubt it. You're not strong enough to defeat me. You have no control over what you can do. You don't even know what you are! You are a child!"

Arthur backed away, and his foot touched something heavy that scraped across the ground. He saw the barghest's eyes glance down and widen, flashing red. The creature stopped its advance. Arthur risked a look. It was the sword gifted to him by the queen and searched for by the knightly brothers. The one Arthur had walked through walls to retrieve from a police station in York. He reached down quickly and snatched it up, and the beast flinched. In the corner of the room, Alexander stirred and tried to speak, but Arthur had no time. The barghest took a step back, the long chain rattling with ominous weight as it stumbled over the shattered doorway.

Arthur pulled the sword from the scabbard and a small part of him thrilled at the motion. He was living every movie he had ever seen—every gladiator and highlander and warrior and knight and ninja. He was all of them and his adversary was afraid. He could see that now. He felt the power from his body rise instantly and pulse into the grip of the weapon, rippling up the blade. Who needed anger when he had this? It was like a lightning rod, a wizard's staff, a magic wand, goddamn, it was the Sword of Grayskull!

"Now who's a fucking child?" he sneered at the barghest and gripped the sword tightly, swinging it in an arc that would have been far more impressive if he hadn't scraped the blade up the wall. He shrugged and raised the weapon above his head as he stepped forward. On the ground at his feet, Alexander raised a shaking hand and tried to speak, but no words came. Arthur wouldn't have heard even if they had. He spread his legs in the stock-standard hero-stance of sword-wielding nutters everywhere and roared out the first thing that came to his mind.

"I have the power!"

He never heard Alexander shout in protest.

He never heard the barghest laugh.

He never heard the Shadowman swear.

CHAPTER 25

Some stories end neatly, and others... don't. Some heroes fall from cliffs while riding Nazi tanks but somehow manage to climb back to safety, and some villains seem to dodge being shot no matter how good an aim the cop has throughout the rest of the movie. And when they do get to the final confrontation, there is always that one moment where the good guy thinks the bad guy has been defeated, but suddenly, they surge back with a vengeance for one desperate, last-gasp, hail-Mary attempt at the prize. It's usually at this point the hero, finally, doesn't miss.

Arthur didn't miss.

But that's not the point. The point is, the barghest didn't dodge. If anything, it leaned in.

The sword carved through the air and hit the beast between the eyes. It was a good hit. And perhaps in another time and place, the blade might have been sharp, and the creature's head would have split in two. But the sword was as blunt as a stick. That, however, is also not the point.

The blade might not have been sharp, but the steel was strong, and so was Arthur. The creature crumpled as its skull shattered in an explosion of blood and gore. The blood sprayed a Jackson Pollock across Mrs. Crazy's tiles. Sudden, blinding, and dazzling flashes of light left Arthur's hands and travelled up the blade, crossing from flesh through steel to flesh. He screamed as the power left him, and the broken body of the barghest rippled with an electric surge as it died. Behind it, in the deep shadows cast by magic fire, something moved.

As the beast fell, a figure rose.

The head was bowed. Long, dank hair hung low, covering naked flesh. Blood and dark fur clung momentarily to white skin, but it fell away as the figure stood and stretched.

Not a girl. Definitely not a girl.

A tall woman emerged from the remains of the barghest and arched her back, running long fingers over her breasts and shoulders and through her hair. Grime and gristle and decay fell from her. Suddenly she looked up, staring at Arthur with jet-black eyes.

She smiled.

And then she laughed.

The story that Arthur thought had ended had only just begun.

In the city of York, the ghost known as Mad Alice wept uncontrollably in her dark and lonely lane. She had never known fear like the surge that just washed over her, assaulting her, tearing at whatever residue of humanity remained.

"The nice young man," she cried.

In King's Manor, the roses beneath the great tree—those strange flowers that inexplicably grow all year round—began to wilt and turn grey.

On the North Yorkshire coast at the top of a cliff overlooking the harbour, the barghest of Whitby whimpered and hid amongst the dark graves standing like sentinels beneath the ruined Abbey. The ocean roared far below, and the wind whipped savagely at the church on the clifftop, screaming in the dying sun as the mist rolled in from the ocean.

Far to the south, behind world-famous stone towers and deep within the great compound recognisable the world over, Mr. Nicholas Lewis, Ravenmaster of the Yeoman Warders and Steward of the Tower of London, knew instinctively something was wrong.

He couldn't explain it, but when you've done a job for as long as he had and as well as he had, you knew deep down when it all changed. He ran through the nearly deserted courtyard, ignoring the quizzical looks from the soldiers with a rising panic scratching at his senses. The soldiers stepped out of line, curious and alert. It was Christmas Day. There were no members of the public to worry about, but the unusual visage of old Mr. Lewis racing through the sudden, cloying mists with his dressing gown billowing out behind him certainly grabbed their attention.

The old man ran past the tower and charged toward the aviary, knowing before he got there what he would see.

When the soldiers caught him, they staggered to a halt and walked the last few steps on nervous legs, rifles cocked and ready. Mr. Lewis was on his knees, cradling Carter Carter's body—a crow so good they named him twice.

In each cage, the bodies of the Tower ravens lay where they fell.

All over Britain, mists rose from the gaps, unnatural and ethereal. They rolled down rivers and across fields, through housing estates and car parks, caressing mansions and council flats alike. Thick and cloying, they fell across the country like sullen clouds, muting the world, and bringing an end to all Christmas cheer. A shroud settled over the land and the shadows it held beneath began to stir, and to move.

CHAPTER 26

"Little people," the woman said with a smile. She stretched her back and arms and looked closely at her hands, turning them over and back. She flexed her fingers and laughed as Alexander clambered to his feet and Arthur staggered backward with the sword grasped loosely in shaking hands, the blade flecked with gristle and bone.

"That's mine," the lady nodded as she stepped out of the mess and took the blade from Arthur's unresisting grip. "Thank you."

"Who?" Arthur began, but she cut him off with a raised hand.

"Oh, don't. You know full well who I am. Don't bother, old man!" she snapped suddenly, her voice full of violent promise as she turned on Alexander who had been moving slowly towards his own sword. She lifted an eyebrow in recognition. "You!" she said. "You were there before. I know you. You and your—" a smile creased the corner of her mouth as the sentence dangled in the air. The lady turned slowly and looked down. Then she looked back to Alexander. "Oh, dear. Did I do that? What a shame. And so *easy* it was, too."

She glanced briefly at Thomas and Maggie Crazy, sniffed, and looked away, back to Alexander, lifting the sword in front of his face.

"Just a load of old rubbish, really," she said. "It was never meant for battle, but you know that; you were there. But my, my, isn't the power of a name something to behold!"

"I'll kill you!" Alexander said in a low, venomous voice.

"Already done that, dear. Didn't care for it. Now, be quiet!" She flicked a hand nonchalantly towards Alexander, and something burst from the stone wall of the dining room to wrap around his head, clamping his mouth shut and pinning him against the stones. It looked like the root of a tree—thick, black, and old—but it moved like a serpent.

The woman smiled.

"Good. I'm glad that little trick still works."

She turned to Arthur. "They're all little tricks, you know. Little tricks for little people. But you—," she stepped closer to him. "You have absolutely no idea what you are or what you are doing, do you?" She brought her face beside Arthur's and sniffed him, wrinkling her nose and sniffing again. "Why you?" she wondered, almost to herself. "Why? I can smell the fear in you. No one this afraid, this pathetic, should have the power you have. You don't deserve it, and I want it."

Arthur stepped back. He was completely and utterly terrified. His mind had gone numb, his thoughts stagnant and broken, there was no desperate planning, no weighing up the options, nothing. He was entirely consumed by fear, and it was all he could do to remain standing. He couldn't speak. He couldn't think. There was nothing he could give.

"You really are pathetic," she sneered. "There is nothing special about you. What a waste!"

"Hey!" Arthur's mum gasped from the floor, cradled in her husband's arms. She was white and panting, struggling to catch her breath as blood seeped from the wound in her shoulder. "You know nothing about my boy!"

"I know everything!" screamed the woman in a sudden and violent fit of rage. "Don't you presume to talk to me! Don't you know who I am?!"

"Why?" Maggie Crazy said in a calm voice, "Have you forgotten? Get the fuck out of my house and leave my family alone!"

"Oh... the mother," sneered the woman, stepping away from Arthur and kneeling down in front of his parents. "You must be so disappointed. But a mother's love, right?" She reached towards the wound on Maggie's shoulder and Thomas slapped her hand away.

"Don't you dare touch my wife!"

"Looks like I already did," the woman grinned. "What a pity—"

She froze.

"Stand up... slowly," Alexander growled, the point of his blade held firmly against the woman's neck. "And drop that sword. You don't deserve to touch it."

"It is mine," she said, calmly, rising to her feet.

"It has never been yours."

"How did you get free?" she asked, sounding genuinely curious.

"You're not the only one with magic," he snarled.

"Interesting."

The woman lifted her arms but held onto the blade. "I remember you," she said in a quiet voice. She turned her head, but Alexander put pressure on the sword. She growled and turned away. "You were there. You and that pathetic brother of yours. You were there, weren't you?"

"Aye, we were there," Alexander said.

"You betrayed me."

"You betrayed *him*!"

"Fool! You have no idea. No idea what could have been. You betrayed me, and you murdered me! Twice!" she roared, spittle flying.

"He gave you a chance!'

"A chance! What chance? I am a queen, and he made me a peasant!"

"Enough talking!"

"Yes," she grinned. "Enough."

The naked woman shivered but it had nothing to do with the cold. The lurid pallor of her skin prickled with gooseflesh, and she closed her eyes in something akin to pleasure.

"Little people," she breathed and flexed the fingers of her free hand. The shadows closed in, and cold swept through the room like a wave before, suddenly, whatever she aimed to do was interrupted by a small dog.

Steve charged from the wreckage of the kitchen and jumped over the top of Mr. and Mrs. Crazy. He launched himself at the woman and sunk his teeth deep into the hand that held the sword. The naked woman yelled in shock and pain, and she cursed as the sword fell to the ground.

In the corner, Arthur blinked and took in the room as if seeing it for the first time. The splintered furniture and detritus of his childhood home, the decapitated body of Archibald, the shattered remains of the barghest. Time slowed as he took it all in: his parents holding each other, Alexander raising his sword to strike the woman's neck, Steve clinging to her hand as she stumbled back, and behind them, in the shadows of the room, two men. One all in black, and one in grey.

And on the floor, the sword.

Arthur moved.

The woman moved.

Arthur was closer. His fingers clasped the hilt of the blade as the woman shook Steve loose. The dog flew through the air and crashed into Arthur, who caught him while spinning back around. The woman ducked below the wild swing from Alexander as his sword carved the air where her neck used to be. She spun on her heel and lashed out with a clenched fist that struck Alexander squarely on the temple, knocking him senseless, and she turned to face Arthur, who pointed the blade at her face. The woman's mouth ripped open in fury as she screamed at him, and Arthur roared back in desperate defiance. There was no pause—no preamble or parlay. Two opposing forces of magic rose up like waves and crashed together. The dark malevolence of the woman and the uncontrolled, terrified force of Arthur smashed into each other, and it was Arthur who staggered backwards into the wall of the dining room.

And vanished.

There was a moment of shocked silence, then the woman screamed again—a primal, guttural noise that was somewhat ruined by the petulant stamp of her foot. Naked, and seething with rage, she turned and ran from the house.

Deep in the shadows, two figures unseen by anyone left alive or conscious looked around at the chaos in the room.

"Well, that was bloody interesting," said the ghost of Archibald, lighting a pipe and taking a deep breath of tobacco, which, in itself was very bloody interesting. Thin grey wisps of smoke rose from the ragged line in his neck where his severed head rested in the mess. Beside him, the Shadowman slammed his book shut and swore.

"There hasn't been this much bloody trouble since Merlin!" he said.

Archibald looked to his right but the space where the Shadowman used to be was now simply... shadow.

"Merlin," he said to himself, sucking on the pipe and shaking his head. He strode over to the unconscious form of his brother and gave him a kick. "Get up, ya lazy sod. There's work to do." It would have been far more effective had his foot not passed straight through the inert form.

"Bugger."

CHAPTER 27

Outside the house, the naked woman sniffed and clawed at the terrace wall in fury. She knew Arthur must be behind it, but where was he? She had expected to find the stubborn creature cowering beside the outer wall of the small home, but there *was* no outer wall. Instead, stone steps lead up the side of the building toward the castle.

Situated on a steep hill, Arthur's parents' house was significantly lower than the road that ran away from it. The front door to the home upstairs was a good ten feet higher than that of Arthur's. Hence, the single window in Arthur's dining room. The other wall —the wall he had vanished through—led underground. Arthur was gone.

The woman howled in the thick mist then raced up the stairs towards the castle, clambering up the steep cobbled street on all fours.

In the relative safety of a stone porch across the street, Bob and Charlie cowered in the shadows as the naked creature skittered away. Bob swore and then swore again to never have another drink. He looked down at Charlie, who was pressing close to his best friend and vibrating with fear. Charlie didn't say a word.

The darkness and pressing silence smothered Arthur and

made him tremble with the weight of nothingness. No matter how many times he blinked or how long he stared into the dark, nothing took shape before him. Nothing moved. Nothing became clear. This was a darkness so complete it consumed him and pushed against him like cold velvet. There was madness in it. The only thing stopping him from toppling over the edge of sanity was the warmth of Steve nestled in his arms, the quiver and vibration of life pressing against life.

Arthur shifted his feet, and the noise of their movement on the stone floor made his heart leap in fright, but the weight of the stone wall bumping against his shoulder made him whimper.

"Can't you go back through?" Steve asked in a whisper, the type of voice you might use in an abandoned church—soft, hushed, and careful about what you might disturb. Arthur shook his head and realised how pointless that was.

"No," he said, his own voice a strangled choke.

Steve thought better than to ask why. Walking through walls took a toll on Arthur. He remembered watching his friend pass through iron railings, and even a few cars when distracted, but consciously pushing himself through stone was something else. Stone has memory. Thousands of years of immovable memory about... well, being immovable. Unknown to Steve, there was a viral video still doing the rounds of Arthur charging head-first into the Eastern wall of York Minster; the giant gothic cathedral in the centre of the city remained entirely unphased by his efforts.

Walking through stone was a bit like standing on the edge of a cliff with vertigo, though it wasn't so much the thought that you might suddenly twitch and throw yourself into oblivion that tormented you. It was that you might twitch and stay exactly where you were.

Arthur could still feel the weight of stone all around him—the pressure. It took all his effort and concentration to convince himself he wasn't still inside the wall. He moved his other arm and the sword he held clattered against stone. The noise made both man and dog jump.

"I'm going to put you down," Arthur said to Steve. "But stay right next to me, okay?"

"Okay."

"You know," said Arthur, needing to talk as he reached into his pocket for his lighter, "I always thought dogs could see in the dark."

"We can, sort of. But there needs to be at least a little light. Not like this," he said.

"What about this?"

Arthur clicked his lighter and the flame flickered to life in the darkness. It took them a few moments of blinking, but when their eyes adjusted, they looked around and saw... more darkness. It stretched away in front of them like a black hole, a dark pit toying with their perception. Arthur moved the lighter slowly from side to side, and dank stones glistened in the flame. They were in a narrow tunnel that fell steeply away, the meagre light unable to penetrate much further than a few feet.

"Funny."

"What is?"

"I always wondered what was behind this wall, but I figured it would just be a sewer running under the road toward the castle." He moved the lighter slowly and peered into the nothingness. "I never thought it would go down."

"What do we do now?"

"I need to get out of here. I can't leave Mum and Dad with that bitch."

"And you can't get through the wall."

"No."

"Then I guess we're going for a walk."

"Stay still," Alexander said to Mrs. Crazy. Arthur's mum was deathly pale and shivering in the arms of her husband. She was in incredible pain and had seen things she never thought possible—could barely even comprehend. Still, the thought that consumed her more than anything was the fact that her son was in danger.

"Arthur—" she gasped.

"Will be fine," Alexander said. He pulled the bloody flaps of the makeshift dressing to the side and looked closely at the wound on her shoulder. He smiled. "Not the worst I've seen," he said.

"'Tis but a scratch," Thomas tried to joke, but the catch in his voice betrayed him.

He stroked his wife's hair and kissed her gently on the head. There was nothing else to do. Alexander had stopped him from calling an ambulance and insisted they would be useless, even if they got to the house in time. The old man was grey and tired, looking older than before and drained of all energy. His hands shook, and he clenched his fists tight to stop the tremors. He was broken. His brother's decapitated body lay to the side, and he tried not to look, but it was right there, in the corner of his vision. Always there. He closed his eyes and focused on what needed to be done. Mrs. Crazy was in danger, but there was still a chance. Thankfully, the barghest was dead—the bloody mess trampled into the floor was a testament to that. So, the wound should heal. *Should*. It was going to take a lot of energy, and he wasn't sure he had enough left to give.

Alexander placed his hand gently over the bloody wound in Maggie's shoulder and felt her tremble beneath his touch. He reached out and felt her pain, clamping his mouth shut against the agony of it. His eyelids fluttered, and he screwed them tight. The pain was tremendous! No one should be able to withstand it, but there was something else there, something else keeping her from letting go completely. Alexander felt the thread of it and held on, using his own power to reach out to her, to spread soothing warmth across the shattered claws of agony. What was it? What kept her going?

He searched, and then he found it.

It was love. Her love for Arthur and her husband. That's what kept Maggie from letting go.

Alexander felt his own body weaken and begin to fail, and he groaned at the effort. He didn't have much left. He nearly fell, but then felt the gentle pressure of hands resting on his shoulders. It was the lightest of touches, but it drew him back from the edge— let him hold on and focus. He reached inside once more and gasped as the power jumped between them. He smiled as he felt the wound closing beneath his fingers, and Mrs. Crazy gasped in agony as the muscles and skin knit slowly together. Alexander grimaced and held on, waiting until he was sure he had leached every last remnant of the barghest and witch from the woman. It was only when her warm hand reached up and stroked his face that Alexander opened his eyes, smiled, and finally let go, collapsing in a heap at their feet.

Mrs. Crazy looked up at the ghost of Archibald standing behind the fallen form of his brother, and she wasn't afraid. She wasn't even surprised. The memory of the dark pain still tormented her, but the burning in her shoulder had soothed. She could breathe freely.

"How?" she asked.

"Magic," Archibald answered.

"I don't believe in magic."

"Doesn't matter."

"Who are you talking to?" Thomas asked, but his wife just continued to look towards the ceiling. Then she glanced at Alexander.

"Is he?" she couldn't bring herself to finish the sentence, but she didn't have to.

"No," Archibald smiled. "He's alive. He's just an old bugger and needs to rest."

"And you?"

Archibald glanced to his left, to the body he felt no attachment to at all, that he didn't even miss. It was a curious thing and probably had something to do with glands. "Oh, I'm very much dead, love," he said with a smile.

"And that doesn't bother you?"

"Well," he said looking at his hands—if he squinted the right way he could see through them— "it's not ideal, I'll grant you. But you know what they say; there's nowt so queer as folk. Although I guess dead folk is a little queerer," he added with a grin.

At the top of Castle Wynd, Mr. Allott had opened the door for a breath of fresh air but instead found a naked woman with filthy black hair and a disconcerting smile standing on his doorstep.

"Hello, love," he said, barely batting an eyelid. "Bit cold, ain't it?"

"Is it?" she said, looking at the curious man. He didn't seem to be afraid of her, but then, he didn't seem to be focusing on her at all. Behind him, a cat cowered beneath a table.

"Aye, it is. You can't be wanderin' around in your nethers. You'll catch your death."

"Oh," she said with a grin, "I don't think so."

A few minutes later, she stepped over Mr. Allott's body to check her reflection in the mirror. She had found an old pair of black jeans in a cupboard and a black button-up shirt that must have been way too small for the odd little man she thought suited her very well. She particularly liked the jeans.

"There shall not be an article of a man upon a woman," she said with a sneer. She ran her fingers through her hair and tied it together behind her neck. Then, running her hands down her sides, she turned and looked at herself. "For these things are an abomination." She smiled again, seeing a reflection she had not seen for centuries.

Before she left the house, she made sure she killed the cat.

From the rooftop of the Market Hall building, the Shadowman

watched the black-clad lady stalk through the mist towards the castle. In his hand, the book quivered. It struggled against his grip as though the contents were fighting to escape, which is, in a curious way, not far from the truth. Everything was wrong. He could feel it in the air. He could practically taste it. Up and down the country, the length and breadth of the land, the world was changing, and the Shadowmen were worried. This was not something any of them had experienced, and they were not dealing with it very well. *This* Shadowman was standing on a pigeon just because.

There is a story that is familiar to everyone who lives in Richmond. In fact, there are a few well-known local myths and legends, but one in particular that is significant to Arthur and his current predicament. The witch woman has no knowledge of this tale, though doubtless it would make her laugh if she knew. Arthur, however, can't get it out of his head.

"Have you heard of Potter Thompson?" he asked Steve as they worked their way slowly through the tunnel. His voice echoed and bounced around in front and behind them, coming back over and over from all directions. Potter Thompson, Potter Thompson, Potter Thompson.

"No," whispered Steve. He was trusting to his nose more than his eyes and was worried about the unfamiliar smells. Rats were bad enough, but it was the stuff behind the rats that made him nervous. He whined, and Arthur called him a good boy. That made him feel better. A bit.

"Apparently," Arthur said, "Potter Thompson found a tunnel beneath the castle—"

"Like this?"

"I guess, like this. He found something at the end of the tunnel as well."

"What?"

"Well..." Arthur said, stepping carefully over something he didn't want to look at. "You're not going to believe this, but the legend says he found King Arthur."

"*King Arthur*?" There was a tone in Steve's voice that Arthur couldn't help but notice, probably because it was full of derision.

"It's not as crazy as it sounds."

"Are you sure about that, because it sounds pretty crazy."

"But what if it's true?"

"Come on! *King* Arthur?!"

"Well, look at everything else! Why not this?"

"What are you saying, that if we keep going down here, we might bump into King Arthur and the Knights of the Round Table?"

"Would that be so strange?"

"Well, fucking yes!"

"Even stranger than being reincarnated as a dog?"

"Well—"

"Stranger than the witch-girl being reincarnated as a devil dog?"

"Erm—"

"Stranger than the fact I can talk to fucking ghosts and walk through walls?"

"Sometimes walk through walls."

"Sometimes walk through walls."

"When you put it like that, I—"

"And I've got this sword," Arthur said, lifting the blade and letting it catch the light of the flame.

"What are you saying?" said Steve, stopping and tilting his head to the side. "Are you saying you think *you're* King Arthur?"

"No, I—"

"Because that would be very fucking strange!"

"You should stop swearing so much. Puppies shouldn't swear. It doesn't feel right."

Steve chose to ignore that.

"Hang on, I thought you said King Arthur was having a nap around here somewhere, so *you* can't be him, can you!"

"No, you're missing the point."

"What is the point, exactly? Do you think *that's* Excalibur?"

"Well, that would be—"

"Crazy! Mental! Abso-fucking-lutely insane!"

"Well, don't you think it's all a little... weird."

Steve looked at Arthur with such withering scorn that it could have felled an oak, but it was entirely wasted because all Arthur could see was the twin yellow reflections of his eyes. "I'm a talking dog," Steve said, slowly. "What would be weird is if I *didn't* think it was weird!"

"No, I mean the Potter Thompson thing. It seems like a big coincidence."

"Who?"

"The guy from the story. Potter Thompson!"

Potter Thompson, Potter Thompson, Potter Thompson.

The echoes danced around in the dark then faded into silence.

"Yes?" a voice replied from somewhere deep in the darkness. "I'm Potter Thompson."

"We need to help Arthur," Maggie Crazy said to Alexander and Archibald. They had moved to the front room of the cottage and were sitting in front of the fire. It seemed like a different world entirely. The fairy lights glowed, the Christmas tree glistened, the fire crackled comfortingly in the grate, and all was well. Yet, in the other room, just on the other side of the wall, all was in chaos and disarray.

"You can't," Alexander said.

"He's right," Archibald agreed. "The lad is on his own and we're in no fit state to help. Not yet."

Alexander looked at Maggie curiously. "Is he talking again?"

"Yes," she said. "Why can't you hear him?"

"I'm not sure."

"It's because he's weak," Archibald said.

"He says it's because you're weak," Maggie said to Alexander.

"Bloody cheek!"

"Idiot," Archibald growled.

Maggie said nothing.

"There must be something we can do to help Arthur," Thomas said as he entered the room. He handed a steaming cup of tea to his wife and another to Alexander. He couldn't see Archibald either but moved to a different seat when Maggie shook her head.

"I'm afraid there isn't. The best thing you can do is to stay out of the way and get some rest."

Maggie snorted at that and shook her head.

"Who was she?" Thomas asked, "that... woman, that came out of the... wolf. Now there's a sentence I never thought I'd say."

"Her name shall not be spoken," Alexander said, and beside him the ghost of his brother rolled his eyes. "For she is evil and there is power in a name."

"Oh, come off it!" Maggie said. "This isn't Lord of the Rings. This is real—I think. What's going on? Who was she and what happened to our son? Why is he involved in all of this?"

"I honestly don't know why Arthur is involved other than what he told us earlier. He has a gift and that led him to her."

"And her to him!"

"He said the girl in York was a child."

"Indeed, she was," sighed Alexander. "But before that, she was something else. It was a last chance at sparing her life. It... did not go well."

"She recognised you, didn't she? She said you were there," Thomas asked. "What did she mean?"

"You have to understand that she has a long history. A history perhaps even longer than I know. The girl in York... the one trapped in the room. That *was* her but what you saw here was also her. In fact," he closed his eyes as a wave of exhaustion threatened to overwhelm him, "what you saw here was her true self. She has somehow managed to defeat death."

"Seems to be catching," the ghost of Archibald said. "I reckon she's been planning this for a long time." Maggie looked at him, but Alexander continued talking.

"She might have been planning this for a while," he said. Archibald grinned. "She was locked away in that room for hundreds of years. It was a cage, of sorts. Then it all went wrong."

"What went wrong?"

"Well, she had been dead for a very long time—almost forgotten. But there were signs that she was trying to break through. It was thought..." he sighed again. "It was thought that given a fresh start she might prove herself. She might even help us. It was a dark time, and she had great power. She could do wondrous things if she wasn't—"

"Such a bitch," Archibald said.

"Archibald didn't like her," Alexander said. "He was dead against it from the start but some of us thought differently. Some of us thought there would be enough of the innocent to counterbalance... the rest."

"You were bloody wrong."

"We were wrong. It *all* went wrong. So, we had to lock her away."

"In the room in York?' Thomas said. "She was the famous girl in the window?"

"It wasn't quite a room in the sense you are familiar with," Alexander said. "It was more of a temporal confinement area interlaced with incorporeal containment runes and—" he stopped as he saw the look on their faces.

"A magic trap," Archibald said.

"—a magic trap," Alexander finished.

Maggie looked from brother to brother. The conversation was very disconcerting. If you had no idea Alexander could not see or hear his twin, you might never have guessed. She wondered how long she would continue to see the ghost of the old warrior and how long Alexander would remain unable. Alexander noticed her looking.

"What does he have to say?" he asked, swaying in his seat.

"You're a ruddy idiot," Archibald said.

"He's worried about you," Maggie said.

Alexander laughed. "I bet he's grumbling about... about..." but he trailed off as his head nodded forward.

"You need to rest, or you'll be no good to anyone," Archibald said.

"He says you need to rest," Maggie said. Alexander nodded again. His whole being ached. He felt thin and stretched to breaking, his body heavy with a weariness that pushed him deeper into the couch. The fire crackled and spat, and the warmth in the room mixed with the warmth of the tea in his belly. The mug he was holding fell from his grasp, and Thomas caught it before it hit the floor. Alexander slumped heavily and fell to the side, passing through the ghostly form of his brother to rest on the couch, long beard and hair falling to the floor. He immediately started snoring. Archibald rose slowly from the seat and walked towards the fire.

"Well, that was right odd," he said.

"What do we do?" Thomas asked his wife.

"Nothing we can do. We leave him here and go find Arthur."

"You can't," said Archibald.

Maggie Crazy spun to him, her eyes blazing. "And why not?"

"There is nothing you can do."

"We have to try!"

"There is nothing," Archibald repeated gently.

"What's he saying?" Thomas asked. He was getting frustrated at only being able to hear one side of the conversation. It was like listening in on an important phone call without speakerphone.

"He says there's nothing we can do for Arthur."

"Like hell there isn't!" Thomas said, rising to his feet and entirely failing to face Archibald with indignation.

"You can see me," Archibald said to Maggie, raising his hands, "but it probably won't last. It's just an echo. A remnant of the magic Alexander used to save you. Believe me when I say there is nothing you can do against this woman. Nothing."

"But I can be there for my boy!" she said.

"And she'll use you against him!" Archibald snapped. "She won't think twice. She'll tear you both apart in front of him just because she can! Just because it will hurt him. Arthur needs you to keep away! That's what you can do! That's the only thing you can do. Keep away and keep safe."

"But why my boy?" Maggie cried, tears rolling down her cheeks. "Why him?"

"I don't know," Archibald said in a low voice. "Sometimes people can do things. They have talent. They tap into something other people can't. It seems that's what happened to Arthur. He has power, and the thing she wants more than anything, the thing she has always wanted, is power."

"But why now?"

"Who knows? He lit up the world like a beacon in a way that hasn't been seen for a very long time."

"But this isn't new, is it? What about when he was a boy? With the ghost in the house?"

"Hundred?" Thomas asked with a confused look. His wife ignored him and continued to direct her conversation to what appeared to him to be the straw Yule goat on the mantelpiece.

"Was it something I did?" she asked. "When he was a baby? When I was pregnant? Is this my fault?"

Archibald stepped towards Maggie and placed an ethereal arm on her shoulder. He'd had very little practice in his new form, so it just slipped right through. He stepped back and awkwardly folded his arms across his chest. He looked straight into Maggie's eyes. "My dear lady. There is nothing you could have done and nothing you did do. The son of a teacher is not always a teacher, and the son of a wizard is not necessarily a wizard. That's not how it works. We are all of us born unique, and we find our own way."

"A wizard?"

"What wizard?" said Thomas.

"Just a figure of speech, my lady," said Archibald. "I mean there is nothing remarkable about the birth of a child that could influence their life in such a way as this."

"Well," said Maggie, after a pause, "he was born backwards."

"Ah."

"At midnight."

"Right."

"On February 29th."

"Well,"—said Archibald, running his hand through his smoke-like beard—"bugger."

CHAPTER 28

Mitchell James Dean, named to be a movie star but lacking any of the necessary requirements, was the curator of Richmond Castle, a job and title he took very seriously. Even now, late in the day on Christmas, he is thinking of his duties. Or, more precisely, he is thinking of the chest freezer in the gift shop and the sheer volume of ice-creams it contains. His wife, Selina, is snoring gently on the couch, but he knows for sure she will appreciate a Nobbly Bobbly or a Peppermint Magnum, and it will give him an excuse to check the grounds. Mitchell took his keys from the hook, pulled on his jacket, and gently closed the door.

English Heritage gift shops are an institution in their own right and attached to almost every listed site in the country. They're treasure-troves of books, tour-guides, knick-knacks, replica weapons, games, toys, and a wide assortment of specially made alcoholic beverages, biscuits, and preserves. They generally adopt the "Swedish Furniture Store" policy of placement by forcing guests to enter and exit via the colourful array of enticing gifts and sweets. In its own way, it's a well-thought-out trap for children and tourists. Mr. Dean was used to the small room being crammed to overflowing with people, flicking through books, ignoring the signs admonishing patrons to not touch the weapons, and trying one too many taster cups of specially made gin and mead without ever actually buying anything. What he was not used to was tall, beautiful women standing barefoot in the dark, covered in chocolate and surrounded by ice cream wrappers.

She was stealing! She must have broken in, today, of all days. Christmas! How dare she!

Inside, Mr. Dean was furious, already mentally compiling a sternly worded letter to the local newspaper decrying the ever-decreasing moral fortitude of millennials (Mr. Dean did not actually know what "millennials" were and so used it as a blanket-term to describe anyone younger than him), but as he took in the scene before him, his inherent Britishness overrode his anger.

"Um, can I help you?" he asked, politely.

The woman turned to him with a smile that contained all the beauty of a tsunami, albeit one with a chocolate coating.

"Oh, yes," she said. "I think you might."

"Who's there?" Arthur asked, hoping the shake in his voice wouldn't echo in the dark and betray his fear. He tried to peer beyond the flame but could make out nothing other than flickering shadows dancing a few feet away and melting into blackness.

"I told you," came the voice. "Potter Thompson. Who are you?"

"I'm—" he hesitated for a moment, "I'm Arthur." He saw no point in lying, which, as it turns out, was probably a mistake.

"Arthur!" cried the voice in the shadows. "It's me! The potter! I found you!" There was the sound of rushing footsteps in the dark and bumps and scrapes as though someone was moving swiftly along while colliding with the wall. Steve began to growl, and Arthur took a few steps back, raising the sword protectively in front of him. He narrowed his eyes, but the darkness of the tunnel was too complete, barely broken by the meagre flame of his lighter. "At long last!" came the voice, closer this time, the sounds of movement louder, the echoes coming from all directions.

"Stop!" Arthur shouted, but all he heard in reply was his own voice rattle back to him, mixing with the footsteps and the brushing, rushing noises as they came closer and closer. Then, suddenly, all was still.

In dark places, there can be a silence so complete that the only sounds to be heard come from within your own body. Steve stopped growling, and Arthur held his breath, but the pounding of his own heart and the roar of the pulse in his ears was so loud as to be almost deafening. Arthur's hand grew sweaty as it gripped the sword handle and his muscles ached with tension. Nothing moved. No one spoke.

And then the flame flickered once and died.

"You're not Arthur," an angry voice whispered behind him. Arthur screamed in a less than manly way and swung round, entirely forgetting the sword he held in his hand, which might have been a problem if the person who surprised him hadn't already been dead for hundreds of years.

The ghost of Potter Thompson looked down at the blade sticking through his stomach. He had no problem seeing in the darkness of the tunnels—he had spent the better part of the last millennium wandering through them, lost and searching. And now, though not as expected, he thought he'd finally found what he was looking for.

Well, almost.

Arthur stepped away, his brain trying to make sense of the things his eyes couldn't see. There was a man standing in front of him, of that he was sure, but the sword had hit nothing more substantial than air. He fumbled with the lighter. Sparks flew but no flame caught, quick flashes of light briefly illuminated an old, bearded man with a bulbous nose and thick eyebrows. His eyes were black holes beneath a heavy brow, his hair a wild, tangled mess. *Flash, flash.* The man's face danced in the quick light, revealing missing teeth in a crusty mouth. Finally, the flame caught, and Arthur and the man called Potter Thompson looked at one another in the flickering light.

"Liar!" the man said, his voice was a hiss, full of anger and bitterness, his face criss-crossed with a mass of wrinkles that moved and rippled in the flame. He looked down at the sword still protruding from his belly and then looked back at Arthur. "Thief!"

Arthur's first instinct was to pull the sword away and mumble an apology. His tired mind had finally tied the tangled ends together, and he realised the man was a ghost. So, the sword wasn't actually causing any harm, but as he pulled the blade away, it resisted. Arthur grimaced, thinking it had indeed caught in the man's guts, that he was wrong about Potter, but when he looked down, he saw the old man's gnarled hands gripping tightly onto the blade.

"That does not belong to you!" Potter hissed.

Arthur pulled again, an instinctive tug like a child with a rope. Potter snarled, his face scrunching into shadow in the flickering flame as he tightened his grip.

"Stop it!" Arthur said.

"Mine."

"You're going to hurt yourself!"

"He's dead," said Steve from somewhere near their feet.

"Doesn't matter," Arthur grimaced, unwilling to let go of either the sword or the lighter, but also worried about the damage he might do to the strange man if he kept grappling with him.

Steve yapped and barked as the two figures struggled in the dark and then the realisation dawned on him as it had with Arthur.

Ghosts can touch the living but it's all about focus and concentration. Potter was focusing on holding the blade but *not* on the fact that it had skewered him like a kebab.

Steve wasn't sure he wanted to find out what would happen if the man's focus suddenly shifted. He narrowed his eyes and growled.

Focus and concentration.

The little dog jumped, and, for the second time that day, sunk his teeth into the arm of a person holding a sword. The sensation was not pleasant, like scratching teeth down a chalkboard, and all of Steve's new instincts rebelled against him, forcing him to let go. Still, it was enough. The ghost roared and lost his grip as Steve dropped to the floor, and Arthur stumbled backwards into the wall. The lighter flew from his hand and plunged them all back into darkness as it skittered away across the dank stones.

"Run!" Steve shouted, tucking his ears back and racing into the dark. After a few moments, he stopped, turned, and ran back. "Run the other way!" he barked at Arthur's stumbling figure. Arthur turned and followed the little dog whilst holding the sword out in front of him.

A brief sensation of icy goose pimples rippled over Arthur's body as he ran through the protesting form of Potter Thompson and then they were away, racing as fast as they dared down the dark tunnel beneath the castle. Arthur followed Steve's excited yaps, and behind them, the ghost of the old potter screamed in fury, the echoes chasing them faster than the old man could.

"Thief!"

Thief thief thief.

As Arthur and Steve raced deeper into the hill, the dark lady moved deeper into the ruined castle far above. Mr. Dean tagged along beside her, carrying ice creams, entirely unable to leave and not sure why.

"Who owns this castle?" the woman demanded, looking up at the towering keep from the main footpath below the gate. It was shrouded in thick mist, but she could make out enough to see that the wide, square stone structure appeared solid and complete.

"No one does, my lady," Mr. Dean stammered. He wasn't sure why he called her that. It just seemed that not doing so would be a terrible mistake.

"No one? Someone must own it. Tell me!"

Mitchell Dean swallowed, though there was no moisture in his throat. He was shivering, and the ice creams weren't helping. He closed his eyes and fell back on years of experience as a tour guide, recalling words that sat like a script in his head. "The castle's construction was begun by Alan Rufus after the Norman Conquest and the Harrowing of the North when the land was granted to him by William the Conqueror," he said. The lady raised her eyes at the mention of William the Conqueror, but she motioned for him to continue. Mitchell was reminded of a cat, toying with a trapped mouse.

He coughed and looked away from her piercing, dark eyes. "Well, the great keep that we stand under was built sometime in the 11th century, probably by the nephews and grandnephews of Alan Rufus. This is the only castle in the country to have such well-preserved architecture from the period," he said, getting into the flow now. There was only one thing he loved more than his castle and that was talking about it. "The rest is mostly in ruins, but the keep is intact, and much of the original curtain wall still exists in fine form, as does the wonderful Scolland's Hall."

"Scolland's Hall?"

"The King's Hall, my lady. Probably finished by Henry II after he took control of the castle. It is named after a fifteenth century steward."

"A King's Hall. That will do me. Show me the way."

"Erm... it is in ruins, my lady. There is no roof."

"Useless!" she snarled. "Do the descendants of these men do nothing to stop their land from falling into disarray?"

"Well," said Mr. Dean, carefully, "as I said—" her withering look bent him into a subservient bow. "My Lady," he stammered, staring at his own feet. "It, erm... the castle, I mean, is not owned by anyone really. It came into the care of English Heritage in 1984, and we have looked after it ever since."

"English Heritage?"

She said the words with such scorn that, despite his fear, the inherent and proudly British part of Mr. Dean shook at the implied meaning.

"A very proud acquisition," he said, standing up straight, shoulders back, chin up... bottom lip quivering.

"There is nothing proud about the Angles or the Saxons," she snarled. "Rapists and thieves and murderers, each and every one of them." Mr. Dean gasped, but she was not done. "They hide behind their false piety, worshipping a nailed god who tells them to love, but they ravage the world in his name, telling their victims it is for their own good! They have no honour, no respect, no understanding! The heritage of the English is nothing but pain!"

"Erm. Well, I suppose there are some football hooligans who—"

"What is that?" she interrupted Mr. Dean's stammering. He looked to where she pointed, a small part of his brain trying and failing to avoid noticing the way the black shirt clung to her as she extended her arm. She clicked her fingers. "The pathetic folly of man," she sneered. "I asked a question."

"That's out of bounds," Mr. Dean said and regretted it immediately.

"To me?"

Mr. Dean fumbled for his keys, dropping ice creams on the path as he did so. It was testament to his fear that he didn't immediately go about cleaning them up. When he found what he was looking for, the frightened man walked over to the heavy wooden door set into the wall beneath the arch of the main entrance of the castle. The iron key rattled as his hands shook, but eventually, he felt the click and turn as the lock released.

"This is a cell block from the 19th century," he said. "It's not open to the public."

"I am not public," the lady said and strode past the shaking man, pushing him roughly out of the way. Then, just inside the threshold of the door, she suddenly stopped and a shiver ran through her body. So far, it seemed to Mr. Dean that the cold of the night had not affected the woman in the slightest, but now, uncontrollable convulsions wracked her slender frame, and she folded her arms tight against her chest. For a moment, just for a brief flicker of a second, he thought he saw hesitation, but she shook it off and stepped forward.

"People have prayed fervently in this place," she said, her voice echoing off the stone.

"This is where they housed the Richmond Sixteen," Mr. Dean said, once again falling into his role as tour-guide. "They were conscientious objectors during the Great War."

"What was so great about it?" the lady asked, moving deeper into the room.

"I... I don't know," the bemused man said. He fumbled in the dark and eventually managed to find the switch on the cold wall. A low hum filled the room and there was a flicker as over-head lights winked to life, banishing the shadows to the corners. It was the first time he had seen the lady in full light, and he could do little but stare as she moved slowly about the strange cell block. She was indeed beautiful. But beautiful in the same way a volcano can be beautiful—great to look at, but preferably from a distance. There was something deeply dangerous about her that he couldn't quite put his finger on. Mr. Dean found himself staring and entirely unable to look away. She was dressed simply enough, black trousers and a black buttoned shirt with the sleeves rolled up. Men's clothes perhaps, but they did very little to disguise the woman wearing them. He knew that *she knew* he was staring, and there was nothing he could do about it. She padded softly about the room on bare feet, perfectly poised, peering closely at the plaster and brick walls and the historical treasure they contained.

"Graffiti," he said, managing to choke the word out and finally tear his eyes away from her body. "The prisoners here graffitied the walls, and we're working to preserve them."

"To preserve the agony of men?"

"To preserve their... experiences."

She laughed at that and ran her fingers along the wall, tracing the lines of the text and the sketches. Passages from the bible, notes to loved ones, prayers, quotes, portraits of lovers and parents, images of the landscapes of home—all etched into the plaster or scribbled onto stone with pencil. She lingered on a drawing of an airplane, something she had seen from the window of her own cell, but of which she had no real comprehension. And there were other things, vaguely familiar and yet completely alien.

Her eyes lowered. "What is this?" she demanded. Mr. Dean stepped closer and tried not to react when she moved near him. He hadn't felt this nervous in front of a woman since high school.

"That's a ship," he said. "The H.M.S. Badger."

"A boat?"

"Yes," he nodded in discomfort. Her mannerisms were strange and unnerving, moving back and forth between confidence and power to almost childlike innocence. Her body and proximity terrified him, but her words put him in mind of the small children who came to the castle on school trips and asked the most bizarre questions.

"How can such a thing float?"

He had no idea what to say, but she had already moved on. He stood up straight as if released and trotted after her.

"God is my keeper," she read, tracing the words with her finger before walking further into the cells, her nail now scraping sharp lines wherever she went as she made hard, angry jabs at the wall. "The banner of Christ, the Lord's cross, shut in with my keeper," her voice took on a sharp edge of scorn and derision and Mr. Dean winced as plaster crumbled away.

"Please," he said.

"Please what?" she snapped, and he cowered before her. "Pathetic," she said, and the man didn't know if she was talking about him or the men who left their marks on the wall. He had a horrible feeling it was both. She turned her back on him and began to read in a mocking voice.

"Midst the darkness, storm and sorrow. One bright gleam I see. Well, I know that on the morrow. Christ will come for me. Well," she laughed, "did he?"

It took the trembling Mr. Dean a few moments to realise that he had been asked a question, and the silence stretched on as she waited for an answer.

"Did... did who?" he stammered.

"Did The Christ come for this poor wretch?"

"I... I guess that depends on what you believe?" he said after a while.

He was growing ever more certain that there was something inherently wrong with this woman. Something—as his wife would say—not quite right, but it was more than that. She wasn't just unusual, she was dangerous. Fear stole over him in a way he had never felt before. He closed his eyes and thought of Selina, offering a little prayer to whoever might be listening that he might see her again. He realised then that he didn't expect to, and he began to tremble. The woman's scornful laughter snapped him back to the world.

"Always the promise of a coming saviour," she said. "Pathetic! No one to blame. No one takes charge. No responsibility or accountability because *he* will come back and take care of everything. Always waiting. Always hoping. Has your great religion really come to this?" she snapped.

Mr. Dean had no real idea if she was talking to him or not. It seemed as though she was ranting to the world at large, and the room grew darker as she got more irate. Some part of his brain still had a modicum of control, and it made his feet take a few tentative steps back.

"Look what it has done to this land!" she snapped, suddenly punching the wall.

Plaster cracked and exploded in dust and part of the wall crumbled to the floor. Mr. Dean sobbed, but the woman was just gearing up. The electric lights flickered, and the shadows danced and moved as though people hid in the dark places.

"You came with fire and sword!" she raged. "You burned everything! You stole everything! You pulled down the sacred places and built your... your churches!" She spat the word and actually spat on a drawing of the cross. Mr. Dean was horrified. "And your crosses! Damn your crosses! You spread your filth with fear and death and poison. And now what? What did you do? What did you become after you killed our gods and raped our lands? Nothing! Too afraid to fight. Too scared of condemnation and damnation! Well, I damn you all! I damn you all!"

The woman screamed in fury and raised her hands to the ceiling. Black shadows leapt like lightning from her fingers. Mist burst into the room through the open door and writhed around Mr. Dean, who screamed and tried to run, but it pushed and pulled at him like a living thing. There were *things* in there. Solid things. Dark things. He felt fingers grip his arms and legs and lift him, sharp nails and claws tore through his clothes and broke the skin in a hundred different places as he was hoisted to the ceiling by unseen forces. The mist rolled and billowed against his body, and he screamed in agony as the woman walked out of the cell without so much as an upward glance. Whatever held him followed her, dragging his body out into the darkness of an unnatural dusk.

CHAPTER 29

Far below, deep in the dark, endless tunnels, the world around Arthur and Steve began to shake. The great stone hill groaned and rumbled as the walls trembled and the floor moved beneath their feet. Both man and dog cried out in fear and raced onward, the thought of millions of tons of rock and stone, castles and homes, crashing down on them driving all caution away. They raced headlong through the darkness, the dog with his ears back and his tail tucked, and the man holding a sword straight out in front. The rumbling grew to a roar, and for a horrible moment, both of them knew this was the end. They could feel the weight of the stones about to crush them, and they knew it would soon be over.

Then, as suddenly as it started, the shaking stopped.

The sudden change caused Arthur to lose his balance, and he fell, tumbling out of the tunnel and into a wide and spacious cavern. Steve stumbled to a halt beside him, his paws skittering on the floor as his back legs tried to overtake the front.

Arthur looked up and blinked in the sharp light. The cavern was a perfect circle, hewn from the rock of the hill itself. Dark tunnels lead away at regular intervals, and between each tunnel, braziers burned brightly against the wall.

In front of each brazier, arranged in a perfect circle with Arthur now in the centre, were twelve large tombs.

"What was that?" Alexander snorted, sitting bolt upright on the couch. Maggie and Thomas Crazy paused in the act of putting their hiking boots on and looked at him. Archibald had tried in vain to stop the parents, but there was little he could do as they dashed about the house making preparations to go find Arthur. Mrs. Crazy had packed a small backpack with a powerful torch, a first aid kit, and a hammer, while her husband gathered their winter clothes and hats.

"No idea," Thomas said, standing up and pulling on his coat. "Earthquake I think."

"Do you often get earthquakes around here?" Alexander asked, stretching and rubbing the side of his face to get the blood flowing.

"Never."

"It was her," Archibald declared.

"Indeed," Alexander said. He stood up with an effort and turned to Mrs. Crazy. "I told you, ma'am There is nothing you can do. I'm sorry."

"We have to try!" she snapped and went back to gathering things she thought they might need—a coil of rope, a handful of cable-ties, a permanent marker, and a bottle of water followed the first-aid kit into the backpack. "Should I make some sandwiches?" she asked her husband.

"Why didn't you talk some sense into them?" Alexander demanded of his brother, who just shrugged and gestured as if to say *what could I do*? There was a long moment of silence as the activity in the room paused, and the strange foursome stared at each other in confusion. Those who couldn't previously see looked at those who previously could not be seen, and it took a long while for the pieces of the puzzle to fall into place. For Thomas, nothing had changed, but it was fascinating to see Alexander's face light up as he called out "Brother!" and then fall onto the couch while trying to hug someone even less substantial than smoke.

"Interesting," Alexander said, standing up and smoothing his robes as though nothing had happened.

"Aye, it's going to take a bit of getting used to, all right," Archibald said, trying and failing to clap his brother on the back.

"Gentlemen," Mrs. Crazy said as politely as she could manage, "if you'll excuse us. We are going to look for our son."

"There is nothing I can do to stop you," Alexander said. It was not a question.

The twins looked at each other though neither spoke. Alexander nodded and turned to the defiant couple. "Where do we start?" he said.

Mrs. Crazy smiled and placed her hand on the old man's arm. "The castle," she said. "And we'll need your sword," she added to Archibald, who grinned and inclined his head.

Mrs. Crazy slung the backpack over her shoulder and lifted the sword. She looked at her husband with steely determination in her eyes.

"We push on," she said, and opened the door.

"I like her," Archibald said to his brother as the men followed her into the dark swirling mists that shrouded the town.

High above, on the roof of the castle keep, the black-clad lady laughed and screamed into the darkening sky as the mists swirled and rolled around her. A tumultuous maelstrom of dark shadows writhed behind the silver veil, as thin and delicate as the wings of a fly, but somehow it held them back. Teeth and claws gnashed and scratched at the night, poking and teasing, trying to find places of weakness. They tore at the unconscious form of Mitchell James Dean, the warmth of his blood splattering onto the stones, giving off tiny wisps of steam that rose into the night and joined the swirling mists. He was naked now, the clothes torn from his body and cast to the ground far below as the creatures behind the mists fought over him. The lady lifted her arms and the spinning stopped. He remained suspended in the sky in front of her as she stood on the battlements high above the blanket of white clouds covering the land. Stars twinkled in the firmament of the cold clear night, and it would have been beautiful if the lady had bothered to look up or even cared about such things. To her, the beauty was in the look of terror on Mr. Dean's face as his eyes flickered open and the pain bit through his body like ice.

"What is left of this once great land?" she snapped, her face a rictus of rage and disgust. "What creatures still roam the dark places? Who remains who remembers the old ways?"

"I don't know. I'm sorry!" gasped Mr. Dean. "Please!"

The woman laughed at him, cruel and mocking. "You think I was talking to you? You insignificant worm—you are nothing to me! I know your thoughts. I see the way you leer. I know how you think! I was talking,"—she turned slowly to look into the deep shadow cast by the moon on the battlements—"to you!"

The Shadowman stepped forward. Darkness fell from him as though he stepped through a waterfall of ink. He was dressed head to toe in a black so deep it seemed as though his clothes were cut from the night itself. But his face was white—deathly white. He carried a pallor of sickness and disease, with eyes sunk deep into the recesses of his skull. Though, the flat cap he wore cast a shadow over much of his face, his thin mouth could be seen, curled into a sneer as he appeared.

"You dare to address me!" he said.

"Quiet!" she demanded and the Shadowman hesitated. No one spoke to him that way. "Don't pretend as though you are anything more than a common caretaker," she snarled. "You have no real power. Not here. You keep things neat, and you clean up after others like a good little dog. I know what you are."

"Then you know it is not wise to test me," the Shadowman said in a voice like iron.

"Test you? How could I test you when there is nothing to test? You are a lackey. You dare not interfere. You *cannot* interfere. All you can do,"—her voice dropped to a dangerous whisper—"is clean up the mess."

Behind her, whatever force that was holding Mitchell James Dean—caretaker, curator and keeper of the keys of Richmond castle—released him.

The scream as he fell was pitiful and desperate and quite long. Though a hell of a lot shorter than he might have liked.

The Shadowman swore and looked to his book, the heavy leather cover falling open to the exact page where the writing danced across the paper, impossible to tie down.

He was still trying to make sense of it when the woman hit him.

There are rules.

There are always rules.

Some rules are written in stone, and some are etched in night-black writing in the books of the Shadowmen. Some rules are older than all forms of the written word and lay across the heart of existence like a tattoo on the soul. Irrefutable and eternal.

The only problem with rules is that there will always be that one person who believes they do not apply—not to them anyway.

Rules can bend. Rules can twist. Rules can break.

But mugging a Shadowman and nicking his book is probably going a tad too far.

A rthur got shakily to his feet and looked around the cavern. "It can't be," he whispered. "It's not possible." His voice was low and hushed, almost reverent, as though speaking at a funeral.

On the floor beside him, Steve shook himself and looked around. From his point of view, all he could see were the flames on the walls and large rectangular stones that rose from the floor, but he could clearly see the puzzled expression on Arthur's face as the man glanced about the room.

"What is it?" Steve asked, but the man didn't answer—instead, he just turned and blinked and then rubbed his eyes. "Arthur?"

"He is not Arthur!" Potter Thompson snapped from one of the dark tunnels as his hunched figure shuffled into the light, leaning heavily on the hewn wall. "He's an imposter! A liar and a thief and —" his voice trailed away as he took in the sight before him.

His eyes widened, and his toothless mouth opened in shock. Arthur looked on in surprise as tears fell from the old man's wrinkled eyes and ran down his cheeks to soak into the scraggly beard.

"It's... I... I've found you!" Potter cried and a great sob escaped from his lips. He held a shaking fist to his mouth and cried as he bit his knuckle and choked out the words. "At long last, I've found you!"

He stepped forward on unsteady legs and reached out to the nearest stone block. He was scared to touch it, his dirty fingers trembling just a few centimetres away from the smooth stone. Arthur blinked and couldn't quite work out what he was seeing. It seemed to him as though the strange cave was blurred and unfocused, like a photograph that hadn't been properly processed. He was exhausted, so he blinked again to clear his vision, but still, the image swam before him.

He saw a cave, that much was true. A cave with a number of exits and with lights on the walls. There were large stone blocks lining the circular wall. They *were* there, *weren't they*? As he stared at Potter Thompson, the world swam and drifted, exactly as it does when you've had too much to drink—when your vision blurs and nothing stays where it is meant to. The stones vibrated in the air, but Potter Thompson did not. Potter Thompson stood as solid and as real and as clearly defined as any man while the world around him struggled to decide what it wanted to be. It put Arthur in mind of the portrait photograph setting on his phone. The picture highlighted the foreground by blurring the background. He stepped towards Potter, but the world around him looked exactly the same. Potter was in focus; the world was not.

Then Potter Thompson finally placed his hand on the stones, and everything changed.

Everything.

CHAPTER 30

Maggie Crazy let out a scream as she saw the body fall through the mists from the castle keep, and she threw herself into her husband's arms as the heavy thud echoed from the closed gates. Thomas pushed her away, and she stood dumbstruck for a moment as her husband left her and raced to the gates, Alexander and Archibald on his heels. It wasn't until she heard Thomas's strangled cry for their son that her mind allowed the same thought to rise. The scream that rose within died in her throat as she dashed to the door of the small office. Thomas was already clambering over the huge wooden gate, but she knew she would never make it that way. It was too high.

Maggie Crazy hit the door at a run, sending it crashing open and knocking down a pile of novelty Viking helmets. She charged through the familiar shop, navigating by the light of the ice cream freezer and aiming for the connecting door at the back.

It can't be him, she thought. *It isn't. It mustn't be. It can't be.*

As she ran into the castle grounds, she saw her husband standing over an inert form on the frosty grass at the base of the keep. The ghost of Archibald stood beside him with his head bowed, and Alexander was still clambering over the gate. Mist swirled around them, and the dazzling security lights lit the scene in a horrendous tableau of sepia. She paused for a second, her hand on the door, not quite able to let go as she took it all in in an instant.

That... shape on the ground might be my son.

But even as the thought entered her mind, she dismissed it. She knew it wasn't Arthur. How she knew, she couldn't explain, but she knew it wasn't her boy. She also knew right then and there that this scene would be forever etched into her brain—that she would wake in the night after seeing this. It would haunt her for the rest of her life with an eternal 'what if?'

This all took no more than a few seconds, but by the time Maggie Crazy made her way up the small slope towards the gathered men, her husband was already calling the police. Maggie glanced briefly at the figure on the ground and wished she hadn't. Without a word, she walked back to the small gift shop and found one of the large tartan picnic blankets from a display table and took it back outside. Without looking at the body, she unfolded the blanket and gently draped it over the shattered form of Mr. Dean.

"They're on their way," Thomas said in a quiet voice.

"Do you think that was wise?" Maggie asked. There was no accusation in her voice, just concern.

Mocking laughter peeled through the mists swirling above them.

"I think we might need all the help we can get," Thomas replied, pushing the phone into his pocket. As one, they tilted their heads heavenwards, but there was nothing to see except the orange glow of the spotlights in the thick fog. "They wanted me to stay on the line," Thomas said quietly, "but I don't think we should wait."

"There are two worlds at play here," Alexander said, his eyes fixed on the churning murk above. He shuddered as he remembered the night before, and the shadows barely held in check. "It is never easy when they collide."

"We don't really have a choice," Thomas said. "Unless you know another number I can call, the police are all we have."

Alexander looked at the ghost of his brother, who shook his head, which, of course, Thomas didn't see. Maggie did.

"We're on our own," Alexander said.

"Fine. Then there's no point standing around here waiting," Thomas declared, hefting Archibald's sword in one hand and reaching for his wife with the other. "Let's go find our son."

Archibald grinned as the two brothers followed Mr. and Mrs. Crazy into the dark maw of the castle keep.

"I like him as well," he said.

The nameless lady watched from high above as the four figures crossed the threshold of the castle. She wasn't watching them in the conventional sense due to the heavy mists obscuring her view, but there are other ways. There was just one more piece of the puzzle. One minor irritant. No matter. It had been a long time since she'd really stretched her legs... metaphorically speaking. She stroked the cover of the dark book in her hands and thought of all she might now achieve.

Finally! She was so close!

The corner of the lady's mouth turned up into what, on another person, might have been a smile, but not even her own face trusted the intent behind it. Her long fingers beat out a steady rhythm on the book's cover, each quick tap like a nail in the spirit of the man who watched.

"That will only lead to your ruin," the Shadowman gasped. He was bound and held by coiling ropes of mist, the shadows within them grasping him tightly. He knew the futility of struggling. He glared at the lady with open malice. "You will pay for this... this abomination. There are rules!"

The lady made a nonchalant motion with her hand, and the mists coiled around the Shadowman's mouth, silencing him. She opened the book and flicked through the pages, peering at the strange shapes as they writhed and twisted, almost as though they didn't want to be read. There was doubt within her—just a flicker, but doubt was a weakness, so she thrust it aside, turning the pages over and over until she found something that caught her eye. She tapped a long finger on the page, and her eyes flashed.

"There you are," she said.

She lay the book down on the parapet of the castle and looked out into the world of shadows and mist. "They never forget in the country," she said, not facing the Shadowman but addressing him anyway. "Not in the deep villages and hamlets. They never forget. Oh, the filth and lies have spread across this land, but people can never let go of the old ways. How can you stand it?" she spat suddenly, turning on the Shadowman.

"You have seen it all, borne witness to it all, and you just let it happen! How can you stand it?"

She didn't wait for or even expect a reply. She was ranting now, caught in a fervour. It had been countless years since she had been this free, felt this much power, and now she must wield it. She *needed* to wield it!

The Lady lifted her hands to the sky and laughed and screamed and whooped as the mists boiled and swirled and tugged at her hair and clothes. She yelled words into the void in a language that had not been spoken in centuries. But words have power, so they darted away through the mists and shadows, spreading across the country and seeking out the dark places and the hidden memories they contained.

Beside her, the Shadowman began to struggle.

Far to the north, beyond the ruins of the Roman wall and over the vast crags, streams, and barren moors of Northumberland, an invisible border runs between two countries. It stretches from one side of the island to the other and within it, the silkies roam, haunting houses, homesteads, and remote farms, but now they are on the move. The silkies are heading south.

On the clifftops of Whitby, the barghest is no longer cowering.

It is a slovenly and thin beast, having not feasted properly in many years. The chain around its neck is worn and rusted and, up until a few moments ago, the creature could do little but shiver in fear among the graves of the church. Now it is running, fresh blood dripping from its maw as it races through the narrow streets and wynds, heading west.

Deep in the murky depths of Lake Windermere, the rocks and silt are churning as the waters above seethe and froth. A creature is rising. It is long and dark and quite blind. It also has no legs. But that won't stop it from breaking the surface and slithering onto the pebbled beach to head east.

The streets of London, Manchester, Birmingham, Cardiff, York, and many others are shrouded in unnatural mist. Those few people who dare to brave the outside—or who do so out of necessity—rush about their business with heads bowed, darting from streetlight to streetlight, not quite sure why the dark places scare them so much. Perhaps it is because there are so many, and they seem to ripple in the shadows? The cities are emptying. The dead are on the move. So are the ones in between. They are all heading north.

In Richmond itself, the small hillside market town is in turmoil. Bright lights bounce from the mists as police cars, fire engines, and ambulances converge on the castle, but the roads there are narrow and so only a few vehicles can push through at a time. The rest crowd into the market square, and the centre of the town is lit up like a disco as red, blue, and orange emergency lights dance in the thick clouds and deep mist surrounding the castle keep. No one is quite sure who called who but the desperate screams of the first officers still haunt those who heard them on the radio. The gates to the castle are locked. The police gather in terrified silence behind the few cars they could squeeze through as they wait for the arrival of A.R.V., S.R.O. and C.T.S.F.O.—anyone with a gun. They called them all.

Above the vehicles and flashing lights, mounted on the iron railings of the castle gate, are the severed heads of their colleagues.

~

Far beneath the chaos unfolding at the castle, Potter Thompson touched the stone of what appeared to be a tomb and dropped to his knees with his head pressed against the rock.

"Potter Thompson, Potter Thompson," he cried to himself. "'If thou had either drawn the sword or blown the horn, thou'd be the luckiest man that ever yet was born!' I'm here," he said, desperately. "I'm here my Lord King, I found you at long last!"

Arthur was still trying to clear his head. He felt nauseous and there was a buzzing in the air, like a swarm of flies he couldn't see. A strange metallic taste flooded his mouth, and no matter what he did, he couldn't get his eyes to focus. The whole cavern appeared to be shrouded in a thin veil of smoke, indistinct yet just enough to make the scene quiver and shake. Steve had absolutely no idea what was going on, but he watched his best friend carefully as Arthur moved towards the strange ghost. Steve whined.

Above Potter Thompson, something moved on the stone slab. The shadows there were shifting and changing, until suddenly—where previously there was only stone—the figure of a man appeared.

Slowly, he sat up.

"Yes!" Potter Thompson cried in ecstasy, stumbling back and then bowing deeply. "I'll not run this time, my lord! I'll not fail you! I *will* draw the sword!"

"Oh, fuck off!" Arthur laughed, somewhat ruining the moment. He glanced from Potter Thompson to the figure on the stone, and back, shaking his head and lifting his arms in resignation. "Nah. I'm not having it. This is complete and utter bollocks! There's no way this is real!"

Slowly, Potter Thompson turned his head to face Arthur, eyes ablaze with fervent passion. His gaze dropped to the sword in Arthur's hand, and his eyes narrowed. The old man went from kneeling to standing and crossed the space between them in an instant. His gnarled and rotten fingers gripped the blade and yanked it free from Arthur's grasp before he had chance to react. With a look of pure ecstasy, Potter Thompson stumbled back and raised the sword above his head, screaming in triumph.

"I've done it! I have it! I'll be the greatest man there ever was!" he crowed.

The whole scene would have been a lot more impressive had he not been holding the sword by the tip of the blade. The unnatural distribution of weight suddenly made itself known and Potter Thompson staggered as he fought to keep the sword upright. For a moment, he moved like a circus-performer balancing plates on a stage, and Arthur saw his chance.

He had never punched anyone before—not really—only himself in the dark streets of York, and he wasn't sure that counted. He wasn't a violent man by nature, and he hated fights. The punches he tried to throw in his dreams always slowed as if thrown through treacle, and they *never* connected. However, the rage, frustration, and fear of the past two days clawed at his nerves and made them raw. The vision of the risen man on the stone slab, the capering Potter Thompson, the terror of the witch-girl, and the all-consuming fear for his parents built within him. He took one step forward on his left foot, drew his right fist back, and thundered all his rage square into Potter Thompson's face.

What Steve saw was the ghost of Potter Thompson crumple to the floor and vanish, the sword falling loose and clattering to the stones.

What Arthur saw was much different.

Arthur saw Potter Thompson. The *real* Potter Thompson.

Peter.

He saw a young man walking along the banks of the river below the castle, throwing stones into the tea-coloured water. He saw him grumbling about his wife, complaining to the night sky about her constant nagging, lamenting the life he thought he could have led if only they hadn't rushed into marriage. Oh, for the folly of youth. Peter Thompson had dreams and ambitions, Arthur could see them—*feel* them. Richmond was too small for the man. He was going to take the old Roman road to London and make his fortune, work in the palace, and impress the royals with his skills. Peter knew in his heart there was more to life than this, more than casting pots for simple village folk by day and putting up with a harridan of a wife by night.

There was more in store for Peter. Life was bigger. He would be remembered for being more than a simple potter, the son of a potter. Arthur watched as the angry young man threw a stone into the thick scrub... and then he paused as he heard it skitter and echo away.

The young man followed the noise and nervously pulled aside a gorse bush to reveal the entrance to a small, hidden tunnel. As he gazed at the mysterious hole, Arthur felt the fear wash over him and he saw the truth. It wasn't his fear. It was Peter's. And there it was, at the very heart of Peter Thompson's character, the one thing that drove him more than anything else—that made him follow in the profession of his father and made him marry the first girl who gave him attention. It was the same thing he knew deep down would stop him from ever taking that road to London. In the core of his being, behind all the pretence, bluster, and blame, Peter Thompson was a coward.

And Arthur saw it all.

The man never even ventured into the tunnel, though he spent the rest of his life wishing he had, even telling people he had, and eventually, *believing* he had.

Peter told tales of it to anyone who would listen and over time those tales grew and changed and shifted to fit a narrative that only existed in his head. He descended into madness, convinced he had been cheated from some great destiny. He stopped working and left the comfort of his home to wander the castle, shouting and raving to all and sundry about the grave of King Arthur hidden beneath them—how it was his destiny to raise the sword of the king and become the greatest man the world had ever known.

Arthur knew the story, of course. Everyone in Richmond, and indeed, everyone who visited the castle, knew the story. It was the same story told in other castles throughout the country. The same story a passing traveller told in a Richmond tavern hundreds of years ago as Peter 'Potter' Thompson sat, drunk and morose, in the corner and listened. It was a good story. So, he stole it.

In the end, half-starved and raving incoherently, the bedraggled and toothless Potter Thompson finally plucked up the courage to enter his cave. He crawled through the vast overgrown gorse, shuffled into the dark entrance… and died.

His ghost had been wandering the underground passages and caves ever since.

Arthur knew all of this the instant his fist crashed into the old man's face. When the connection was made, the ghost of Potter Thompson snapped back and fell, vanishing through purple light as he hit the ground. Arthur blinked and opened his eyes, but it made no difference. There was nothing but inky black. He blinked again and again but saw nothing.

The room was gone.

He stood, panting in the dark, trapped in a hill beneath a castle with only a talking dog and the ghost of ghosts for company.

"There he is," the nameless lady said as she leaned over the battlements, looking into—and beyond—the mists that flashed red and blue far below. She had felt Arthur's power and now she was definitely smiling, though it was not a smile that would give anyone comfort or cheer.

She cocked her head to the side and her eyes flashed as the winds whipped around her, plucking at her hair and clothes.

"And here come mummy and daddy!"

CHAPTER 31

Thomas Crazy raced up the narrow stone steps inside the castle with the sword in one hand and a torch in the other. It had taken them a long time to batter down the door to the first floor, so they had missed the chaos from the front of the castle as the police arrived. This was one of the few things they might be very grateful for this Christmas.

Thomas and Maggie might never have got through the door at all had Archibald not drifted through the wood and used all his power of concentration to slide back one of the bolts. It had been enough to weaken the rest of the door, and with a rending crash that drowned out the screams of the dying police officers, they fell through the opening and into the cold interior of the castle keep.

Arthur's parents knew the castle like the backs of their hands, having lived below it for nearly thirty years, so they charged straight up the narrow stone stairway that led to the second floor. Then all four of them—mum, dad, the breathing twin, and the mortally challenged one—stumbled to a halt when they entered the grand room.

The high stone walls, vaulted oak ceiling, and double high-set windows were enough to make any visitor pause in wonder, but it was the lady dressed all in black that brought Thomas, Maggie, and the twins to a crashing stop. She stood beneath the two windows, barefoot on the wooden floorboards, and apparently entirely unconcerned by their presence. She spread her arms wide and bowed theatrically, a dangerous smile curling the edges of her mouth.

The twins spread out, one on either side of Arthur's parents, Alexander had drawn his sword, and beside him, Maggie was hefting the weight of the hammer in her hand. It had come in very useful on the door, and she had no reservations about using the same technique on the woman in front of them. Thomas held Archibald's sword in two hands and the ghost of the old warrior stood beside him. The four companions faced the woman who did nothing more than smile... until she clicked her fingers.

Dark mist billowed through the high windows and swirled about the rafters, but it was the creatures that came through the two doors on either side of her that were the immediate problem. They tumbled from the shadows and the dark openings in a mass of limbs and teeth and claws. Most were no bigger than children, and all seemed to be vaguely human in shape. But it was as though their creator had heard what humans looked like and then put them together in the dark without paying any attention to the instructions.

"Look how the little ones have suffered," the lady said in mock pity as the creatures swarmed around her. Ten, twenty, thirty, maybe more. Some stood upright, some shuffled on all-fours, and in some cases, all-sixes. "They are the forgotten ones," she said, "but I called them back from the shadows, from their holes, from beneath the bridges and cellars and deep old forests. The boggarts and the hobgoblins and all those sacred creatures who were once feared, even revered. Back when there was respect!" She spat the last word and the mass of creatures around her writhed and clamoured, gibbering, and slathering in anticipation, but they would not go beyond the woman in black. They pushed against each other as though pressed against glass, a tangle of limbs covered in decay and dirt and grime; they thrashed and tore at an invisible barrier, yellow teeth flashing and claws ripping into the wood of the floor. Still, they did not come any closer.

"Where is my son?" Maggie Crazy demanded. She was terrified and on the precipice of complete and total panic, but the thought of her boys kept her going. Her Arthur, lost somewhere in the castle or below it, and brave Thomas standing beside her and slightly in front, brandishing a dead warrior's sword. Always protecting her—always her knight in shining armour.

Or, in this case, her knight in woolly hat with a fluffy pom pom on top.

"Your son?" sneered the woman. "Your son is a disgrace! You should have drowned him at birth! You—" but whatever she was about to say was cut off as Maggie Crazy screamed in fury and threw the hammer with all her might. It spun in the air and hit the woman square in the face, smashing her nose, and splashing bright red blood everywhere. The woman in black roared in pain and staggered backwards, cracking her head hard against the stone wall where she stayed, arms spread to steady herself.

There was a moment of silence as the three men cast quick glances at Maggie Crazy and Archibald whispered, "Well... fuck."

Then, all hell broke loose.

This is not, necessarily, a metaphor.

The dark lady turned her head and laughed, her teeth flashed savage white from behind the mask of blood, and whatever force it was that held the creatures back was released. They surged and tumbled over each other like water building up and breaking down a fence. The four companions roared in defiance and stepped forward to meet the onslaught.

There are stories where the heroes make a last valiant stand and defeat the bad guy against insurmountable odds.

This is not one of those stories.

Sorry.

The fight was over in seconds.

Thomas was strong, but he had never wielded a sword before. His first wide sweep took the head clean off a snarling, single-toothed hobgoblin, and severed the hand of another. But the wild swing dragged his body around by the weight of the blade, and he was brought crashing to the ground before he could even think about a backswing. The last thing he saw before he was knocked unconscious was his weapon-less wife headbutting a creature that looked oddly like a tall, leathery koala.

Alexander fared a little better, but even he was overwhelmed by the sheer number of adversaries and was eventually tackled to submission as boggarts pinned his arms and legs and jumped up and down on his body.

Archibald was useless.

He's a ghost.

He did manage to push one boggart in the back, but it just turned around and punched a confused goblin in the face.

He stood there as the creatures swarmed over his companions... and *through* him.

"Fuck," he said for the second time.

"Use your power," Steve said in the dark. Arthur was glad it was pitch black because he jumped a mile when the little dog spoke.

"What do you mean?" he hissed.

"The purple light thingy," Steve said. "Make a torch."

"I don't think it's supposed to be used like that," Arthur said but then fell quiet. He had no idea how it was supposed to be used, or where it had come from, or what it even was, for that matter. He knew he could access something unusual and powerful, but he really had no clue about what he should and shouldn't do with it. It's not like it came with a rule book, which, he thought, would have been very handy.

Arthur closed his eyes and clicked his fingers. He felt the familiar rippling up his arm, and when he opened his eyes again there was a ball of purple flame dancing on his palm casting bright light around the room.

"That's better," said Steve. "What the hell was all that about? Who was that man?"

"He was Potter Thompson," Arthur said, casting his hand around the cave and looking at the "tombs." He paused and blinked in the light. They were nothing more than rock ledges—natural layers of stone probably shaped by millennia of rising water. Everything was smooth, but it wasn't the smoothness of man, it was nature.

"I... I don't understand," Arthur said, moving over to the rock on which he saw the rising man. He touched it and had to fight down the urge to flinch. It was just a rock. "There's nothing here."

"What did you want there to be?"

"Did you see the man?"

"Potter?"

"No, the other man."

"There was no other man. What are you talking about?"

"When Potter was kneeling beside this rock, there was another man lying on it. He sat up. He... he was right there!"

Arthur seemed desperate and scared—more so than usual. Steve trotted over to him and sniffed the rock. Then, because he's a dog, he cocked a leg and peed on it.

"Mine. Sorry mate, but I didn't see anything."

"It was definitely there. I think it was supposed to be..." he trailed off.

"Supposed to be...?" said Steve. Arthur looked down at him and the dog looked back with big, innocent eyes.

"King Arthur," he said.

"Fuck off!" said the puppy.

"I know it sounds crazy, but that's the whole deal with Potter Thompson, he's supposed to have found a tunnel beneath this castle that led to the resting place of King Arthur and his men! But when I punched him, I saw... well... it was all bollocks! He'd made the whole thing up."

"Then why do *you* think you saw King Arthur?" Steve asked.

"I don't know! I don't get it at all. It was like I was seeing what Potter *believed*." There was a long moment of silence while they both thought of the implications.

"Well, that could cause a few problems," Steve said finally.

"You're telling me!"

"Imagine..."

"Don't!"

"What?"

"Whatever you're going to say, don't say it! My head is already fucked up enough as it is, and that bitch is still with my Mum and Dad, and I—" Arthur broke off as a sob strangled his words, and he started to shake. Steve trotted over. Unable to do anything else, he butted his head against Arthur's shin.

"Hey, it'll be okay, okay?" he said. "They'll be fine. Those two old blokes seem like they can handle themselves."

"One."

"Pardon?"

"One old bloke. The other one got his head bitten off, remember."

"Well, I'm sure they'll be okay." Which just goes to demonstrate the relentless and charming optimism of dogs.

"Are you? Because I'm not! I need to get out of here!" Arthur raised his hand and concentrated. The purple light pulsed and grew and illuminated the cavern. He turned in a full circle, but there wasn't much to see. A few stone shelves he had mistaken for tombs and only two dark tunnels.

"Do we go back the way we came or try the other one?" Steve asked.

Arthur headed towards the new tunnel. "Keep pushing on," he said, repeating the words his mother used whenever things got tough, which, in turn, were words from her own father: Just keep pushing on. You'll get there eventually.

With Steve on his heels and the sword in his hand, Arthur Crazy strode into the dark.

CHAPTER 32

Constable Melanie Gangadoo had been with the police for just over two years and excelled at everything the job threw at her. She finished top of her class in training, graduated with distinction, and achieved multiple awards along the way. The reports from her two years of active service were a testament to her character and her drive to succeed. She thought she had been given a small taste of damn near everything the job had to offer but she was not prepared at all for the sight of three severed heads above the gate of the castle.

The whole scenario was like a dream. The mist, the castle, the flashing lights of the emergency vehicles, the shouts and commands thrown back and forth through the narrow streets as officers took positions to surround the castle. Houses and pubs were entered and rooftops climbed, but the castle wall itself was huge. It clung to the very edge of the hill, and for much of the circumference, it provided a thirty, forty, even fifty-foot vertical barrier from the nearest path. There was no way the police could effectively encircle the whole area. They were stretched too thin, and they desperately needed back-up.

A sharp cry broke the night, louder than most, and a hive of activity descended upon the squat, white-walled cottage at the top of the tiny castle car park. Word spread quickly.

Another body.

A man had been murdered in his own living room. His cat impaled to the wall with a bread knife.

This had to be a dream. Nothing about this was real. This sort of thing just did not happen in sleepy Yorkshire towns.

Powerful searchlights were dragged into place and generators kicked to life, though the arcing beams of white light did nothing to pierce the thick mist. If anything, they just made the small car park glow like a false day and the ceiling of mist seem even lower.

Constable Gangadoo stepped forward into the open area in front of the castle and looked around. No police had approached the gates or the gift shop attached to the castle. They all hung back behind cars or in the narrow alleys and roads. Those who arrived first were being interviewed, but most were in hysterics and sitting in the back of waiting cars unable to talk. There was a rumour of helicopters and the military, but as far as the constable could tell, no one else had actually approached the gate to see what they were dealing with.

She swallowed her own fear and loosened the clasp on both her taser and baton. If no one else was going to do it, and no orders said otherwise, then she was going to have a look herself.

She moved cautiously towards the gate while hugging the wall of the nearest house. She wasn't going to approach it head on but rather come in from the side. That way, whoever was inside might not see her. The talk among the other officers was that whoever had committed the murders was now inside the castle itself.

There had been no sign of movement for some time. One of the more coherent first responders mentioned something about chains, so the assumption was made that there were hostages. If any were in view from the gate, that information would be invaluable to command.

Constable Gangadoo slowed down as she approached the tall

wooden gates and leaned back against the wall, taking a few moments to control her breathing. She moved slowly, creeping forward inch by nervous inch, trying not to make a sound. The gates were bolted to the walls with heavy iron hinges, and there was a gap of a few inches between wood and stone, enough to peer inside and maybe see something useful. Gangadoo quietened the nervousness in her heart and leaned forward to look through the gap. Mists shrouded the courtyard of the castle, as it did everywhere, but the heritage spotlights illuminated the lower section of the keep and the arched gateway that connected the cell block to the main building. Movement caught her eye in the darkness of the archway, and she watched as a line of figures made their way to a door set in the cell-block wall. There seemed to be three adults and a number of children, but they were too far away and the mists too thick. Officer Gangadoo had always trusted in her instincts, but she didn't know what to think here. It was all wrong.

The *adults* looked like they were prisoners being escorted by the smaller figures. That couldn't be right. It made no sense at all.

She peered closer, pressing her face against the gap but the mists swirled, and the figures were lost to shadows. A sudden scream from behind made her turn in place, her hand automatically reaching for her baton. She never saw the giant form that stepped into view behind the gates. She felt it though, as it reached over the top of the wall and grabbed her by the head in one giant hand. Chains rattled in the night and the world filled with screams.

She struggled.

Briefly.

Somewhere high above, the sound of laughter drifted through the sky.

Down by the river, the ghost of John Snell glanced momentarily at the glow coming from the top of the hill. It looked as though the castle itself was on fire, but he didn't care. He turned his back on the town and stepped to the edge of the raging waterfall, letting the roaring waters tug and pull at his feet. Tears rolled down his cheeks and he angrily brushed them away.

"What's another lost promise in a world of traitors and sin?" he said and stepped into the river.

Arthur and Steve ran through the never-ending tunnels. They twisted and turned and went up and down and around, completely losing any sense of direction. Arthur thought they had to be below the town rather than the castle, but he couldn't be sure. There was no telling what direction they were taking or where they were heading.

The only thing they could do was to keep on running—to push on.

Steve was panting heavily by now, and so Arthur reached down and scooped him up and tucked him under an arm. The little dog licked his face in appreciation, and then apologised. But Arthur didn't mind. The affection was nice. It made him feel ever so slightly less frantic and insane. He was trapped in a labyrinth with no end in sight, holding a talking dog and a sword, and lighting the way with fire from his free hand. His parents were at the mercy of a naked woman who used to be a giant wolf—who also used to be a little girl—and he could talk to ghosts and walk through walls. Correction, *sometimes* walk through walls.

He wondered what the shrinks would make of the latest addition to his story.

Arthur imagined them sharpening their pencils and thinking about their PhDs as he jogged on. His mind, like his body, was exhausted.

These sorts of things do not happen to normal people, he thought. Maybe he was actually insane and, somehow, he was dragging everyone else along with him? Maybe, like Potter Thompson, he had created a delusional reality that had nothing to do with the real world? Or, more likely, this was the biggest cliché in the book, and everything he was experiencing was some strangely vivid fever dream.

Arthur considered this as he jogged through the underworld. Whenever he ran in his dreams, he never seemed to get anywhere, and he was getting nowhere now. So, perhaps that was it? He was at home in bed, fast asleep, and he just couldn't wake up. He'd had plenty of dreams in the past that seemed real enough. What if you were in a dream that seemed real, and you couldn't tell the difference?

He stopped suddenly and Steve whined.

"Nope, definitely not a dream," Arthur said, lifting his hand to illuminate the tunnel... and its occupant... in front.

"What isn't?" asked Steve.

"This isn't."

"How do you know?" the little dog asked, who had been thinking along the same lines.

"Because I grew up in Richmond, and I never once dreamed about the Little Drummer Boy."

Standing in front of them with a big smile on his face, was a small boy with scruffy blonde hair, and a pristine military uniform. Over his shoulders he carried a drum on a harness and in his hands, he held two sticks.

The boy bowed his head politely and began to tap out a slow rhythm on the drum.

Traat-tatt, traat-tatt.

He turned on his heel and marched away into the darkness, the drumbeat echoing off the walls.

Traat-tatt, traat-tatt.

"Come on," Arthur said. "He's going to show us the way out."

"How do you know?"

"I just do. Trust me."

"Always," said Steve.

They followed the drummer boy as he led them deeper into the tunnels, never saying a word, but waiting patiently for them to catch up if he took a different tunnel or changed direction. He never hesitated and he never faltered.

Traat-tatt, traat-tatt.

Along the way, they picked up other people, ghosts and spirits from around the town that drifted out of dark doorways and connecting tunnels. Some came straight through the walls, fleeing the chaos in the town and searching for refuge below ground. For many, it was the first time they had ever broken the bonds of their haunting, but witches tend to have that effect on people—living and dead.

Arthur and Steve watched in awe as the procession grew. The Drummer Boy seemed to sense where the lost souls were and gathered them to him.

With each new companion, he did the same thing: he smiled, bowed, and then went back to drumming. Arthur stuck close to the boy, and Steve shivered in his arms, nervous at the line of ghosts forming behind them, but on they marched.

Traat-tatt, traat-tatt.

Soon enough, the air changed. A cold breeze drifted down into the tunnel, and Arthur could smell the frost and the trees of the world outside. A dim light appeared, and the strange procession suddenly left the cave and entered a room, the ground giving way from stone to grass—though, there were still stones above their heads. An opening at the far end looked out to the world where thick fog glowed dimly in the night sky.

Arthur smiled. He knew exactly where they were.

He had played hide and seek in this spot many times when he was a kid, and he had played other games here when he was a bit older.

They were at Easby Abbey, the grand ruins of a monastery that sat a mile downriver on a wide curving bank of the Swale. So, all the legends were true. The castle and the abbey were indeed connected by underground tunnels. His mum would be thrilled to hear this.

His mum.

Arthur pushed the thought away for a moment and turned around slowly, noticing for the first time the sheer number of ghosts and the way they all stared at him. They may have followed the Drummer Boy, but it was Arthur they were focused on. Or rather, the glowing fire at the end of his hand.

Slowly, he started to connect the dots. They weren't just running *from* something, they were running towards something.

Towards him. Towards hope. Towards the memory of a door they were denied.

"I... I can free you all," Arthur stammered, casting his eye over the crowd. There were so many of them—young and old, men and women, many dressed in clothes that belonged to another time. Arthur saw the robes of monks, uniforms of soldiers, and overalls of labourers. There were figures in chainmail standing next to men in suits and wide-eyed children from all times and places. He saw one young girl wearing a Nirvana t-shirt with a flannel shirt tied around her waist, and he backed away.

He knew her. Well, he knew of her.

Arthur remembered the story from school. The strange assembly in the middle of the day with the crying teachers. The girl on the bridge. She smiled at him.

"I can end all of this," he stammered, tears spilling from his eyes. "I can help you, but, but I can't do it yet." There was a moan from the gathered figures, and they pressed closer to him like starving children, some hands reaching, grasping in the dark. "I will," he said, backing away. "I promise! But I have to go back. I have to make sure my parents are safe. And if I free you all now, I might not have the strength to help my mum and dad." Arthur stepped towards the opening and the mass of ghosts followed like hipsters heading towards a food truck. "I'm sorry," he said with tears in his eyes. "I just, I don't know how all this works, but I'll come back for you. I promise! I swear!"

And with that, he extinguished the flame and fled from the ruins of the abbey.

The girl in the Nirvana t-shirt moved to the stone archway and watched him vanish into the dark.

Arthur had always been a strong runner, but it had been a very long day on top of a very long night, and he was already tired. Shifting Steve to his other arm helped, but he wished he had a scabbard for the sword. The weight of it interfered with his balance as he jogged along the familiar riverside path towards the town. He was cold, but he didn't really feel it. Memories of his dad teaching him how to run, how to control his body on this very path, flitted through his mind as he matched his breathing to the rhythm of his steps.

Before long, he passed The Drummer Boy Stone, and he realised he had come this exact way the night before after making another promise to another ghost.

"I will keep them," he gasped to himself. But his parents came first. He had to prioritise the living over the dead. He needed to get back home.

As Arthur and Steve burst from the cover of the trees and ran below the large houses on Easby Low Road, they saw the glow coming from the town. Arthur stumbled to a halt at the end of the wynd and looked up the hill and back. To his left was the main bridge over the river with the old train station on the far side. In front of him lay The Batts and the old grammar school. But up the hill to his right was St. Mary's and the town. Was it really last night he sat between his parents singing Christmas Carols? How can one life change so much in such a short space of time?

Arthur shook his head, trying to clear his mind.

The quickest way to his house was up the steep road, he knew, past the church, and through to the marketplace. He glanced that way and shivered, the thought of a hill run filling him with dread, However, the thought of something happening to his mum and dad while he stopped to catch his breath was unbearable.

Making a silent promise to give up the cigarettes if they got out of this in one piece, Arthur put his head down and started the ascent, knowing even as he did that it was a promise he probably wouldn't keep.

I f Arthur had been thinking straight, he might have given his current situation a bit more thought before charging into the marketplace, sword (and dog) in hand, but he wasn't and he didn't. Arthur thought he was racing to his parents' rescue through streets as familiar with him as they were to him. This was home. *His* home.

What the police thought, as they stood at the hastily erected barricades in the main square and watched him bear down on them from out of the mist, was, *Holy shit! That man is charging us with a drawn sword, get the tasers out!* This thought was swiftly followed by, *Try not to hit the dog!*

Because everyone likes a scruffy dog.

CHAPTER 33

Tasers hurt. Getting tasered by three nervous cops who have seen things that shook the very fabric of their perceived reality *really* hurts—quite possibly three times as much.

Arthur's body still twitched as he lay in the back of a dark police van. Spasms rippled through his muscles, and it felt as though he had been repeatedly stabbed by red-hot pitchforks. He was pretty sure he'd pissed himself, but as he couldn't really feel anything other than white-hot pain, he didn't care.

As far as heroic charges go, his had not shaped up as expected.

Arthur rolled over and groaned. The deep *thrum-thrum-thrum* of approaching helicopters filled the night, and he could hear people rushing around outside. There were screams and shouts, as well as the sharp crack of gunfire, running feet, and roaring engines.

Living so close to one of the largest army barracks in the country, the residents of Richmond were familiar with the sound of weapons being discharged on gun-ranges across the moors, but the rattle of powerful rifles in the confines of the town cracked like thunder.

And above it all, shrill and full of malice, was the laughter.

In the back of the van, alone and afraid, Arthur knew it was directed at him.

"Get up," he muttered to himself, tears streaming down his face. His hands were tied behind his back with cables that bit painfully into his skin. It was the least of his problems. He forced himself into a sitting position with a cry and sat there sobbing, trying to control the spasms that still rippled through his back and down his arms and legs.

"Arthur?" a voice called in the darkness, making him jump. There was a dim light in the back of the police van, and he twisted and turned but was very much alone. "Arthur, it's Steve! Can you hear me?"

"Yeah, I can hear you," said Arthur. "Where are you?"

"Under the van."

Arthur struggled against his restraints and fought a wave of panic that rose from his belly to his chest, threatening to overwhelm him.

"I can't get out!" he sobbed, and the words burst a dam inside. He kicked and screamed and thrashed against the side of the van in desperate panic. "Let me out!" he screamed over and over. "Let me out! You don't know what you're doing! Let me out!" but none of the police heard him. Even if they had, they were used to that sort of reaction from the back of a paddy-wagon. It made no difference, and it certainly never convinced a single copper to change their mind. Beneath the van, Steve put his paws over his ears and waited for it to stop.

"Are you done?" he asked when the banging subsided and the shouts turned into muted sobs. "Look, Arthur," he said, trying hard to make his voice sound more like a man and less like a cute little puppy. "You're going to have to get out of this yourself. You know you can do it. You've done it before. You just need to concentrate, and use your power."

"It's not as easy as that!" Arthur snapped back, taking deep breaths and trying to push down the soaring panic that was making his heart race. "When I did it before, I was either so drunk

I didn't know what I was doing or so scared I... didn't know what I was doing!"

"Aren't you scared now?"

"Bloody terrified, but it's not the same."

Steve padded around in a circle, wracking his brain to think of a way he could help his friend.

"What about the sword?" he said.

"The police took it."

"No, you idiot. What about when you got the sword from the police station in York. You were sober then, weren't you? You weren't running for your life or anything."

"Yeah, but, well, I don't know. I sort of did that in a daze. I don't really remember much about it. One minute, I was in a hospital bed in York, and the next, I was on a train with the sword in a cricket bag. There are flashes of bits in between, but I don't really know."

"Well, maybe that's the key," Steve said.

"What do you mean?"

"Don't concentrate so hard on making it happen. Maybe you need to concentrate on not concentrating?" Even as he said the words, he knew it sounded bloody ridiculous. Arthur's muffled "oh fuck off" confirmed it.

Steve paced around again, thinking hard, then he stopped and sat down close to the rear wheel. He closed his eyes for a second then whispered to himself, "The greater good."

"Look," Steve snapped suddenly and inside the van, Arthur lifted his head from his knees at the sharpness of the tone. "Stop being so fucking pathetic!"

"What?"

"Oh, shut up and listen, you whiny little bitch! All you do is complain, and you've got this magnificent gift that others would kill for—*have* killed for—and you're just sitting there and wallowing in self-pity because you're too much of a fanny to do anything about it!"

"Hang on—"

"Shut up!" Steve growled, and then he steeled himself to keep going. "Sarah died because of you! Lord Acaster died because of you! I'm a fucking dog because of you!" He heard Arthur standing up in the van and kept going. "Are you going to let your parents die as well? Are you? Are you going to break your promise to them like you've broken it to every other ghost you've met in the last two days?"

"Shut up, Steve!"

"You shut up! If your mum and dad die it will be your fault! There's no one else to blame but you!"

He heard Arthur shout and the van shook as a loud bang sounded from above.

"Oh yeah, that'll help. Just smash the doors down because no one has tried that in a police van before! Are you really that pathetic? Your parents are probably already dead, and—"

There was no bang. No crash. No dramatic roar of rage or need to exclaim that you're only supposed to blow the bloody doors off. Arthur simply fell through the side of the van and landed in a heap on the cobbled street. He rolled over with a groan and stared at Steve, who backed away behind the wheel and whined. Arthur was breathing heavily and glaring at the dog, his eyes fierce and rimmed with tears. His chest rose and fell as he gasped for air. Slowly, he got it under control. His face softened, and a smile curled the corner of his lips as his eyes lost some of their intensity.

"Was that your 'with great power comes great responsibility' speech?" he asked, sitting on the road.

Steve stepped out from under the shadows and whined.

"Yeah. Did you like it?"

"It could use a little work," Arthur said, struggling to his knees and rubbing his wrists. His hands were free from the restraints, which, he imagined, would raise quite a few questions when the police looked in the back of the van. "Thanks," he muttered to the small dog.

"What do we do now?" Steve asked.

"I need to get the sword back. It's important. I don't know why but I think it's the key to all of this. Did you see where they put it?"

"In the van."

Arthur paused.

"Seriously?"

Steve nodded.

Arthur looked around, but there were no police officers near them. They were all crowded along the streets close to the castle. He walked over to the door and looked through the window. There, on the front seat, lay the sword.

"Can you reach through and get it?" Steve asked.

"Maybe," said Arthur, peering closer. Walking through things was the strangest part of his power, and it left him feeling nauseated and with a taste of tin in his mouth. Though, that could well have been the after-effects of the tasers. If he could help it, he didn't want to do it again. He wondered if British police vans had bullet proof windows. If not, maybe a brick?

He looked down and smiled.

"What is it?" asked Steve.

Arthur opened the unlocked door of the police van, reached in, and took the sword.

"Well, that was easy," Steve said. "Now what?"

Arthur gripped the sword tightly and looked up at the castle. "Now the hard part," he said. "But first, I need to change my pants."

CHAPTER 34

Arthur's sense of relief that his parents weren't in the house was swiftly replaced with a worrying question: where were they? This, in turn, was promptly taken over by the realisation that they had most likely been taken to the castle. The inevitability of what he had to do thundered around Arthur as he sat on his childhood bed and changed his jeans. It would be so easy to lie back, fall asleep, and wait for it to all blow over. That's what childhood was all about, letting the adults take care of the big stuff while you went to your bedroom for a nap. That's why he had come home after all the chaos in York—to let the grown-ups take care of him for a while.

But now he was on his own.

Well, he had Steve, but Steve was a puppy, and that just raised more questions.

To really add to his frustration, Arthur fumbled while tying the shoelaces of his Vans and swore as the knot fell apart. He closed his eyes and breathed deeply.

"I need an adultier adult," he said.

When he was ready, he made his way downstairs where Steve was waiting beside the fire that still crackled with red coals. The sword lay on the couch where he had left it. He smiled at the scene; it could have been any normal day. Then he noticed the coffee cups, his mother's shoes, and his dad's slippers, Arthur paused. The slippers were unmistakable. They, like the Christmas jumper, had Rudolph the red-nosed reindeer on them, and his dad had been wearing them all day.

"If *she* took them, I doubt she would have paused to let them have a cup of tea and put their shoes on first," Arthur said. Steve looked around the room and joined the dots for himself.

"You're right. So, that means they left of their own free will. Where would they go?"

"To look for me," Arthur said. Of that, he was certain. He had got lost in the woods a few times when he was a child, and he knew his mum and dad would stop at nothing to find him.

"Where would they look?" Steve asked, but he already knew the answer.

"The castle," they both said at the same time.

"Different path, same destination," Arthur said, "I guess it's destiny or some shit?"

"What do you mean?"

"If you can see the castle, you can always find your way home," Arthur said. "Something my dad used to say when I was little. If I ever got lost, all I had to do was head to the castle and I'd find my way back."

"That's deep," Steve said, which is an odd statement to hear from a puppy.

"Only one problem," Arthur declared, lifting the sword, and looking down the blade, "I don't believe in destiny."

This would have been a really heroic thing to say before setting out on a dangerous adventure if the protagonist hadn't then walked to the door, paused, and had what can only be described as an overwhelming panic attack.

Thankfully, Steve was no stranger to such things and recognised it for what it was. He coached Arthur through a series of breathing exercises, and, after a time, the shaking subsided. The two figures sat beside the radiator where Arthur had collapsed looking at the door that should already have been closed behind them.

"What good am I going to be if I can't even get out the door?" Arthur said. Steve knew better than to answer. "I mean, I'm so scared. I'm terrified, mate! It was easier in York. I was drunk for most of it, and it all happened so fast. It was like a whirlwind that picked me up and carried me. I didn't really have a choice, I just acted—did the next thing that needed to be done."

"That's all any of us do," Steve interjected.

"But it was different then. I didn't really know what I was getting myself in for, and now I do. I don't know if I can do it. She's so strong. And so... so fucking evil! The whole bloody police force is out there shitting themselves, and it sounds like the army is there as well. What the hell can *I* do that they can't?"

"You know what you can do," Steve said.

"But I don't, do I? That's the thing. I don't. Not really. It's not like I was given an instruction book or some mysterious mentor to guide me in the use of my powers. Where's my fucking Obi-Wan Kenobi?"

"I guess you'll just have to figure it out for yourself,"—Steve placed a paw on his friend's thigh—"but you won't be alone."

"You're a good boy," Arthur said and laughed a little as Steve's tail wagged furiously and tongue lolled. "God, this is so weird."

He stood up.

"A man-child and a dog-man, huh? Against the forces of darkness." He reached for the sword.

"Could be worse."

"Oh, yeah, how?"

"I could be a cat."

Arthur gripped the door handle and closed his eyes for a moment. None of the big adventures he had ever read or seen in the movies told the truth about crossing the threshold. For one thing, they were usually metaphorical. Yet, here he stood, literally on the threshold of the safest place he knew, about to step over into the dark. He was terrified, and the pain in his chest from the rawness of the panic attack was still there. There was something else beside it, though—the cast-iron certainty that he could not stand idly by while his loved ones were in danger. Arthur simply did not have a choice, and that was the certainty he needed.

"We push on," he whispered to himself. Then he opened the door and stepped into the night.

"About time," the lady in the castle grinned. "I was about to send someone to get you." She ran her finger through the small pool of blood on the floorboards of the grand room and the image of Arthur disappeared.

She stood up and looked around. She had been busy. The whole floor of the great hall was covered with similar pools of dark, sticky liquid. Within them were visions of people and places and creatures on the move.

"I like this place," she said, picking her way carefully through the pools. "I think I will be comfortable here."

She walked to the end of the hall where some of her creatures had dragged furniture from... well, she had no idea where, and neither did she care. The long seat was incredibly comfortable, though, and she settled herself down with a contented sigh.

"I am hungry," she announced, knowing that she need not say more. In the corner, there was a frantic scurrying as hobgoblins, boggarts, and shadow-creatures raced to the stairs to satisfy her desires. She laughed. This was turning out to be a very pleasant day, though there were things she did not understand, and that was a source of irritation.

The lady drummed her fingers on the arm of the couch (stolen, as it happens, from one of the nice hotels in town) and considered her options. She needed the man Arthur so she could take the power he did not deserve—that had been denied her for so long—but she didn't necessarily want to dispose of him just yet.

It could be useful to keep him alive for a short while, just to... fill in the blanks.

Who knows? He might even be fun. For a little sport, perhaps? Then again, she was getting ahead of herself. She turned her head sharply at a loud clatter and smiled as rows of bottles and jars appeared on a small table beside her. One of the bottles was still wobbling. Boggarts are remarkably handy creatures to have around.

"I like the iced creams," she said, and there they were, the whole chest freezer suddenly appearing at the other end of the low couch. Two dark creatures slunk back into the shadows with their heads bowed. "Excellent," she said, but then the gunfire started again, and she sighed.

The lady stood and stretched before sauntering over to one of the many pools of blood on the floor of the great hall. Kneeling, she clicked her fingers above it, and an image of the castle gates appeared. Her pet prowled along the perimeter, keeping all at bay, and it looked like he had been having some fun.

"Good," she smiled. "You spent far too long in the other place, my Jack-in-Irons. You all have." She saw flashes then from the strange black tubes held in the hands of men. More gunfire. Like the crack of thunder. She knew what guns were, but these did not fit with her knowledge. The sheer force and power fascinated and thrilled her. She moved her fingers, and the image focused on her pet—the giant creature at the gates—as it roared in pain and lumbered away into the relative safety of the castle grounds. "Most unusual," she said as though it was nothing more than a mild distraction.

She sauntered over to the chest freezer and reached inside.

"Nobbly Bobbly," she read and laughed, biting into the ice-cream without removing the wrapper. "What an interesting world."

Arthur knew the way to the castle gates would be blocked, and anyway, only an idiot would storm a castle through the main entrance. Thankfully, he had something the police officers trying their best to surround the keep did not: years of experience playing hide and seek. He raced to the end of the terrace with Steve hot on his heels. The short road ended at the wall of the last house and turned into the footpath known as Castle Walk. This narrow path followed the top of the mount with a sharp drop to the river on one side and the high castle walls on the other. Whenever they walked this way, Arthur's mum would always comment on how Richmond had a perfect castle, impossible to attack from anywhere but the main gate.

Unless you knew a way in.

Right on the corner, under cover of the tall trees that clung to the side of the cliff, there was a spot where the garden wall of the last house met the great wall of the castle. The height discrepancy between the two was hidden by thick hedges, which are surprisingly easy to squeeze through for curious—and horny—teens.

Arthur—a few years older now, though perhaps not a whole lot wiser—hoisted Steve into the gap and pushed the sword in after him. It had been a few years since he'd climbed into the castle this way, and he was significantly bigger than he used to be, but he put his head down and forced his way through, pushing the sword in front and scrambling along behind. Within moments, he'd burst through to the other side and paused for a moment to catch his breath.

The southeast corner of the castle grounds had been converted into what was known as the Cockpit Gardens, an area of well-manicured lawns surrounded by neatly tended gardens and hedgerows for people to picnic in, relax with a coffee, or, in Arthur's case, sneak into with girlfriends during his mid-teens to lay on the grass and 'look at the stars.'

It is amazing the way in which memories of youth choose to pop into your mind at the most inopportune times. Thankfully,

Steve had leapt from the short wall and was noisily pissing in the bushes, and this snapped Arthur right back to reality.

He hopped down and joined the little puppy on the bottom path of the gardens and ruffled the dog between the ears.

"Good boy, let's go."

It was the dead of night by now, and the mist clung heavy to the world, blocking out all light from the stars and moon. The eerie glow from the front of the castle was enough to light their way, and Arthur ran up the path through manicured garden beds and darted between ornate hedgerows. He half expected to stumble into the police, but there was no one in sight. They were probably trying to climb in from Castle Walk or sneak through the houses on the other side of the keep. Either way, Arthur and Steve had the gardens to themselves. This didn't turn out to be particularly useful, however, because when they got to the rear gates of the castle, they found them locked and barred.

"Shit," Arthur said.

"What?" Steve asked.

"What do we do now?"

"Seriously? Steve barked at the metal bars and wagged his tail. "Just walk through them."

But Arthur couldn't. He knew he couldn't. Not now; not again. Walking through solid objects was not something he could control, and they didn't have time to make him angry. He was scared, for sure, and that had worked before, but he was also excited, and that tipped the balance somewhat. Climbing a castle wall in the middle of the night and racing through the grounds with a sword in his hand had tapped into all sorts of latent feelings deep within Arthur, not to mention many that sat right there on the surface. It was so cool! He was scared, but he was also pumped! He'd just have to think of a different plan that didn't involve abusing the laws of physics. Yet again, his childhood came to the rescue.

"Come on," he said. "This way." He ran back along the path, tracing the imposing inner wall of the castle until he found what he was looking for—a narrow hole at the base that led from one side to the other. It had probably been a drain, though he had no real idea, but crawling through it had been his favourite trick as a kid. He loved showing friends and family, when they came to visit, how easy it was to squeeze through to the other side. The only problem was, where the bushes had a bit of give for a man who had grown a bit, hundreds of tons of stone were a touch more stubborn. Steve, on the other hand, was a lot smaller, and darted through to the other side yapping excitedly.

"Do you think you can make it?" he asked, running back and looking up at Arthur from the small hole.

"Only one way to find out," he said, getting to his hands and knees. "Here, you grab the sword."

He shoved the weapon handle-first through the gap and then crawled onto his belly. It was a tight squeeze. He tried to put both arms through at once like he did when he was a kid, but his shoulders stopped him almost immediately. He heard Steve growling as the small dog used his teeth to drag the sword through the tunnel. Arthur struggled backwards to free himself before trying again with both arms by his sides, thinking he might push himself through with his feet. That was just as useless as the first way, and he never did like doing 'the worm' at the school disco.

Arthur didn't want to be found three days after this was all over, a starved husk trapped beneath the castle wall. He swore and thrust one arm through and then squeezed his head in after, tilting his body to the side. His shoulders slid through, and he clawed with the outstretched hand while pushing with his feet. There was a moment of near panic when his whole body lay beneath the massive inner wall, but then his head poked through the other side, and he dragged himself out, panting and grinning at Steve.

The grin died on his face when he saw the scene before him.

It is all too easy to become self-obsessed and focus solely on your own experiences when caught in difficult circumstances. So, sometimes, it does us well to look at things from a different point of view. Take, for example, the point of view of Captain Amy Le

Roux of the Royal Airforce, who has served two tours of duty as a combat pilot in Afghanistan and is a decorated veteran of many conflicts. She has faced gunfire, enemy rockets, helicopters, and warplanes. She is no stranger to combat, but having just dropped an S.A.S. squad into the open grasslands inside a castle and then watched helplessly as all six men were instantly torn apart by clambering shadows, she is definitely experiencing something new.

Right now, the lumbering giant thundering across the grasslands has all her attention.

She watched as the ten-foot beast that looked vaguely human but massively over-exaggerated with bulging muscles and a bald head steamed in the night as it raced out of the mist and roared at her. There was nothing in her vast experience that even came close to this.

For one thing, it had tusks. Like a pig.

And around its neck was a great chain from which hung the heads of two police officers. Captain Le Roux knew this because the distinct helmets were somehow still attached.

The beast's body was covered in bullet wounds and blood poured from the grey flesh, but it moved with terrifying agility. Apart from the chain, it wore nothing else, and here is a detail that is unique from the point of view of Captain Amy Le Roux; the creature was male.

It is a strange thing that dark creatures who live in deep shadows and realms slightly to the side of our own are often depicted with such quintessentially human items as clothing. It is as though we are okay to have demons and devils under the bridge and in the cellar but, for the love of God, hide their shame!

Captain Le Roux took all of this in instantly. She didn't understand a lot of what she saw, but she was trained to react on instinct, so she did.

Arthur watched as a sleek black helicopter hung in the air and the lumbering giant leaped for the cockpit. The twin guns mounted to the sides opened fire, and flames roared from them as time slowed. The rotors chopped through the mist, kicking eddies and swirls into the night, and the giant was stopped in mid-air by huge bullets ripping into its body. A desperate swipe from a great claw hit the front of the chopper and sent it into a spin as the bullets tore through the torso and head of the beast, finally killing it.

The machine and giant were frozen in the air for a moment, stark against the backdrop of the mist-shrouded castle. Even from this distance, Arthur saw the pilot wrestling with the controls, fighting to pull the ailing helicopter away from the castle walls. It tilted to the side and vanished suddenly over the edge of the cliff, down towards the river. The beast fell to the ground and Arthur felt the impact as it hit the earth.

A scream echoed through the night.

"That. Was. Awesome!" Steve gasped.

"Come on," Arthur said. "We need to keep going."

The man and dog raced across the wet grass, hugging the inner wall of the castle. Arthur was very aware of the dead soldiers lying on the open field he played on as a child, and he was even more aware of the creatures keeping pace with them. But nothing stood in their way. None of the creatures came close, and they made it across the castle grounds to the base of the old cellblock without obstruction.

"That seemed... a little easy," Steve said, and Arthur nodded in agreement. They rested under cover of the cell-block wall, and the clambering shapes kept their distance—watching, moving. But coming no closer.

"This feels like a trap," Arthur said.

"It is," came a voice from beside them and they both jumped away from the cold stone wall. Arthur swung the sword up protectively, and Steve began to growl but there was no one there.

Behind them, on the open grasslands of the castle, the black shapes seethed and clamoured within the mists but stayed where they were.

"Why else would they hold back?" the voice spoke again, and

Arthur paused. It sounded familiar, but he couldn't quite place it. Then it spoke again, and he knew instantly who it was. "Bloody wall! I can't get through the bugger!"

"Archibald?!"

"Aye, lad."

"I thought you were dead?" Even as he said it, he knew what a ridiculous thing it was for him, of all people, to say.

"Aye well, turns out there's more to life than meets the eye. But then, you already knew that."

"Where are you?" Arthur asked, stepping closer and placing his hand on the cold stone. At his feet, Steve sniffed the wall. "Where are my parents?"

"They're in here, lad. In these cells. That woman's sealed the walls though and I can't get through."

"Are you all okay?"

"Aye, we're fine. I mean, I'm dead and my head keeps falling off, but other than that, we're all just gravy."

"Mum! Dad!" Arthur hissed loudly.

"Oh, they can't hear you, lad," Archibald's voice said. "They took a bit of a beating, but they're all right."

"What do you mean?" Arthur snapped, his voice rising in anger. "What happened?"

"*She* happened!" Archibald said.

"But they're okay?"

"They're unconscious, but they're breathing."

"I'll kill her!" Arthur snapped. Now that he knew for certain his parents were at the mercy of the witch, the anger surged within him.

"Hold on, boy! Don't do anything daft. Wait—"

The voice trailed away, and there was some muffled swearing and cursing and what sounded like straining. "Hang on!" the voice said again, although it sounded as though it was far away and muffled. Then, all of a sudden, Archibald's head drifted through the wall. This would have been disconcerting enough without the fact it was being held by the hair and swinging slightly as ethereal fingers tightened their grip.

Arthur stepped back and let out a little giggle. He couldn't help it. It just happened. It was either giggle, pass out cold, or run away screaming.

"Sorry, lad," the disembodied head of Archibald said, "I can't seem to get out and I don't know how long I can hold this for. It… hurts," he grimaced. "There's a door round the back there," he nodded, and his head swung gently back and forth, the long white beard trailing below. He grunted once more, and the ghostly hand dragged the head back through the wall.

Arthur raced off to the archway that connected the cell block to the castle keep. He stopped at the corner and peered around it. They were behind the main gate of the castle and could see bright flashing lights and dark shadows racing back and forth as the police and soldiers on the far side took positions. More helicopters roared in the sky above, but they were deep in the thickness of the mists and couldn't be seen. Searchlights tried to pierce the fog, but they just cast eerie glows through the night and illuminated the dark shadows that swam inside. No one seemed to be in a hurry to come any closer. The loss of an entire S.A.S. squad probably saw to that.

Arthur crept forward, hugging the wall and trying to keep to the shadows. After everything that had happened, he really didn't want to get shot by a frightened copper. He reached the door and then paused. He had absolutely no idea what to do. He tried the handle because, well, why not? But of course, it was locked. The door was huge and made of wood so old it was like steel. What did he think he was going to do, huff and puff and blow it down? He knew just by looking at it that he would never be able to kick it open. That sort of thing only happened in the movies. In real life, the police used hefty battering-rams, and despite the over-abundance of police, there was a distinct lack of rams. Below him, Steve cocked a leg and peed on the door. Arthur was about to shoo him away when the poor little dog yelped and jumped back as if struck.

"Something bit me!" Steve said. "On my... on little Steve."

Arthur knelt and peered closer. There, along the bottom of the door, rippling and shimmering like ink, was a thin, black line that filled the gap between wood and stone. He stood up and traced it with his finger, touching it gently and feeling the familiar electric prickle up his arm.

"Magic," he hissed.

CHAPTER 35

Above them, in the great hall of the castle, the dark woman leaned closer to the pool of blood and watched intently as Arthur rested the sword against the stone wall and stared at the gate.

"Fool," she hissed, tapping her long-nailed fingers against the wooden floor. There was the sword, right there! She could command a boggart to get it for her, and it would be within her grasp and out of harm's way in an instant. But the man was so curious, what was he doing? There was no way he could...

"No!" she gasped and stumbled backwards, landing with an unceremonious bump on the floor.

When she scrambled back to the pool Arthur was gone and the door was open. She screamed in rage.

Below, Arthur lit a purple flare in the palm of his hand and raised it above his head as he entered the dark cell block. The door had been far easier to bypass than he'd expected. One small blast, and the black lines vanished into smoke, and the door swung open.

Slowly, the room came into focus, and Arthur's heart stuttered as the vision of three slumped bodies eased out of the shadows and into his soul. A strangled sob ripped through his chest, and the flame in his hand pulsed a blinding white, feeding off his emotion. It blazed like a camera flash, dazzling him, Steve, Archibald, and... the Shadowman. But Arthur had no time to digest that vision. He tossed the ball of light into the air, and it hung there—exactly where he wanted it to—like a lightbulb in the middle of the cell. He didn't even have to think about it.

Arthur fell to his knees between his parents, looking first to his mother and then his father. Their chests rose and fell with uneasy breaths, and they were beaten and bleeding. His mother's nose was broken and her forehead bloody and bruised. His dad's arm was twisted at an unnatural angle, his short dark beard matted with blood.

Arthur fell back onto the floor, cross-legged like a school kid and stared from one to the other. There is something fundamentally wrong about a child having to see their parents this way. No matter how old the 'child' is. It goes against all natural reason and logic, and Arthur felt the instant shock and sorrow give over to boiling rage. It surged within him, deep inside—a simmering darkness that threatened to rise up and spill over everything.

"They'll be all right, lad," Archibald said, carefully, stepping closer. He could see the young man shaking and the way his fists and jaw clenched. He tried to reach out to Arthur's shoulder, but it took him a couple of goes and Arthur didn't really feel anything.

"Why is this happening?" Arthur said in a low, dangerous voice, forcing the words out one by one. "Why them?" He looked up at Archibald, who, despite himself, took a step back. The ghost shrugged, which was a slightly tricky procedure, all things considered, and held onto his head as he nodded.

"Ask him."

Arthur turned. To Archibald, he seemed like a different man. His face had changed. His eyes were hard and unforgiving. They blazed as they landed upon the Shadowman.

"You!" he snarled, full of hate. Steve whined and backed away. Archibald folded his arms and kicked the inert form of his brother to no effect.

The Shadowman raised his head but didn't move. He stood still with his arms slightly away from his sides, like a cowboy in a duel. Arthur looked closely and saw more black lines shackling the man's wrists to the iron bars of the cell, they shimmered like wet ink.

"You're trapped," said Arthur, a slow smile twisting the corner of his mouth. "I didn't know you could be trapped."

"You know nothing of us," the man said. His voice was level and calm, without the least hint of emotion.

"I know I got rid of one of you," Arthur said, moving closer, raising the sword. "He looked just like you. A different hat. But just like you. What *are* you?" he said.

"Shadows," said the man.

"Don't play fucking games with me!" Arthur shouted, and his face contorted with anger. "You were there, weren't you! You were there in York, and you were there when that bitch did this to my mum and dad! You were there, and you just watched! You did nothing!"

Above them the light of Arthur's magic pulsed and rippled across the stone ceiling.

"There are larger concerns than yours," the Shadowman said.

"Not to me!" Arthur shouted.

"Pathetic human!" another voice snapped, but it was distant and muffled. The Shadowman and Arthur stared at one another for a moment. The voice did not belong to anyone in the room. The lights rippled across the ceiling again, and Arthur suppressed a shudder that spread over his shoulders and down his spine. He was full of anger, but his mind was racing. He was trying to tie all the pieces together.

"She's right" the Shadowman echoed the strange voice. "You are just a pathetic human."

"You know nothing about what it means to be human!" Arthur snapped.

"You are animals, just like the rest."

"And what are you? You're useless! You do nothing! You have power but you don't use it to help people. You just watch!"

"That is our job."

"Your job is to watch darkness spread and demons devour?!"

"We fix the... mistakes," the man said in a low voice, his gaze flicking to the ceiling for a moment.

"You fix the mistakes!" Arthur roared. He raised the sword and stared into the eyes of the Shadowman as the light above him blazed.

"Fix this, you cunt!"

The lady smiled as she watched Arthur bring the sword crashing down. The pool of blood flashed a dazzling white as the sword connected, and the picture vanished. She rose slowly and stretched. Things were far more complicated and infinitely more interesting than she expected. She walked slowly across the room to the dark book, which sat with brooding malice on a small table near the couch. She ran her fingers over the strange patterns on the cover.

"Oh, I think the rules have just been thrown out," she laughed.

Outside, the police continued to surround the castle.

"Where is she?" Arthur demanded, turning from the slumped form of the Shadowman to Archibald.

"You know where she is, lad," the man answered, his eyes wide. "She's up there, but you can't do this!"

"I have to!"

"No, you don't! You need to run. You need to get away and hide. You're playing with fire! You don't know how to use those powers, and if she gets hold of them, she'll be unstoppable!"

"If I don't stop her, who will?"

"The one who is destined!"

"And where is he?!" Arthur demanded.

Archibald paused and couldn't meet the young man's gaze. "He is... somewhere else," he said.

Arthur tried his best to control his anger but the sight of his parents lying beaten and bruised on the floor was seared into him. He wanted answers. "And *who* is he?" he demanded.

"Arthur!"

"*King* Arthur?"

"He wasn't a king," Archibald said, quietly.

"And this sword?" Arthur asked, lifting it in front of Archibald's face. The grey warrior took a step back.

"His."

Arthur gasped, his eyes wide and wild. Despite the anger—despite the danger and the pain—that one simple word and all its implied meaning hit him like a half-brick in a sock. There are some revelations that can cut through anything, that's why they're called revelations.

Arthur Benedict Crazy, son of Thomas Arthur Crazy and Martha Margaret Crazy lifted the blade as if seeing it for the first time, and a lifetime of reading fantasy stories and watching movies roared to the surface.

"Excalibur!" he exclaimed. And it *was* an exclamation, full of all the awed and fervent passion such a moment deserved. Until Archibald spoke.

"It's not Excalibur," he said.

"But you—"

"It's not bloody Excalibur! Ruddy hell! This is why we never mention the man's name! One bloody cleric writes a book and forgets to put 'this is a work of fiction' on the front and suddenly everyone is an expert on early British mythology. Think clearly, boy!"

The sword fell, Arthur's shoulders sagged, and the anger returned. He glared at the twin.

"So, what's your plan, then," he said, "if this belongs to 'the one who is destined' I mean? You're going to take the sword, hop in your car, and go find King Arthur?"

"He's not a king," Archibald mumbled, "but yes, something like that."

"I don't believe you."

"I don't care, boy!" Archibald snapped. He, too, was beginning to simmer. None of this had gone according to plan, least of all dying.

"And how long will it take you?" Arthur said. "You tell me to think clearly, but what about you? Do you think you can get back here before she lays waste to the whole town? Who knows what she's doing up there! In York, it took her just a few hours to gather a whole army of ghosts. You've seen what she's done already—the creatures in the shadows, the ones pushing against the mist, the bloody giant! I'm asking you, how long?"

Archibald didn't say anything, and to Arthur's amazement, he looked away. If he wasn't dead—and therefore no longer possessing the necessary equipment—Arthur would have said the old man was blushing. The silence stretched on, and in it, Arthur slowly realised the truth.

"You don't actually know where he is, do you?" he said. Archibald looked at him briefly then looked away again.

"Fucksake! I knew this was all bollocks! Fucking Arthur and Excalibur!" Arthur shouted, turning in the room. "You're no better than Potter Thompson! Well, that settles it," he said, pointing the sword at the slumped figure of the Shadowman. "My plan is better."

CHAPTER 36

A phrase often used in times like these goes something along the lines of 'never in his wildest dreams,' but to say this of Arthur Crazy—that never in his wildest dreams did he think he'd be storming Richmond Castle with a sword—would be entirely inaccurate. When you spend your childhood living in the shadows of a castle, when its walls and ruins are your playground, when the towering keep is a symbol of home, the extraordinary thing would be to *not* have those dreams.

Arthur had a plan, and parts of it had been in place for over twenty years.

The best way into the castle wasn't up the stone steps and the rooftop walkway of the cell block. That was the easy route for elderly tourists.

The *best* way was through the great rear arch of the keep itself, past the stone well, and up the incredibly narrow spiral staircase. This led straight to the first floor, and from there, the only option was the flight of steep stairs that rose sharply to the Grand Hall.

Arthur was certain that's where he'd find the woman. She'd either be in the hall or on the roof. As the helicopters were still circling—no doubt fighting against the high winds and thick mist in an attempt to land men up there—he'd put money on the Grand Hall. It seemed more *her*.

As he ran through the castle, Arthur also knew, with a certainty he couldn't explain, that he'd be in no danger until he found her. He had sensed her eyes on him for some time and knew she watched his every move. It was the only way to explain how easy it was to enter the castle grounds in the first place.

She was expecting him.

He probably should have given this more thought.

Getting into the castle was easy. Getting Steve to stay behind was not. And so, as Arthur ran across the first floor with his footsteps echoing in the cavernous room, he swung himself up the stairs and raced as fast as he could to the top, trying to put as much space between him and the dog as possible. He figured if he could deal with the woman quickly, then Steve wouldn't come to any harm. It would take the poor little fella a long time to climb all those stairs with his tiny legs.

This was the next part of his plan, such as it was.

Run in, all guns blazing, and don't give her a chance. There would be none of that monologuing nonsense, no chance to explain, no offer of surrender, no bargaining. Just a sudden charge and then hit her with all the power he could muster.

I've beaten her before, Arthur thought. I can do it again.

As he approached the top of the stairs, he saw lights flickering against the stones, and so he dug deep down inside to bring all his power to bear. The sword in his hands flamed purple, and a tiny, disconnected part of his brain did a little happy dance at what appeared in the dark of the stairwell to be a lightsaber.

There was no way this could possibly go wrong.

Arthur rounded the corner, raised the sword, and screamed a challenge as he raced into the room.

He made it halfway across the floor before the lady clicked her fingers.

"Poor little Arthur," she said, walking slowly towards him on bare feet, the thin black jeans and shirt clinging to her body, her hair unbound and falling loose about her shoulders. "I can see your thoughts, you know. I've been watching you. I know exactly what you want to do. You and that little sword of yours. I know what you want to do to me."

Arthur was suspended in the centre of the room, held by hundreds of thin black threads anchored in the pools of blood, pinning him in place. They coiled around him, moving and pulsing over his body, holding him tin a rigid—crucified pose two feet off the ground. The lady leaned in and whispered. "I might let you."

Arthur stared into the woman's eyes and saw the depth within them. Deep, black pools of nothingness. It was like teetering on the edge of an abyss and looking into the void.

"I should thank you," she said, placing a hand on his chest. "You freed me. Twice!" She laughed then. "Oh, what would I do without my little Arthur?"

She moved behind him, her hand caressing as she went, he struggled to see and gasped for breath. He was in agony.

"More to the point, dear. What should I do *with* you?"

"I... I can help you," Arthur stammered. The coils around his chest were crushing him and he could barely breathe. Some of the black lines were inside his body, passing straight through his flesh and holding him still. The police tasers were nothing compared to this.

"Help me?" she laughed. "Do I look like I need any help?"

Arthur spoke through gritted teeth, tears of pain falling from his eyes. "I can... free you," he managed to say, and was rewarded with more laughter.

"Oh, I do like that little trick of yours, but I'm not dead, dear," the woman crooned, coming around him from the other side and moving even closer. She pressed her body against his and whispered in his ear. "As you can see, I'm very much alive."

"You... you..." Arthur tried.

"Me. Me," the woman said, mocking him.

"I..."

"Oh, this is getting tedious," she snapped. She stepped away from him and pointed a finger directly in his face. "Now, you behave yourself, and I'll let you go." She clicked her fingers, and the restraints vanished. Arthur fell to his knees and the sword clattered to the ground beside him, landing with the blade in one of the many pools of blood. The woman tutted and beckoned with a red-painted nail (where she had got the nail-polish from, or the time for a manicure, was anybody's guess). The sword flew through the air, and she caught it by the handle. It was an undeniably impressive move.

"Naughty boys don't get to play with toys," she said. She turned the blade back and forth and looked at Arthur. "Do you even know what *this is,* or are you just blundering around with it like you are with *his* powers? All excited, full of vim and vigour, and absolutely no idea what to do!"

"It's Excalibur," Arthur mumbled, trying to give himself time to think. Plan A hadn't exactly been a raging success. He needed time.

"Ha! Arthur and Excalibur!" she laughed. "What nonsense! Excalibur was nothing more than a butcher's tool. But this... this is special." She wiped the sword on the sleeve of her shirt, high on the arm, leaving a smear of blood beneath her shoulder.

"This isn't for fighting," she said, running her thumb along the edge of the blade. "You wouldn't do much damage with an edge like this. No, this is a ceremonial sword. It confers status." She pointed the blade at Arthur, and suddenly her face changed, contorting into a mask of fury. "Status!" she screamed. "Do you understand status?! It is earned! Not given! Not stolen! Earned!"

As she shouted, the shadows in the corners of the room jumped in excitement. Arthur saw the vague shapes of arms and legs and heads, but they were all on the edge of his vision. Not quite there—not quite real. Not yet anyway.

"Status!" she screamed at him again, taking three quick steps forward and placing the blade at his throat before he even had a chance to move. "Like this!" She lifted the sword and Arthur closed his eyes in fear, this was it, the moment of his death. He was frozen and incapable of fighting back.

Some hero, he thought. Some Jedi.

Arthur swallowed the sob that threatened to spill from his lips, and his heart rose up to meet it. One last desperate pulse of blood around his body before the end.

Make it quick, he thought, but then he felt the gentle tap of the blade on his shoulder and the whisper of air as the sword moved over his head to tap the other.

He opened his eyes, and the lady smiled down at him. Her eyes were entirely black.

"I knight you, Sir Arthur," she said. "Arise, a knight."

Arthur did as he was told, completely unable to do anything else. He staggered upright on trembling feet.

"Please stop," he said.

"Please stop!" she mocked. "By the gods! Were you so whiny in Eboracum? I seem to remember you taking charge and being…" she waved her hand, "…more! But you're just a little boy aren't you. A little boy who needs his mummy and daddy to fight his battles for him."

"Stop!" he said, harder this time.

"Ohh! That's better! There's some fire!" She moved around him —pacing, stalking, a predator toying with a meal. "There's the man who was so willing to sacrifice his friends! Tell me"—she lifted the blade to his throat again and resting the cold steel against his flesh—"did you love her?"

"I said stop!" Arthur gasped, staring down at those cold eyes. He could feel his temper rising, but he also knew this was what she wanted. He tried to control it, but it was hard not to listen to her. Not when she spoke the truth.

"She loved *you*, you know. Deeply. She loved you so much, it was enough to break the bonds and ties of hundreds of years of death. Imagine falling in love so deeply in just two days? And you killed her. She died for you. At your hands! It's all very dramatic," she added.

"I—"

"You what? You know it's true. You saw it when you *set her free*. Do you think she's free? Do you wonder where she is now? Burning in hell perhaps, or floating on clouds, singing with the angels? That sounds like hell to me. No, much more fun to be here. Alive and kicking!"

"What do you want?" Arthur said, trying to keep his anger under control. He needed to act. He needed to do something.

"Everything!" she screamed suddenly, her eyes growing wide and her face contorting in rage. Spittle flew from her mouth as she ranted and raved. Arthur tried to back away, but she kept the sword point right on his throat, digging in. Her hand didn't shake at all, and the blade remained perfectly still.

"I want everything! I want it all. I want this land as it should have been before all the old ones were pushed into the shadows and before the truth was forgotten and bastardised and broken. I want those churches pulled down and the old sacred sites washed clean with blood. I want sacrifices!"

She lifted her head to the sky, and the blade moved away from Arthur's throat. He took his chance.

He ducked to the right and brought his left arm up in an arc to push the sword away. Then, twisting his legs to kneel, he punched a purple fireball into the woman's stomach. He screamed as he made contact and let the fire raging within him pour out through his closed fist. The woman doubled over, and he pushed her back, screaming the whole time as he forced her over the pools of blood. They slammed against the stone wall together, and Arthur was roaring at her, pushing and straining, forcing the fire into her with all that he had. It took him a long while to realise she was laughing.

He turned his head slowly. The woman's face was right next to his, looking down and straining against the man, with tears of laughter rolling down her cheeks.

"Yes, Arthur!" she cried, her eyes close to his. "Do it! Feel the power! Isn't it glorious!"

Arthur gasped and hesitated, and that was all she needed. The woman pushed him back and slapped him hard across the face. A resounding smack that rocked his head to the side and made his skin burn. Arthur staggered but stood up to face her, his ear ringing and his left eye watering. If that's all she had, he could handle it. He took a deep breath, set his feet, raised his hand, and...

The woman stepped in close, driving the sword deep into his side, ripping through shirt and flesh as though they were alike.

Arthur blinked. There was no pain at first.

He looked down and laughed, and then he looked up, deep into her eyes. The darkness of her pupils seemed endless and void, drawing him in. She smiled, and to his shame, he found her beautiful. Then he coughed and blood fell from his mouth. Arthur gasped, and then the agony hit.

"Don't you ever lay a hand on me!" the woman roared and pushed, forcing Arthur back. She followed him, keeping the sword in a firm grip, not letting it leave his body.

Arthur's eyes widened, and his mouth dropped open as the blade cut deeper. He staggered again, and she moved with him, pushing and pulling the blade, steering him, toying with him.

"A blade doesn't have to be sharp, boy!" she spat. "You just have to know how to use it!" They moved in a macabre waltz through the pools of blood, the woman leading. The wound seeped down the blade and onto the floor, tracing a pattern across the stones.

Arthur had never felt anything like it. The pain washed over him, emanating from the wound and pulsing through his whole being. It was cold, but it burned with a fierceness that took his breath away. Every time his stomach moved—every time he gasped or even breathed—it was as though she stabbed him again. He could feel the blade inside him, feel the metal tearing flesh and ripping muscle. Worse than that was the magic. It was there too, leaking out and mixing with the malevolence of the woman, turning it into poison.

"Do you know what the secret of this sword is, boy?" she

hissed, pushing the sword further and smiling at Arthur's cry of agony. "It is as simple as the truth. You can feel it, can't you! Feel it spreading through you, feel the power. Only the worthy or the damned can unlock the secret of this blade! And I am both!"

She forced Arthur to his knees by lifting the pommel and pushing down. He cried out in a desperate gasp of pain as he collapsed.

"Kneel!" she sneered. "All will kneel before me in the end. You might as well get used to it! You should be grateful! There was a time when the people who touched this blade made vows to defend this land, but they were weak. They refused to do what was necessary, and they paid the price. All *you* have to do, dear Arthur, is watch."

Arthur looked into her flashing eyes and tried to summon the power, but he had nothing left to give. He raised his fist, and small sparks flickered from his fingers and died like the last breath of a candle.

"Pathetic," she said. "Look at how you manifest such a gift! Electricity and balls of fire. Are you really so unimaginative?"

"You don't have to do this," he managed to gasp and then he winced as she laughed and knelt down in front of him.

"Oh, I know I don't have to, but here's the big secret..." She leaned in over the sword and looked deep into his eyes before hissing, "I want to."

Arthur groaned and looked down.

"Look at you, Arthur," she said. "You're pathetic. But we're connected. Can you feel the bond between us now? Is this how you felt when you 'saved' me? You saw the *true me* back in the city, isn't that so? And tell me, did you like what you saw?"

"You murdered your family," Arthur gasped, remembering the moment he first made a connection with her, back when she was a girl during the plague. He witnessed her parents tremble in fear, locking their own child away and caging her with iron and magic so she couldn't hurt anyone else.

"They weren't my family," the woman sneered, "and they

murdered me first! They murdered me long ago, Arthur. You know it's true. You can see it now, can't you, the real me! Who I *really* am! I should have been a queen, but they were too scared to do what needed to be done, and so they murdered me. All because I had the strength they lacked. Then they brought me back, Arthur. They brought me back to a time of disease and pain! They brought me back when they needed me. I was a queen, and they made me a peasant. Again, they were too afraid. I was just a little girl, and they locked me away in that room, trapped me beneath the shadow of their church for four hundred years." She thrust the sword deeper into Arthur, and he screamed.

"I can help you!" he cried out.

"Oh... oh, my saviour!" she crowed. "And now we get to it, don't we Arthur. Now we get to the truth. Big brave Arthur saving the sweet, innocent girl in the window." She spat on the floor by his feet. "We both know you didn't save me because you wanted to make sure your power was safe, to help your friends, to release them into whatever comes next. You didn't save me because you thought I needed saving. There was no grand and noble gesture. You used your power on me because saving the sweet innocent girl would impress the beautiful woman!"

"I—" but it wasn't pain that stopped Arthur from finishing his sentence. Not physical pain anyway, and the woman knew it.

"You know it's true, Arthur. That's what this sword does. Just like your power! I imagine the combination of the two inside you right now is quite the thing. I *know* you can feel it, Arthur. I know it. Don't argue now. Don't plead. You're only arguing with yourself! All their deaths are on you! The queen's death is on you! The guardian's death is on you! Your parents' deaths are on you!"

"Fuck you!" Arthur spat.

"Yes, Arthur! Fight! Rage! Feel it! Live and die and do it all again. You're so scared. All of you in this strange world are so scared. You live in a straight line, racing from cradle to grave, and your churches point the way, telling you this is how it must be.

Live our way, and wait for the end! Wait for the saviour to come! It will be better after. Wait. Wait .Wait!"

Arthur struggled and fought, but the pain was too much. He sank down and gasped for air that wouldn't come. She was right, of course. Everything she said was true. He knew it now, or he had always known it, but now it was crystal clear in front of him. Who did he think he was, running around waving a sword and believing he was powerful? What had he done with it? What had he accomplished in the six months since these gifts came upon him? Nothing but death and destruction and broken promises.

Sarah was gone. Lord Acaster and the Queen were gone. He had no idea where poor Steve was. He let the puppy-man who adored him follow him all this way. He raced up the last steps in his arrogance thinking he could end everything before Steve arrived, and then what? He'd walk out of the castle the conquering hero? The saviour with his faithful companion by his side? But the truth—the painful, awful truth—was that he let Steve come because he wanted the company. Because he was scared to go alone, and he knew he wasn't good enough.

It had been Steve who told him the truth in the first place, Steve who unlocked his powers, Steve who jumped in the river after him, and Steve who attacked the lady to give him time to escape.

Steve was there in the darkness beneath the castle and there to rescue him from the police van... and from his own searing panic at the door of his house.

Arthur couldn't have done any of it without Steve, yet, in the end, he had abandoned him. Why? For glory?! Arsehole!

And where was Steve now? As Arthur charged into the room so certain of his own ability to take care of the woman in black, he didn't even think of Steve racing up the stairs behind him.

A puppy, come to face a devil.

"Hurts, doesn't it," the lady hissed, and he knew she wasn't talking about the blade. He needed to keep his thoughts guarded, somehow, but he was being laid bare.

The rippling, pulsing sensation that swarmed like poison had taken over everything: every facet of his personality, all the lies and manipulations, all the times he told himself he was doing something for the benefit of others when in truth it was all about him. Arthur. Arthur. Arthur.

He saw friends he'd lied to, girlfriends he'd left for no reason —manipulating the situation to make them think it was their fault. He saw the image he tried so hard to maintain in front of other people fall away and all the faults of his character laid bare. He hung his head and slumped over the sword, tears rolling down his cheeks as he saw his parents, their bruised and battered bodies in the cells below. They would do anything for him, and he knew it. They had the scars, the breaks, and the bruises to show for it. They were there because of him. It was all his fault.

"Yes," said the woman softly. "It *is* all your fault, Arthur."

Arthur glanced to the side, and something caught his eye, darting across the shadows. He dropped his head quickly. Think! He needed to think!

"Why?" he gasped. "Why are you doing this?"

"Oh, please. You're better than that. So, you want my truth now, do you? Now we've had yours. What shall it be?" she sneered. "What circumstances made me this way? The poor tortured little girl—there must be a reason, surely? Will that make it better for you? Will it make more sense if I was beaten and abused or had some traumatic life-altering event that shaped my destiny? You're pathetic! Even now, you don't really care. I can tell, you know. You're just getting me to talk. I can only assume it's to make you feel better in your last moments."

"Well, don't worry, Arthur. I'm not going to let you go. Oh, you'll die all right, but it isn't going to be easy, and it isn't going to be quick. There will be no 'happily ever after' for you." She pointed to the table at the end of the hall. "I have the Shadowman's book and you... you killed him!" she said. 'All I have to do is tear out a page and you're trapped forever. And you know what, Arthur? Once I've taken your power—once I've used this sword to take every last scrap from you—at the moment of your death, I will bind you to me. You'll be mine forever." She paused, then smiled. "Or I might just throw you down a dark pit and forget you," she said, patting him on the face.

Arthur took a deep breath and wept at the pain coursing through his body. He couldn't find the words, but he lifted his eyes to peer around the room.

"Don't worry," the woman crooned, "it will all be over soon. Well, it won't. But you did want the truth." She leaned in close to him, her lips hot on his ear. "Here's my truth, little man," she whispered. "Sometimes there *are* no reasons. Sometimes there *is* no catalyst. Sometimes..." she gripped the blade tighter and twisted. Arthur gasped in agony and cried out, lifting his head. He caught another glimpse of movement, but the woman wasn't done. "Sometimes we stab because it feels good!" she said.

"I can help you," he begged. She sneered at him, ignoring the words. Good. He looked at her and tried to seem defeated. It wasn't hard. "Why?" he asked.

"Because I want to," she said, simply. "People steal because they want what others have. They tread the weak beneath their feet because that is where they deserve to be. And maybe, just maybe, it's because I've been doing this for a very long time,"—she leaned in closer and lowered her voice—"and I'm really good at it. *We* are all the heroes of our own story!"

"I'm glad you think so," Arthur said, and there was something in his voice that caught her off guard. She sat back and looked at him. Arthur lifted his head and spoke again, his eyes glancing to the shadows behind. "Because heroes come in all different shapes and sizes," he said.

Steve leapt from the couch and sunk his teeth into the crouching woman. He wasn't aiming for her flesh this time but her hair. His sharp little teeth clamped tight over a great mass of it as he landed on her back, and then he kicked for the floor.

You can have all the dark powers in the universe, but if you have long hair and someone pulls on it hard enough, you're going down.

The woman toppled backwards with a shout of anger and sprawled across the floor, the sword ripping from Arthur's body. He gasped in agony, but he only had this one chance. Arthur summoned his power and sent bolt after bolt of purple flame into the woman, forcing her back as Steve tugged and pulled for all he was worth—growling and struggling against her. Arthur knew now that the power couldn't harm the woman but that didn't matter.

He just needed to get her off balance.

Purple balls of light exploded like fireworks, and the woman screamed in rage, throwing herself backward at the dog. She cannoned into Steve and forced him to let go, batting him away and clambering to her feet. She turned swiftly to face Arthur, her hands up, ready to shoot dark magic at him, but Arthur was already there.

Right in front of her face.

She coughed and looked down.

The blade stuck out of her chest, all the way to the hilt.

"I think I know how this works now," he said through gritted, blood-stained teeth.

"You think that's enough to end me!" she snarled.

"No," Arthur said, "but this should do the trick."

He let go of the sword as the Shadowman emerged from the dark and threw a thick chain around the woman's neck. Her eyes widened in shock, and then she screamed as the man tightened the loop.

It was a scream to end all screams.

It built and spread and blasted out from the castle keep, raging across the country. Through towns and fields and mountains and lakes, it rippled and grew, touching all corners of the island. It spread from Land's End to John O'Groats, Middlesbrough to Mayfair, Waitrose to Aldi. Whatever creatures were heading towards the castle turned tail or talon and fled as the noise washed over them. They ran, scurried, crawled, and flew, fleeing back to the safety of the dark places.

When it ended, the woman stood panting, held fast by the Shadowman and the chains of the barghest. Blood poured from the wound in her chest, soaking her dark shirt and dripping to the floor. Arthur moved closer and wrenched the sword free, but she remained upright, swaying slightly.

"You know what my truth is?" Arthur said, throwing the sword away and stepping closer. "The real truth?" Steve joined him, standing beside his best friend, his tail wagging. "Yes, I've made mistakes. Lots of them. But that's life, and life is simple. You try your best, you push on, and, really, just don't be a dick."

"I—" she began, blood pouring from her mouth.

"Yes?"

The woman stepped forward against the bonds and lashed out in the only way she could, violently kicking Steve in the side of the head. He yelped and scurried away howling to the back of the room. Before the woman could say anything more, the Shadowman dragged her to the ground by the chain, pinning her to the floor.

"That was a bit much," he said, and the black-bladed knife flashed in his hand. Just once.

Arthur stared, speechless, holding his own wound and feeling dizzy as the room began to spin. "Wha—?" he managed. The Shadowman reached over to the table and grabbed his book. It vanished somewhere about his person, then he turned back to the woman and gathered the long chain around his arm. He turned to Arthur.

"I like dogs," he said simply and stepped into shadow, dragging the body of the nameless woman after him.

Arthur stared for a moment and then looked around the room. The shadows and dark shapes were leaching away, fading into the gaps between wood and stone. He stumbled and fell to one knee with a grunt.

"Steve?" he said.

"Arthur?"

The puppy limped over to him, avoiding the pools of blood.

"Are you okay, mate?"

"Yeah, are you okay?"

"I'll be all right."

"Arthur?"

"Yeah?"

"Did you really say, 'because heroes come in all shapes and sizes?'"

Arthur smiled. He started to reply, but fell over instead.

PART III
NEW YEAR

CHAPTER 37

It was New Year's Eve, and the Crazy family walked slowly down the path from Easby Abbey towards town. They were in no rush. Well, the humans were in no rush as they were still recovering from some pretty serious wounds, but Steve the dog had discovered the joy of squirrels and was currently racing hell-for-leather around the base of a large oak tree in a blur of excited yapping.

Thomas's arm was in a sling, Maggie had two black eyes and a swollen nose, and Arthur's whole stomach was wrapped in tight bandages and braces to keep the stitches from bursting.

It had been slow going, but it was tradition, and traditions are important. The Crazy family always went for a walk on New Year's Eve. It was the way they saw the old year out and prepared to let the new year in, though this walk had been slightly different for a number of reasons.

To begin with, they had Steve. The Crazy's hadn't had a dog since Arthur was a kid, and he was a joy to be with, even if he did see sheep as more of a challenge than something to avoid.

Secondly, they had stopped by the river, and Mrs. Crazy handed cigarettes around and they all had an awkward yet companionable smoke together. Though, Arthur declared he was quitting.

The big difference, however, was probably the conversation they'd just had with a large number of ghosts in the ruins of the abbey. That bit definitely wasn't part of the usual routine.

The Crazies arrived home to the cottage below the castle to find three cups of tea ready and waiting for them. Alexander was passing the steaming mugs to Archibald, who was practising his telekinesis by adding sugar. To Arthur and Maggie, it looked perfectly natural, but for the third day in a row, Thomas was having trouble processing the floating cutlery.

"Thank you," he stammered when Alexander handed him a mug.

"You know,"—and all the men in the room did know, for it was going to be the same thing Maggie had said every day since Christmas—"I still don't understand how anything hasn't been made out of what happened."

They rattled off the many reasons they had discussed throughout the course of the week and added a few more just for the sake of the thing.

"It was too big; people can't handle things like that."

"They said it was a training exercise by the army."

"I heard a man in the pub say it was just kids letting off fireworks to celebrate Christmas day."

"Drunks."

"Teenagers."

"Government conspiracy."

"Yes." Mrs. Crazy said, and they all knew what was coming next. "But people died! Real people. Flesh and blood. Poor Mr. Allott was butchered in his own home... along with his cat!"

"They said he died of a heart attack," Thomas said.

"And the cat?"

"Well, no one really knew he had one, that's just rumour. He kept himself to himself, didn't he."

"Yes, but what about the poor people who had to go in and

clean up? What about the police who investigated it? And what about those poor police officers at the castle and the soldiers from the helicopter?"

"I told you, love, the army will take care of their families. They're good like that."

"Actually,"—Alexander reached over to place a newspaper in front of Mrs. Crazy—"there was an article about that today. It says the helicopter pilot lost her bearings in the thick fog, and the instruments failed. They're hailing her a hero for missing the houses and bringing the helicopter safely to land on the football pitch over the river. She's going to get a medal."

"Well, that's something, but I can't help but feel for those poor soldiers and those poor police. And did no one else in the town see the giant lumbering around the castle or the monsters in the shadows?"

"It was Christmas Day, Mam," Arthur said. "Most people were inside. It was only us lot running around like nutters."

"But there are so many questions!"

"Perhaps I can provide some answers?" a voice said, and they all jumped. The Shadowman was standing in the corner of the room near the curtains. He stepped forward, and Archibald jumped to his feet.

"You'll not take me, ya bugger!"

The Shadowman raised his hands, they contained neither a book nor a blade. "I have not come to take anyone," he said. "I have come to speak to you," he looked at Arthur. "But first an answer to your questions. It is the job of the Shadowmen to clear up the mistakes. The events of this past week were... big. One of the biggest. We have had everyone working to put things right. This has included,"—he paused, clearly searching for the right words—"making *alterations*."

There was something in the way he said the word that made none of them question him.

"It is perhaps best," he continued, "to simply, as you say, move on."

There was a long moment of silence, and then Arthur stood up.

"You wanted to speak to me?" he asked. The Shadowman nodded.

"Now, hang on!" Archibald said. "How do we know we can trust this bugger?"

"Yes," agreed Maggie. "Sorry, son, but I think we've got to be careful here. Too much has happened. Are you sure this is wise?"

"I set him free. He saved us."

"It is true, your son cut the bonds that tied me," the Shadowman said. "He could have killed me, but he didn't."

"I don't know. I still don't know if we can trust you."

At that moment, Steve walked into the room and padded straight over to the Shadowman. The night-clad man leaned down and scratched the tiny dog behind the ears. Steve wagged his tail and licked his hand.

Arthur looked at his mum. "I think I'll be all right," he said.

CHAPTER 38

The procession weaved a solemn path through the marketplace into the wide cobbled street of Newbiggin. Tall, leafless oaks marked the route like soldiers standing to attention, watching them pass. A large, portly priest led the way, wiping his brow and rubbing a lace handkerchief over his neck and bald head. He was flanked by guards and twelve halberdiers. Behind them came the bailiffs, butchers, castle guards, jailers, churchmen, and townsfolk. It seemed as though the whole town had turned out to bear witness.

Slowly, the procession came to a halt and formed a circle in the middle of the cobbled street. They waited in silence. There was the occasional cough and scuffle of feet, but other than that, the morning was quiet and still... until a sudden drumbeat echoed from the tall buildings of the town.

The crowd turned as one and a man appeared.

He was tall and well-built and walked with his head held high, the iron collar around his neck visible for all to see, but he would not be bowed. He marched ahead of his guard and made his way to the centre of the circle, looking neither left nor right but focusing on what lay ahead. When he reached the middle of the crowd, he paused for a moment and then clambered onto the platform. He climbed over bundles of thickly chopped wood and wagons of twigs, pushing aside heaped greenery as he reached the central pole and turned his back to it.

A young man dashed up and tied his hands behind his back, then quickly darted away.

The drumbeats stopped.

The priest stepped from out of the crowd and held out a large crucifix on the end of a pole.

"Kiss it," he said, his voice weak and shaking. "Kiss it, and this will all be over."

The man on the pyre spat and glared. "Do your worst, false priest!" he said. His voice was strong and carried across the gathered people. There were gasps and exclamations, a few cheers even, though they died quickly as the soldiers turned to face the crowd.

"So be it," said the priest and stepped away, nodding to a group of young men. "Light it," he commanded.

The flames caught quickly, and soon, the smoke billowed, thick and dark as the greenery smouldered. The man in the centre was lost but his voice could be heard loud and clear as he cried out.

"Christ, help me!"

Suddenly, another man stepped forward from among the shocked townspeople and strode to the pyre. He stood as close to the fire as he could get, shielding his face against the heat, and raised his voice to be heard over the roar of the flames.

"Hold fast there, Richard Snell," he said. "And we will all pray for thee!"

The man clasped his hands together in supplication and knelt down. All around the square, people joined him, falling to their knees and adding their voices to the murmured prayers.

The priest shouted and raged and tried to drag the soldiers and the guards out of their lines to do something about the insubordination, but soon enough, some of them were kneeling too, and the priest was left, coughing and spluttering in the smoke.

"It is time," the Shadowman said, and Arthur stepped from behind one of the oaks, the weeping ghost of John Snell clinging to his arm.

"Your brother died a valiant death," Arthur said, but the old ghost was too overcome to respond. He lifted shaking fingers to Arthur's face and patted him once. Arthur stepped away and strode towards the fire. No one tried to stop him. No one could see him. The Shadowman had made his alterations.

When Arthur got to the blazing inferno he didn't hesitate, he simply stepped inside the flames and vanished.

A moment passed and the pyre began to flicker more brightly and reach higher, roaring into the sky. The smoke burned out as the flames got hotter, then they turned white, and, finally, purple.

"You may go now," the Shadowman said, and John Snell limped forward, his head bowed, his back bent, but the closer he got to the fire, the taller he walked. By the time he vanished into the flames, John Snell was running, his arms out wide... ready.

The crowd began to drift away but many lingered. They were different. Dressed different. Young and old. At first they just watched, but then, one by one, others stepped towards the fire.

Arthur had given them a choice. He told the ghosts of Richmond what he could do and how he planned to do it, but the choice would have to be theirs and theirs alone. He couldn't make the decision for them.

The Shadowman watched as more and more ghosts walked from the town and vanished into the flames, he flicked through the pages of his book, trying his best to keep up. There were soldiers, knights, officer workers and slaves. Peasants walked beside lawyers and used car salesmen, and children raced through them all to be first into the light.

"Not this much trouble since Merlin," he grumbled to himself as a girl in a Nirvana t-shirt stepped into the flame and vanished.

"Oh," he said.

She was the last one.

The street was empty. The work was done.

The crowd had gone, and suddenly, there was only the Shadowman, the fire, and then, stepping from the shelter of a doorway, one small boy. He carried a drum.

The Shadowman watched as Arthur reappeared and gestured to the child, but the drummer boy simply smiled, shook his head, and walked away. The sound of his drum echoed from the walls and faded into nothing as he slowly vanished, fading out of sight.

The Shadowman watched as the supernatural fire died, and the morning turned from light to dark. Wooden carts disappeared, and parked cars came into view. The buildings changed and grew as the world reset itself, until only Arthur remained, standing alone in the middle of the street, his head hung low, and his shoulders slumped. A small dog ran out from beneath a car and joined him.

The Shadowman watched.

CHAPTER 39

Three vehicles were parked side by side in front of Tan Hill Inn, the highest pub in Britain. One was a brand new, state-of-the-art Volkswagen campervan. Thomas Crazy was polishing the lights for the third time in ten minutes. The car in the middle was a well-looked-after Mark II Jaguar, one owner from new. Aside from a broken left headlamp, It was in pristine condition and had recently been fitted with a new sound system. The third car was considerably smaller than the others. It was a 1972 Mini Cooper S in British Racing Green with a Union Flag on the roof and white stripes on the bonnet. Thomas Crazy thought it was a bit much. Arthur Crazy was in love.

Steve the dog, sitting in the front seat with his head hanging out of the window, was just happy to be there.

"So, you're really doing this then?" Arthur said to his parents. They had just had their last meal together before parting ways for, as his mother put it, new adventures.

"Just try and stop us," Maggie Crazy said, giving her son another tight squeeze.

"I love you, Mam," he said, leaning down and kissing her on the head.

"I love you too, darling."

"Be careful, okay."

"I'm always careful."

"I'm serious! This talking to the dead thing is no joke!"

Maggie sighed and looked up at her son. "I told you I won't go looking for anything, but if something finds me, that's a different story."

"Well, just be careful."

"Yes, *Mum!*" she said in a mock teenage voice, but then she saw the look on his face and laughed. "Oh, Arthur, don't worry. All I can do is talk. I can't do any of the things you can do. It'll be like that TV show where the woman with the big boobs helps ghosts with the things they've left unfinished."

"Except you'll repeat what they say verbatim, right love?" said Thomas Crazy, coming over and wrapping his family in a big bear hug. "Always drove me mad, that show. She'd ask the ghost what they wanted to say to the people they'd left behind, and then she'd say something completely different. Always got on my nerves."

"And what are you going to do, Dad,"—Arthur laughed— "while mum is off talking to dead people?"

Thomas stepped back and grinned, twirling the keys on the end of his finger. "Me, son? I'm going to drive!"

There were a few more hugs and kisses, and a lot more *I love yous* and promises to call regularly and meet in two months. Then, there were two cars left.

Alexander, Archibald, Arthur, and Steve watched as the campervan slowly disappeared over the moors.

"Well, gentlemen," Arthur said, trying to find the right words to sum up everything he needed to say. He looked from one man to the other. "I... thank you," he said.

"Don't mention it, lad. Our pleasure."

"Aye, piece of cake," said Archibald.

Arthur couldn't help himself. "Piece of cake? You died!"

"Aye, well, it doesn't screw your career up like it used to."

"So, what are you going to do now?"

"We're away south," Alexander said. "It is long past time we rested."

"Aye, and we need to get the sword back to its rightful owner, yer ken?"

"And that would be?"

"Arthur!"

"What? I was only asking!"

Arthur shook hands with the twins and commented on how much better Archibald was getting, he almost felt him that time, and then he watched as they drove away. There was an awkward moment where they climbed in the car, paused, got back out again and swapped sides but after that they were off, vanishing over the moors in the same direction as the Crazy people.

"Just me and you then, bud," Arthur said, climbing into the mini and patting Steve on the head. "You're going to love York, I promise. Lots of squirrels."

"You remember I used to live there, right?" Steve said. "It's where we met."

"Oh, aye, but that was then, and this is now. It's all going to be different from now on, yer ken?"

"Don't do that."

"Sorry."

"Good boy."

Some stories end with the hero driving off into the sunset. That would be a fitting final note to this story, too, except York is in the east and the sun sets in the west. Ah, well, you can't have everything. But you should probably know those roses outside King's Manor bloomed wonderfully this spring, and that's something, in the end.

ACKNOWLEDGMENTS

To everyone at Parliament House Books, past and present, but especially Mike Feeney. This book may never have happened without Mike first believing in, and fighting for, The Book and the Blade. You're a gentleman. And to Brianna, Erica, Amanda, Chantal, Cindy, Jennifer, Jessica, Alyssa, Shayne, and, of course, Malorie who has edited both *The Book and the Blade* and *The Sword and the Hounds*. I also want to say a special thank you to Alexandra who has been a total legend this last year. Stephen King said "to write is human, to edit is divine." He's not wrong. Thank you.

To my friend, Andrew McLaren, whose knowledge of cars was invaluable to this story. We could talk for hours about music, Lord of the Rings, scotch, red wine, and the merits of playing Articulate with the love of your life, or whatever else took our fancy. Who knew our long conversations about the Jaguar MK II would be some of our last? Every man should have a friend like Andrew. He was a gentleman and a mentor. I miss you, mate.

To our friends on Castle Terrace. Thank you for welcoming us and making us feel part of the community. It was amazing to live in such a beautiful place among such wonderful people. To Peter and Christine, in particular, for many shared Speckled Hens, glasses of wine, and good times. Your names are not mentioned in this story, but your spirit and kindness definitely embody some of the characters. I'll leave you to guess who. And to Heather, for telling us the story of Hundred. We love you and miss you all.

ABOUT THE AUTHOR

A.B. Finlayson makes things up and occasionally writes them down. He's been a fighter, a poet, and a preacher. He went to school and then became the teacher (only some of these things are true). He's a Yorkshireman living in the sun and can usually be found hugging the air-conditioning when he's not playing bass guitar (poorly). He has an awesome wife, two amazing kids, two cats who apparently own his house and tolerate his presence, a loyal dog with the world's saddest face, and his wife's bloody bird (which he pretends to hate). His real name is Alexander but only his mum calls him that...when he's in trouble. He doesn't like writing about himself in the third person and frequently makes mistakes when trying. In the immortal words of Paul Simon, you can call me Al.

WWW.ABFINLAYSON.COM

 facebook.com/abfinlaysonauthor
x.com/ABFinlayson1
instagram.com/a.b.finlayson

9 781956 136753